THE EMBERS OF SIWA

THE EMBERS OF SIWA

NICK THACKER

The Embers of Siwa: Harvey Bennett Thrillers, Book #12
Copyright © 2022 by Nick Thacker
Published by Conundrum Publishing

WANT FREE BOOKS?

HEAD OVER TO NICKTHACKER.COM/FREE-BOOKS to download three full-length thriller novels!

ACT I

"Hateful to me as the gates of Hades is that man who hides one thing in his heart and speaks another. It lies in the lap of the gods. Tell me, Muse, of the man of many devices, who wandered far and wide after he had sacked Troy's sacred city, and saw the towns of many men and knew their mind."

— Homer, *The Iliad*

CHAPTER 1
PRISONER 348

Imrali Island, Turkey

"Do you know how to incite a rebellion? How to start a revolution?"

I shake my head.

"With one hand on the heart and the other on the trigger."

The Poet stands to his wiry, six-foot-three frame and leans over the minuscule metal bunk bed. I lay on top, over the single sheet rather than under it, to separate my bare back from the crusted remains of whatever's stuck to the once-shiny plastic mattress.

The mattress can hardly be called one: it seems to have been crapped out of an automotive factory after some designer re-jiggered the controls to change the shape of car's backseat cushions. A rounded rectangle, a couple of inches thick, and it does almost nothing to cover the sharp metal wiring of the bedframe itself.

I look over at The Poet, his head hunched so it doesn't contact the stone ceiling and offer him a slight grin. "Cute."

I don't feel like talking. I don't feel like doing much of anything, for that matter. Pretty soon, I probably won't feel at all. Most of my desires went away a week after I arrived. Most of my longings, my

5

sufferings, my carings — even about my own well-being — they all died after the first month.

"You do not agree?" The Poet asks.

His English is good, but I'm not sure what his first language is. Something similar to Russian, I'd guess. As far as roommates go, he's as good as any. Probably one of the better ones in a place like this. My eyes roll to the side and peer at his eyes — the hazel in them twinkling even in the low light of our cell.

"No, I don't disagree," I tell him. "I just... uh, I just don't give a shit."

He looks at me like he wants to smack me, but I know better. The Poet has never shown any signs of physicality. Never expressed himself with anything but words. And he's good at words, even though the words I understand aren't his first language, which tells me he's even better with them than I can ever know. I'm no linguist — I'm barely considered 'traveled,' and only then because I had the gall to stick my neck out and get involved in matters I should never have even known about.

The Poet waits there for another long moment, either waiting for me to continue — I'm not going to — or trying to translate whatever it was he was going to equip next. Finally, after a few more seconds, he turns on a heel and stomps out of our cell.

I turn back and let my eyes focus once again on the ceiling. It's close to lunchtime, and I'm starving, but I'll never let them know it.

That's a new thing for me. Something I never thought I'd be capable of. Fighting's not an option, and I shudder as I remember what trying it led to. Now, the fight has to come from within, but it has to stay within as well. Another real fight with them would only lead to the same cycle. Pain, loss, rehabilitation, reeducation, and on and on. Turns out I'm not going out in a blaze of glory like I'd sort of always imagined. There's not going to be some miraculous plan, some awesome plot hatched out of some brilliant place of my mind that's been hidden from me until this moment.

I'm not going to beat my way through these guards and commanders.

No, but I *am* going to take myself away from them, all without leaving.

Do I have it in me? Does it even matter?

I'm hungry, but that's pretty common now. It's been two days since I've last eaten. A bit of water keeps me strung along, and I know I'm only a few days away from feeling the first pangs of true, actual hunger. The clinical sort of starvation, not the American kind. They'll try to force-feed me — I've seen it happen — but I'm stronger than everyone here. I've already proven it to myself, but have I really ever proven how long that strength would last?

No, I have not. This is going to be my final salvo. My parting gift to my dear suitors.

I finally give in. I slide off the top bunk, moving slower these days on account of my weakening musculature and atrophied core, realizing that I'm going to have to ask The Poet to switch with me at some point. It's going to be too much to get out of the top bunk. Eventually, the bottom as well. I'll just sleep in a fetal position in the corner of our cell.

Now I understand why. Just the thought of pulling myself up, rung over rung, back up into my bed, agonizes me. I can feel the pain, the soreness in my shoulders and arms and fingers and even toes as they press down into the stone to launch my body just mere inches up to the first rung. I feel the soreness, knowing it won't abate for days, perhaps longer now.

The mere thought of it all makes me shudder. I hit the cold stone floor with my bare feet, not bothering to grab my single pair of socks. Shirtless, wearing only boxers and ripped shorts over them, I stumble out of our cell. I'm sure my haggard face terrifies the others across from me, but if it does, no one shouts about it. No one speaks at all, actually.

This is my solemn march, my statement. One I have been making for weeks, one I will continue to make for at least a few more weeks. My statement is simple, and it's final. It requires no spoken words, hardly any thought, but all the willpower and determination I have.

Hopefully I have enough left.

I walk down the narrow hallway, knowing my way around well enough to do it with my eyes closed.

At least I still have eyes. The same can't be said for Giorgio. He's missing an ear too, apparently our keepers' sign that by using our mouths too much, our other parts will be cleaved off as necessary.

Two eyes, an ear, and a few fingers was apparently the cost for Giorgio to finally keep his mouth shut.

I consider myself lucky in that regard. No one is afraid of my voice. No one thought I could be capable of Giorgio's whimsical prose, his stirring and inspiring oration. The commanders think there is no danger from me in organizing a rebellion like Giorgio did.

They were right. My rebellion is internal. My rebellion is silent, like my soul.

CHAPTER 2
RAOUL

SEPTEMBER 14, **2020 | local time 6:21 pm**
London, England

Raoul stepped forward and prepared to open the chopper's door. *This is insane*, he thought. *I'm not military. I've never even flown in a helicopter before, and now I'm jumping out of a perfectly good one?* As terrified as he was, he had to admit there was a pang of excitement lying just beneath the surface.

He had barely graduated college when he had joined the group known as The Faction, eager to lend his brilliant mind to solving the world's critical economic issues.

The Faction, however, didn't need economists. It needed soldiers. Apparently, it needed them to jump out of helicopters.

After a harrowing experience at *Campo de' Fiori Plaza* in Rome six months ago, Raoul had finally accepted the inevitable: he was going to have to work his way up through the chain of command just like everyone else who claimed loyalty to The Faction.

There were no shortcuts. He was not special, and his brilliant mind would just have to sit on the sidelines while he earned his way.

The Faction was a secretive, international organization that ruled in the cracks of society. Orders were handed down via whispers, the loose hierarchy completely unknown to most low-level members. No one even knew the names of their own superiors, much less those at the top of the organization.

For as conspiratorial and mysterious as the shadowy organization was, it represented one thing to Raoul above all else: *hope*.

The Faction's ways were certainly questionable, at least by societal standards. But there was no denying the effectiveness of those ways. Raoul had seen firsthand the corruption and disease in society, the money that exchanges hands between the silent power brokers who craftily stab each other in the back once the money was settled on the other end.

It was a cycle of voracious greed, a lust for control and power that had plagued humanity since the dawn of civilization.

The Faction was going to change all of that. Money could buy power, and intelligence could earn money.

But The Faction had a much simpler, much more straightforward plan: steal the power.

Other than playing the duplicitous games of money mongers and rich warlords, rather than accepting the rules of modern societal politics, The Faction existed for one purpose alone: to grab and hold whatever power it could, wherever it could.

That was the plan he had bought into — to help his organization control and gain power. A better world could only be earned through determination and struggle, by wresting control of the power from those who did not deserve to wield it.

He sensed someone looking at him, and he jumped back into action.

On his partner's signal, Raoul threw the helicopter's side door open. He was still strapped inside the chopper's cabin, the line safely taut on his belt, but the sudden windstorm inside the small craft nearly made him lose his stomach.

"Coming over the drop zone in twenty seconds," the pilot yelled

into his ear. The built-in noise-canceling headset Raoul had donned early in the flight had been switched with the in-ear wireless system he had donned about ten minutes ago. They were currently flying over restricted airspace above London, and the pilot and copilot expected interference at any moment from any direction, so it was critical that their communication lines not be severed.

And since Raoul and his partner were about to jump out of the aircraft, wireless radio transmission was the chosen way to keep that line intact.

Even still, Raoul knew the first tenets of this job well, and he would be able to perform his duties without needing to call back to the chopper. He waited for the copilot's countdown to begin at five seconds, already noticing the chopper's slowed descent over the downtown city skyline.

He saw the Thames in the distance, the black snake winding through the busy evening streets on its way to the North Sea. He tried to find their next checkpoint amidst the inky blackness but came up short. They were moving too quickly, their next destination still out of sight.

Raoul echoed the countdown alongside the copilot, one of the ways The Faction had coached them in order to steady their nerves. They had been trained well — as well as Raoul imagined nonmilitary personnel could be trained — but the real thing was nothing like the exercises.

He heard the countdown in his in-air headset. *"Four, three, two."*

As soon as the copilot said the final count, Raoul was out the open side of the chopper. He felt his legs and feet stiffen as they landed on the helicopter's landing gear rail, feeling the auto belay line cinching tight with the rope's new length.

Another countdown began, this one in his own mind. *Three, two, one.*

When his countdown finished, the earth below Raoul exploded in a ball of flame and light. The pressure wave was not quite strong enough to change the chopper's hover, but Raoul heard the deafening roar of the blast even over the rotor wash, through the noise-canceling monitors.

He pushed off the foot of the rail and allowed his body to freefall, directly into the explosion.

CHAPTER 3
PRISONER 348

LOCAL TIME **unknown**

Imrali Island, Turkey

The Poet's watching me as I sit across from him. He's looking into my eyes, trying to examine my soul or something. He must have been a shrink in a past life, I don't know.

Maybe trained to help people, maybe trained to hurt people.

I have no idea though, and I don't care. That life — the one where I care — is over, and it's becoming more and more difficult to even remember it.

I still remember the big things — the people, the settings, the general emotions. I know them like I read them in a book, like I skimmed over them and the feeling of knowing them once is what remains.

All the nuance has left me, all the details gone. It's probably the biggest irony that God thought fit to give me senses like taste and smell and sight and touch, and our keepers here have thought it prudent to allow me to keep them, while every hour that passes I feel the loss of another memory I thought was stuck in my brain forever.

I have forgotten touch — what it feels like. A caress on my lower back, or lips on my cheek, or the way the breeze blew as she walked past. I remember those things, but I don't remember the detail of it. If I try hard enough, I can almost feel those things again, but then the hunger screams for attention and all the memory is as good as gone.

I remember making chili, my mom's way — I can still rattle off the shopping list to acquire all the ingredients, I can still feel starting the range top in the kitchen. I can almost smell the slow-cooked deliciousness, but that deliciousness is really only a word.

That deliciousness is almost completely lost to me now. I don't remember what it tasted like. I know my lips sometimes crave it in the middle of the night, when the hunger wakes me up. But even when I try to push out everything else in my mind but that taste, I'm lost to it.

I've forgotten how white the snow was against the green of the pines outside my window. I've forgotten the feel of the sun, the depth of color it provides the world. The only sun I see is the mandated admittance per day during which we are allowed to circle the grounds as few or as many times as we are able. Some of us run laps. I tried that, but I still hate running. I run when I'm being chased, I used to joke.

No one's chasing me anymore.

The Poet's still staring at me.

"What," I croak. I don't even inflect the question, but it seems he gets the gist.

"You," he says. "Need to eat."

At the mention of eating, my stomach does a backflip and I nearly vomit the remaining bile I've got inside me. Not sure why it has that effect on me — eating doesn't scare me; in fact it should entice me. It should be the *only* thing I want.

I must have trained my mind better than I thought I could.

I'm frail, gaunt in my cheeks and neck, places I never thought weight could be lost. Even the webbing between my fingers seems to hang lifeless, like skin growing on my body just hasn't gotten the message yet.

Even my teeth hurt, as if they're adjusting to a generally smaller human than they were promised.

I shake my head at The Poet, my lips part, the cracking on them not even quelled by water anymore.

His bright eyes flick toward my chest, the rest of me hidden from view beneath the metal table. The metal chair is cold under me, and I wonder if those two feelings — cold and hot — will be the last to leave me. Will I be able to feel those two basic feelings until the very end? Or will I just slowly turn into a corpse, awaiting mummification?

"Must eat," The Poet repeats, his voice hardening. I know he's trying to order me, trying to frighten me into compliance. But he, like me, is weak. Whatever aggressiveness may have existed in him previously, whatever will to prevail used to live inside the stick figure of a body he's in, is long gone. And he's no dictator. He's not a confident person by nature. Hell, it seems like half the time we've spent in here together he's looked up to *me* for strength, even though he got here first.

I almost chuckle, expending valuable calories my body would prefer to hold on to.

He reaches out suddenly, grabs my wrist. Holds it hard, though I'm not sure I would be able to tell the difference between somebody putting it in a vice grip and a toddler grasping it. I look down at it, then back up at him.

He moves his mouth to speak again, but there's no noise.

I sense movement, sense the changing of the guard. It's dinnertime, so it makes sense they are changing shifts. This one will be on duty in here until tomorrow morning. Ironic, as none of us prisoners are even allowed to come into this room until breakfast tomorrow.

The guards roll around their pre-programmed route like magnetic chess pieces moved by an invisible force. I can barely see their feet moving as they slide around us and land in their destinations, then continue watching everything and nothing at the same time. Other prisoners ramble, droning on. Their voices are low, but some of them are talking fast.

Suddenly I understand why The Poet waited to speak again. The guard closest to us settles into his long watch, immediately checking out and becoming the lifeless soldier they all eventually turn into. The Poet looks at me again, his eyes different this time.

Finally, his mouth falls open. "Hold."

My face stays on his, unmoving.

"*Hold*," he repeats.

What the hell is that supposed to mean?

"Hope. Hold."

I shake my head, just the slightest of side-to-side motions.

He repeats the motion, contradicting me. "Hold. Hope. *Hold. Hope.*"

Hold hope? He's gone mad. That's it, my only friend — if I could even call him that — has been lost to me. Can't say I blame him — I did the same thing to him by choosing to starve myself to death.

Maybe he's telling me *he* held on, maybe *he* held hope while I lost it. Maybe this is his way of forgiving me, of understanding me.

The guards move again. I notice there are more of them than usual. They are preparing for something, but what?

I looked back at The Poet. His bright, lively eyes haven't shifted.

Or maybe this is his way of condemning me.

CHAPTER 4
FREDDIE

SEPTEMBER 14, **2020 | local time 1:15 pm**
Washington, D.C.

"Son, I know we haven't always seen eye to eye..."

The man paced; hands clasped behind his back as if he were auditioning for a role in an old military drama. He fit the bill far more than any actor could — he was one of the highest-ranking military officers in the United States, after all. General Nathaniel Rollins looked up at his nephew as he spoke.

Freddie knew he was one of the few men his uncle had to crane his neck upward to see. His uncle was not a short man, and it seemed the apple had not fallen far from the tree.

"Seems like you're about to say something like, 'I miss you, son.'"

The general chuckled, and Freddie smiled. "Maybe I do miss you."

"Well, I'm no longer serving."

"Doesn't change the fact that now and then, a man wants to see his nephew. Is that so hard to believe?"

"You want the truth, sir?"

Freddie's uncle stared him down — or up, technically — for a moment, then arched his lips in a slight smile. It wasn't much, but it was far more than most men serving under him had ever seen.

Freddie couldn't help himself. He laughed out loud. "Never thought you to be the sentimental type, sir."

"Tell anyone outside this room and I will discharge you all over again."

"Humor, as well? Damn, you're almost unrecognizable."

The general extended a hand and offered Freddie a seat in the older man's well-appointed office. The general was a soldier, but Freddie knew he had grown accustomed to the class and pomp of political life in modern-day Washington, D.C. He would never admit to it, but Freddie suspected he actually enjoyed this work. Everyone knew the man could have retired a decade ago, but no one dared ask him why he had chosen to stay.

Freddie sat down, rapping his knuckles on the wooden arms of the upholstered chair. It was stiff, as if no one had ever sat in it before. Knowing his uncle, perhaps no one had. "You know, when I said I was in the area and would just swing by, I was just being nice."

General Rollins smiled again. "I know that's not true. You were on your way out to Alaska, by way of Chicago. D.C.'s a bit out of the way, so I know you got my email. Either way, I appreciate your willingness to come see me. These days, I can barely get out of the office for lunch, let alone meetings, even if they *are* with my own family."

Freddie waited, wishing he would elaborate a bit more. His mother had passed away about twelve years ago from breast cancer, and he knew her brother had never been quite the same since then. This new sentimental streak might even be a sign of his recognition of mortality. Freddie shook the thought away. *I'm not even sure time itself can kill this guy.*

"Anyway, I know you're out to see your group. Seem like good people. I'm terribly sorry for what happened."

Freddie nodded his head and sighed in acknowledgment. He pulled his eyes back up, fixed them on his uncle, and waited for the man to get to the point. As always, there was a reason for the general's email. There was an ulterior motive. Sure, he might want to see him, but Freddie knew there was *something* else on his mind.

Finally, General Rollins spoke, his voice uncharacteristically low. "I have information. About where he might be."

Freddie could not hide his shock. He let his mouth fall down, no longer caring about the silent song and dance of proper military etiquette. "The hell? Where? How —"

His uncle held up a hand. He shook his head. "You know I've already overstepped my bounds. Handing this stuff over to a civilian can land me in the slammer, son."

Freddie gritted his teeth. "I'm not a civilian. And I have a feeling you wouldn't bring me all the way out here just to scold me, so I feel bad for you."

"Affirmative," the man said. "I merely need to remind you, since it's been a while since you were active duty."

"Eleven months and three weeks."

His uncle arched an eyebrow, no doubt questioning whether Freddie was missing active service.

As it turned out, Freddie was not, but he *did* miss the camaraderie, the rhythm of it all. He enjoyed being a part of a team, and while the CSO was a capable group of men and women, they operated with a particular disdain for military procedure. Almost by definition, they were decidedly *not* military.

He was still getting used to that part, as much as he enjoyed their company.

Freddie's eyes glanced once more around the room, then he spoke. "You said you have information. What sort?"

"The sort that you're going to need."

"Need for what?"

The general sighed, then smiled. "You can't make me spell it out for you," he said. "Got to leave me with just a taste of the old days."

"You were never a spy."

19

His smile grew. "I never *told* you I was a spy."

Freddie rolled his eyes. "Right, and I'm the Queen's Crown Jewels. Anyway, you got information that I'll need in order to — I'm assuming — find him?"

The brief respite of humor in the room vanished. His uncle nodded. "And I do hope you find him, son."

CHAPTER 5
RAOUL

London, England

Raoul felt the wind of the rotors pushing down even as the explosive debris and remnants pushed upward, meeting in the middle in a sort of strange, antigravity bubble. Pieces of glass, metal, and wood hit his body, but his bodysuit of light armor prevented any injury.

The light from the explosion dissipated and Raoul saw his target — a gaping hole in the ceiling of the British Museum, floor two, section 61. The grotesque maw had been blasted open by the impact grenade his partner had dropped out the chopper's open door as soon as they had hovered over the museum.

This brings new meaning to the term 'smash and grab,' Raoul thought.

His freefall was aborted suddenly by the grip of the belay line, which tightened and shifted the fall to an easy descent. There was enough line to make a drop twice this far, but The Faction had not altered the chopper's military specifications upon its acquisition.

More was certainly better than not enough.

He flew feet-first through the open hole in the museum's ceiling alongside his partner, mirroring his motions. They fell together through the smoke as the dust and debris itself settled, once again trapped by gravity's tug, and five seconds later he felt his feet on the floor.

Raoul unclasped the carabiner and let the line hang loose as the chopper hovered far overhead. He saw their new target about ten feet away, barely perched on the perimeter of the hole they had blown through the museum's top.

It wasn't exactly where they'd hoped it would be, but it was enough to work with. He jogged over with his partner, who carried two extra lines clipped to his belt. When they reached the object, his partner unclasped the two extra straps and handed one to Raoul. Together they worked silently, careful to place the lines underneath the object's vaulted base, threading the carabiners and straps beneath the feet of the heavy stone box.

Raoul ran back to the center atrium where the two personnel lines were still hanging, and he grabbed both of them and tugged, signaling to the copilot to release some slack for them. A second later, more line fell from the heavens and Raoul ran back over to his partner and their target. The two men repeated their motions, and the four vinyl straps were soon threaded together in a four-fingered hand, strong enough to pull this heavy object upward. Each strap looped around the object's base and connected at a point overhead.

"Phase two," his partner said calmly. He had never worked with this older man, known only to him as Stinson, but he guessed the man was ex-military. They had given him more responsibility than they had Raoul, for one. Stinson had also seemed completely at ease jumping out of a helicopter and strapping up a 1500-pound artifact to the bottom of it.

Raoul was about to jump into the open top of the stone box — the next phase of this mission, — when he heard commotion from somewhere inside the museum.

"Looks like we made too much noise," Stinson said.

Raoul forced a smile, once again surprised at the man's ability to make light of any situation. He wished he could understand how to manifest that. He certainly hadn't felt the man's ease when he had been marching through the plaza with a flamethrower six months ago.

He didn't feel at ease now.

He wanted to duck, to hide within the protection and confines of the open stone box, but he knew that was not his mission.

If I am to die today, so be it. As long as The Faction gets its price. As long as it continues its struggle against oppression, its victory march toward ultimate power.

He locked eyes with Stinson.

"You're unarmed, I'm not," Stinson said. "Stay inside, but make sure the tension doesn't go sideways."

There wasn't much Raoul could do other than shift his weight accordingly as the chopper pulled against the ancient object's mass. And since it was a bit off from the direct center of the atrium, he knew that it was going to first slide sideways along the floor, simultaneously pulling the chopper to the side. Too much at once, too fast, and the vinyl straps would be yanked against the sharp reinforcement of the ceiling that had been twisted and bent in the explosion.

One wrong move and the entire thing could snap, allowing it to tumble back down and their plan to fail.

Raoul nodded, eyes wide, as Stinson ducked and ran across the room, immediately out of sight in the shadows.

He heard shouts and footsteps pounding on the hard floors of the museum, saw two of the facility's night crew coming into the wide atrium.

"What the —"

The first security guard's words were cut off as Stinson broke cover, taking him down without another sound. The second guard whirled around to see what had become of his counterpart, but

Stinson had already lifted his pistol and fired two shots into the man's chest before he could even pull his own weapon.

As he fell, Raoul saw that it wasn't a weapon the man had been trying to pull out — it was a radio.

He once again remembered his mission. Once again remembered why he had joined The Faction. *It is shameful how safe and secure these people have all come to feel*, he thought. *Even the sound of an explosion was not enough to alert these men that something was wrong.*

People were complacent, Raoul knew. Trained to seek homeostasis. Trained to not care about the world around them.

These two men had paid the ultimate price for that complacency, and there would be more.

Raoul's job was to make sure those payments were all worthwhile.

The chopper pulled abruptly, a gust of wind or burst of warm air carrying it sideways. The stone feet of the object strapped beneath it ground beneath his feet as Raoul rode inside the box like sitting in a bathtub. They moved a foot forward, then six inches up, then another couple of feet before the whole thing came crashing to the floor.

He didn't need to see it to know that was going to leave a mark.

Raoul felt the lurching in his stomach once again, but he had no time to react to it. Stinson raced toward him, tucking the pistol behind his back once more and jumping feetfirst into the box.

Even as he landed, barely out of breath, he spoke calmly, as if simply talking on the phone while he strolled to the park. "Let's move. Up and out," he said.

The helicopter didn't need more invitation than that — Raoul suddenly felt the ground disappear as the box hung freely in the air as it listed through the new hole in the museum's ceiling.

Raoul had not considered what these missions for The Faction might be, but if he were honest, he never would have suspected it would be this.

He never would have thought he'd be balancing in an ancient sarcophagus through an exploded hole in the ceiling, hanging by a thread to the bottom of a helicopter.

He swallowed, then saw Stinson looking at him. He forced a smile.

"Phase two complete," he shouted. "Phase three to begin shortly."

CHAPTER 6
JOHNSON

SEPTEMBER 14, 2020 | local time 6:26 pm
London, England

Officer Blake Johnson tracked the chopper from his squad car. He had been thirty minutes away from the end of his last shift before an extended vacation when the radio in his squad car crackled to life. He had let out a deep sigh from inside the cruiser, hearing the dispatcher dropping the codes for *explosion* and *break-in*. He had rolled his eyes and shaken his head then.

Please don't be anywhere near me, he had thought. *Please don't make me work late.*

And then the dispatcher had delivered the worst news of his night: *"...location near the British Museum, standby for street address."*

At that point, he had smacked the steering wheel and thrust the car into gear, flying through the roundabout to head back toward the museum, where he had been only moments earlier. He knew he was the closest patrol officer on duty, and the chief would not find it amusing if he had simply ignored it and claimed he hadn't heard the dispatch.

He enjoyed the job, but he also enjoyed his well-earned time off.

The thought of spending the long weekend at the lake, casting a line out to the water with his niece and nephew, quickly began to fade as he felt the adrenaline starting to raise questions in his mind.

He had gotten back to the museum only half a minute after the dispatcher's call, and even from the street level he could see smoke rising from the second-floor of the building.

Besides onlookers and bystanders who happened to be out around this area of town this evening, there was no commotion or noise coming from the museum. He decided to take it easy, to wait for backup before jumping into the fray. He drove a quick loop around the front and eastern side of the museum, then parked and brought the radio up to his mouth. "Johnson here. Checking in — nothing noteworthy out front, but I do see smoke rising from one of the back buildings. Should I investigate?"

The answer came immediately. *"Negative, Officer Johnson. Stay put and wait for backup; we've got eyes in the sky inbound from your six."*

He heard helicopter rotor wash from somewhere in the distance as the dispatcher finished the command, and he turned and looked lazily out the side window to see it rising over the horizon.

The rotor wash sound suddenly began phasing with a similar-sounding noise from the opposite direction, this one even louder. He flicked his eyes to the right and they widened as he saw another helicopter — this one obviously military, bigger, faster, and meaner-looking than the smaller police chopper. It pushed away from the top of the building, moving slower than he knew it was capable of. He frowned and pulled the radio back up to his lips. "I've got a bit of an update here... uh, not sure what's happening. I see a chopper — looks military, not sure the make or model. But, uh, it's moving away from the museum. Slowly."

He watched as the helicopter rose higher and higher into the night sky over London, its location only revealed to him by the lights from the nearby buildings.

But then he saw something else. The chopper wasn't alone — something moved with it. Something about twenty or thirty feet *beneath* the chopper's belly. It floated in the air for a moment as the chopper started to change direction, and when the moonlight caught it just right he could see bright orange vinyl straps connecting it to the chopper.

"What the *bloody* hell..."

He made the snap decision to follow the chopper — this thing was clearly part of the reason for the explosion at the museum, and he wasn't sure if their own police helicopter would be able to spot this one. It was flying with no lights, and Johnson knew that if it got out over the quieter suburbs or near the channel, it would disappear completely.

He threw the car into reverse and backed up quickly, only realizing too late that he had nearly caused two oncoming cars to collide with him. He waved a quick apology but threw the stick back once again and sped up. He tried to line up the chopper's vector, knowing the streets of this district as well as anyone. As long as it continued in this direction, he could follow the street to the bridge where it would intersect with the Thames.

As long as there was light enough traffic this evening, Johnson knew it would not be an issue to stay on the chopper's tail, especially at the slow speed it was currently flying.

But even as he considered this and developed the plan, the chopper began speeding up. He guessed that the pilot only needed to steady that massive object hanging beneath it as it lifted it from the museum, then it could afford to increase its speed and let the object trail diagonally behind it a bit. No sudden movements, and it would eventually be able to fly at nearly top speed.

At that point, he would be toast. There was no way he would be able to catch up to the flying machine with a terrestrial vehicle, no matter how much weight it was carrying. And especially not being able to travel in a straight line like the helicopter.

He called in the update to the dispatcher, hoping the man on the other end would have already passed him through to their police helo. In situations like this, repeating instructions so multiple parties could be engaged only led to delays and setbacks, and eventually failed missions.

The dispatcher on duty confirmed his travel plans and even offered him a route allotment, meaning that any other officers currently on duty would work to keep traffic out of his way, and if the chase got to be more intense, he had Transport for London on call as well.

The pilot of the helicopter he was chasing was apparently not taking any risks. The chopper had sped up little after leaving the museum, and Johnson was surprised to see how easily he was able to keep it in sight, using the long stretches of straight highway between it and his patrol car to stay on its tail. About three blocks north of the museum, it slid to the right and made a line for the river.

"Shit," Johnson mumbled as he examined the options laid out before him. The bridge he had plans to cross, if it came to that, was still half a mile away, and he wasn't sure there was a better option closer to him.

If it gets across the river... he knew there was no chance to pick up the helicopter's location if he couldn't get across the river with it.

He pulled the cruiser to the right, ignoring safe driving procedure. His head and body flew toward the center console, but he recovered and swerved the car over a side street and into a narrow alley that paralleled the Thames. He lost the chopper between the taller buildings while in the alley, but fifteen seconds later he was out the other side and once again caught its black silhouette, the smaller rectangular shape hanging beneath it. It had gained a bit on him, and he hoped he could make it up with a left turn to follow the new street bordering the river.

The helicopter veered left as the dispatcher crackled through the radio again, informing Johnson that there were three patrol units on standby on the other side of the Thames, awaiting instruction.

He floored the accelerator, weaving around cars as he barked commands into the radio in response, telling them where the chopper currently was and its direction.

It now appeared to him that the helicopter would be following the Thames River itself, potentially all the way to the sea. They had to have a plan to apprehend it before then. An aircraft like that could easily make it through the North Sea and across the channel into France, or even head northward up to Scotland — or, of course, one of the many uninhabited islands there. At this hour, their movements would be invisible to anyone on the shore, and he had a feeling the chopper was equipped with some sort of stealth technology that would easily foil their plans to track it.

He raced along the Thames, his car gaining speed as he barreled through intersections, cars honking their disapproval to his right. Either he was getting very lucky, or Transport for London had already marked his route for green lights. The streets were quiet, thankfully, so he didn't have to worry about any pedestrians with their noses in their phones getting in his way.

Johnson saw the chopper slow a bit over one of the wider sections of the river in this area. Suddenly, the object hanging beneath it snapped off. The chopper shifted in the air a bit before gaining some more altitude. He watched the object as it fell straight down, the heavy box crashing against the still waters of the inky river. He blinked and it was gone, nothing but a cascading ripple of concentric circles falling out in all directions to mark its impact.

"Dispatch," he said into the radio, "looks like it just cut its load. It snapped loose over the Thames. I will send my current GPS coordinates in case you don't have them, and I'm noting that the impact site is about a hundred yards to the south and about fifty east from my location."

The affirmative response came immediately. He waited, unsure of whether they wanted Johnson to continue tracking the chopper or to focus on the object it had dropped. Whatever it was now sinking to the bottom of the river, it had been of high enough value to someone who had enough resources to commandeer a military helicopter to retrieve it.

And whatever it was, Johnson had a feeling the museum would be wanting it back.

CHAPTER 7
FREDDIE

SEPTEMBER 14, 2020 | local time 1:26 pm
Washington, D.C.

"What is it? What did you find?"

Freddie could hardly contain his excitement. He had almost lost hope, and now a spark of it had suddenly reignited. He had spent the last six months in a state of funk, a state of pessimism and worry. He was unsure how to react to his uncle's news — he didn't want to get overly excited, to get his hopes up — but then again, they had nothing else.

There had been nothing even remotely useful revealed to them in months. All their leads had long since dried up.

General Rollins cleared his throat as he walked behind his desk once more. "Got most of the details in a report. You know how things go. As of this morning at 0837, these files no longer exist on any hard drive, as per the official record. I trust you understand what that means."

His uncle slid a manila envelope over the great oak desk toward Freddie.

Freddie swallowed as he sat. *So this is it, then. This is what optimism feels like.*

He grabbed the envelope and pulled it toward him, lifting the cover before the folder had even hit his lap. He previewed the first document inside, a simple printout of a map with an area on it circled in red marker. It appeared to depict a location just off the coast of Turkey. Aside from a small peninsula of protruding land on the map's right edge with a city labeled *Armutlu*, the rest of the map showed nothing but blue — ocean, labeled *Sea of Marmara*. A small key in the bottom left corner of the page showed that the circled area covered about five square miles of ocean.

He frowned but slid the paper over to the left side of the folder as he saw the second item behind it. It was an identical map on another sheet of computer paper, save for one small feature.

"Is that —"

"An island," his uncle said, finishing the sentence. "Just off the coast, about six miles from the north shore of the Turkish mainland."

But he shook his head. "What is this map from? I thought —"

"The first map is from a public maps website. It doesn't matter which one — they're all the same. They all show the same thing here — empty ocean. They all depict the same stretch of water in the Sea of Marmara, devoid of any islands or landmasses whatsoever besides the few that dot the area to the west."

Freddie understood now where his uncle was going with this.

"The second map, on the other hand, was taken from our own defense satellites, which is why I am considering this highly sensitive information. There is currently a blacked-out stretch over this portion of the globe, so direct imaging by public satellite and most military paraphernalia is expressly forbidden, according to more than one worldwide treaty."

"But this is the United States of America."

General Rollins smiled for the third time. "*But* this is the United States of America, exactly. And I happen to be pretty close to the top of the food chain in this grand old country, son."

"And... you think he's here?"

His uncle nodded. "Keep reading."

He pulled out the third page, titled *Brief and Overview*, and when Freddie had reached the bottom of the first paragraph, he felt his hands shaking. "This is... this is a hell of a favor. I don't think I can —"

"I'm going to stop you right there," the general's booming voice began. "If you are about to say you don't think you can ever repay me, don't worry — you can't. But I don't need you to, and I don't *want* you to. This is *highly classified* information, but I don't know a better man whose hands I could put it in. You just promise me you will not let this intel go to waste, and — possibly more importantly — promise me that *no one* ever knows where you got it from, and I'll die a happy man."

Freddie wanted to hug him. Hell, he wanted to kiss him on the cheek. As long as he could remember, he had never felt any emotion toward his uncle — or his own father, for that matter — besides anger, confusion, and frustration. Whatever familial love had existed when Freddie was a boy had quickly morphed into something of an ideal rather than an overt feeling, likely around the time Freddie was old enough to even remember that sort of thing. He vaguely recalled a few times his father had given him a quick hug or slap on the back for a job well done, but for the vast majority of his life his father had ignored him completely until the day he died. Besides that, General Rollins — when he was even around — treated Freddie like the future soldier he would become.

As an adult now, Freddie understood their relationship a bit more, though he would still consider it strained. But his uncle seemed to be making strides, or at least trying to.

And this was no small thing. He nodded down at the folder in his lap, still in disbelief. *This could be a breakthrough.*

"You have my word," Freddie said. "General — again: *thank you*." He continued reading through the rest of the brief. It was a simple typed document, likely written by his uncle earlier that day, explaining the known characteristics of the area in question.

His head shot back up when he reached the bottom of the last paragraph. It didn't make sense. "Wait a minute," he said. "I don't... I don't understand. I thought this was going to be — well, something different."

"What *did* you think it was going to be?" His uncle asked.

"I don't know," Freddie stammered. "I figured there would be a mention of some company or something. Like some evil billionaire who bought the island so he could keep it out of the public eye. I mean, how else do you completely erase its existence — that would cost a ton of money."

"Don't rule that out just yet," General Rollins said. "But yeah, this does seem strange. Still, I think it's your best bet."

Freddie knew that was true, and he knew it didn't matter *what* was on this tiny island off the coast of Turkey.

He was going to pay it a visit.

CHAPTER 8
STINSON

London, England

The stone sarcophagus sank quickly, surprising even Stinson. He lunged down in the inky water, toggling on his wrist-mounted flashlight.

He was still wearing the clothing he had donned before the mission, leaving his arms exposed to the river water as debris and fish swam past. It was chilling, both physically and mentally — every dive brought with it new, unforeseeable outcomes. Every dive offered a chance at success, and plenty of chances of failure. But none of these chances bothered Stinson. He was a well-trained diver, even making it through the Norwegian equivalent of the US Navy SEALs BUD/S training. Being in the water was second nature to him.

He could not say the same for his assigned partner on this mission. Raoul was a good kid, he supposed, but he was exactly that — a kid. The guy was barely out of college, and the only thing they had talked about after their briefing was his desire to do something with his 'hard-earned economics degree.'

Stinson did not think highly of academic types. To them, their self-assigned brilliance and worldly wisdom had been handed to them on a silver platter, and that silver platter had *actually* been 'hard-earned' by folks like Stinson. When a society had enough spare time to begin investing in their own personal mental progress, it meant they had become soft. They had lost sight of the sweat, blood, and lives paid to secure that lethargy.

And yet he couldn't fault Raoul — the kid might be young and dumb, but he was at least in the right place. The Faction was going to change the world, top to bottom, and he had enough smarts in him to join forces with them, academic brainiac or not.

This was the first mission they had served on together, and, as all Faction missions had proven, his organization had kept the details under wraps until the last possible second. He had met Raoul about an hour prior, just before entering the helicopter that would take them to the British Museum. There was no training together, no long planning sessions, no brainstorming backup options — that had all been done days and weeks ago, wherever The Faction did those sorts of things.

Stinson's and Raoul's job was to *act*, not to *think*. They were proving their loyalty and value to the organization they had claimed to be committed to, and this was just one of many missions Stinson had taken part in. He had served for a decade with the Forsvarets Spesialkommando, then had opted to turn his training and experience into a more lucrative career.

He felt tapping on his arm. The kid was swimming next to him, following his lead, as he had been instructed. He wanted to turn and smack him, to force Raoul to just pay attention and follow suit, but it seemed the kid was frantic about something.

What?

He pushed forward, toward the direction Raoul was pointing in.

Then he saw it.

Tied to an anchor that had been discarded, now lying somewhere in the darkness of the deeper waters of the Thames, was a line. The rope ascended upward to about ten feet beneath Stinson's belly, about five feet ahead.

He smiled underwater, then pushed ahead once again. He knew Raoul would be coming up on the end of his air, fighting against the pressures of the increasing depths, and the desire to give in and float upward.

But their safety lie in deeper waters, not the surface.

He kicked hard, letting his lithe, muscular frame do what it did best, and he reached the bag tied to the line in another ten seconds. He pulled on the drawstring holding the contents inside, pushing the floats on the outside of the bag around to the back to give him access to the opening.

From within the bag spilled out four black canisters — each containing 3.6 cubic feet of air, each fitted with a small pressure gauge.

Stinson's smile grew wider. He had not been sure what to expect for this part of the mission. The Faction was notoriously good at playing its proverbial cards close to its chest, and from his previous missions — one in Cozumel, Mexico, that was similar in some ways to this one — he knew only to expect the unexpected.

Stinson could not be sure The Faction intended to strand him and Raoul out here. Any mission for them could be the last. He had known members who had made a mistake during one engagement, thought they had been forgiven later, and then simply vanished during the next outing. In a way, The Faction's handling of members who did not make the cut was a crude but effective — and useful — tool. Rather than go through rigamarole of meetings, appointments, debriefings, and dismissals, The Faction simply designed another mission that would accomplish another goal of theirs, then sent the offending member on it without a plan to retrieve them when completed.

He had hoped that was not going to be the outcome of this mission. When he had heard that they were to follow the cut line holding the sarcophagus into the Thames river without breathing or swimming gear, he wondered. Surely at that point the British authorities would have eyes on them and would simply arrest them — or worse — if their heads breached the surface.

But now, he could see that was not going to be the case. He pulled one of the canisters out and secured the mouthpiece over his mouth. He handed a second canister to Raoul, who copied his motions. He left the two remaining canisters inside the bag, knowing that it meant they were going to need them later, and pulled the bag from the anchored line holding it.

Then he frowned. *What next?* he wondered.

There had been no further instructions. Usually these Faction missions were dead-simple, or at least straightforward enough that untrained newcomers like Raoul could even complete them. For this mission, however, their instructions had ended with 'follow the sarcophagus into the Thames.'

And so he waited.

Raoul floated next to him, the younger man obviously more uncomfortable than anyone had a right to be, and Stinson shook his head and nearly laughed, watching him struggle with the canister in his mouth.

How long are we supposed to wait? he wondered.

As it turned out, not long.

He heard a faint *zing* reaching his ears, the high-pitched whine growing in volume as it neared. Raoul's eyes widened, but Stinson calmly turned and pointed his arm-light at the oncoming sound.

The noise's cause came into view. Three more divers, each wearing full scuba gear, each dragging behind them something that almost made Stinson wet his already very wet pants.

The F5S SEABOBs puttered along behind the divers, four in total. They had somehow wired them together to create a series of underwater propulsion systems that could be controlled from any of the four devices.

Stinson had seen propulsion systems like these — he had trained on their older, smaller predecessors in the FSK. But he had never had the opportunity — or the cash — to try out the sleekest, most powerful versions on the planet.

Each device could pull a full-grown human male along at a speed of over nine miles per hour underwater, and the gyro-enabled computing system would react to slight changes in bodyweight for pinpoint-accurate steering.

And it seemed they were heading to deeper waters.

Stinson followed them down another fifteen feet, where the divers flicked on powerful headlamps and lit up the riverbed. He saw artifacts of all ages and sizes, but one new item in particular caught his eye.

The sarcophagus.

The divers immediately got to work threading a new set of vinyl straps around the cinched straps Stinson and Raoul had installed up at the museum, and within minutes they were ready. They tested the torque and tension of the SEABOBs and the straps, made a few adjustments, and then one of the men turned and gave Stinson a thumbs-up, pointing with his other hand.

Stinson got the message, and he hustled to reach the straps. Raoul, a far slower swimmer, had only just reached the riverbed, but he too grabbed hold of one of the vinyl straps rising from the sarcophagus' corners.

The four SEABOBs pulled upward in unison, guided along by the three pilots, and together they lifted the sarcophagus and the two men up and away from the gritty river floor.

Once again, Stinson smiled. He was not going to die here. Not today.

And whatever The Faction wanted with this sarcophagus; it was more than to simply dispose of it in a river.

ACT II

"My doom has come upon me; let me not then die ingloriously and without a struggle, but let me first do some great thing that shall be told among men hereafter."

— Homer, *The Iliad*

CHAPTER 9
PRISONER 348

Imrali Island, Turkey

I'm about done now, I suppose.

It's been a good run, far better than I would've expected. Far better than I could've hoped.

Hope. Hold hope.

And there it is again. The Poet's damned incantation. Spoken like a crazed lunatic while we were at dinner so many days ago.

Days? Or hours? I don't even know anymore; all I know is that I'm about used up. My stomach has begun to do that thing stomachs do when they *truly* begin to starve, that weird twisting and groaning and then expanding, as if trying to talk itself into not being completely empty. What's funny to me is how little it hurts.

The physical pain, of course, is excruciating, but I can't really *feel* it. I just know it's bad. Almost unbelievably bad. But, then again, everything about my situation is unbelievable. The fact that I can even recognize that pain still exists within my body and is possible within my psyche is another one of God's twisted ironies, I suppose. Everything else has been lost to me — my own ability to think clearly, my memories of sights and feelings and smells and tastes all gone.

But I'm left with pain, or at least the acknowledgement of it.

This is my fate. They've got me strapped down again, another metal table. In some weird echo chamber deep in my brain, I jokingly wonder if there is some sort of prison surplus store these guys all purchased their shit from. Metal tables, metal chairs, all shiny and cold and clinical. *Prison Surplus Superstore,* they might call it.

Maybe these guards are from there, as well. All the same, all with cold eyes and dead faces. Probably mirroring my own.

The straps are far tighter and far stronger than necessary, and I wonder if the plan here is to simply keep tightening them until my wrists are severed and my hands just flop off the table like the dumb, useless appendages they are. Ditto with my feet. If they wanted to kill me, they could have done it a thousand times over by now. If they wanted to torture me, they could have come up with a million creative methods to do just that.

Maybe they have — tortured me, that is. I can't really remember the details of my imprisonment, aside from The Poet and the starving.

But no, I've chosen this fate myself. I've been starving myself for months now, — The Poet keeps me informed of how long each of my sprees goes on — and, inevitably at some point, one of the robot guards notices and calls to one of the masters. Then they shove me along into another corridor they don't allow anyone else to walk through, strap me down, pull my jaw open and force-feed me with the tube. It does nothing to sate the hunger, but I suppose it does sate their desire to keep me alive longer.

I suppose it makes them feel better about themselves.

I actually manage to chuckle out loud. I didn't think I was capable of such a thing anymore, didn't think it was even possible for the air to squeeze up my lungs to vibrate my vocal cords, my mouth to provide a proper reverberation chamber, and for actual human speech to come tumbling from my chapped, dry husks of lips, but there it is. A real chuckle.

I'm not even sure why I'm laughing. Perhaps I find something funny, but I can't remember.

I sneer then at the guards. My final hope is that I'll get to see them on the other side, see them blubbering and sputtering through their excuses and apologies outside the pearly gates.

It gives me a slight bit of respite to think that, except when I realize I'm not quite sure which side of the pearly gates I'll be on myself. Will I be sputtering alongside them? Enemies on earth, allies above? Will we be arguing with one another, contradicting each other as we try to one-up the other's sins?

I don't care anymore. *Take it from me,* I try to say. *Take it from me.*

No more words. No more voice.

A chuckle — that was the last of his earthly words, they'll say. *He had no final words, nothing wise or impactful to leave us with. Just a chuckle at some unknown joke only he could hear.*

I see the tube, see the scientist or doctor or whatever the hell he calls himself walking it over to me, a ritual we are both intimately familiar with now. It will work, of course. They will shove it inside me and pump me full of goo that will keep me alive for another month, another two, another three. I will continue to starve myself, continue to take myself out of their control, continue to withhold whatever it is they want to extract from me. To keep from them, forever and ever, the locations, the names, the details, the weaknesses and strengths, the truths.

They want *them,* much like they got *me.* They want to know where *they* are, they want to know how they might be able to find *them,* to trick them as they tricked me, they want to be able to use them — if not to achieve their final purpose, to bring them one step closer.

Whatever that may be.

But they won't get them. My loved ones, my friends, the last bastions of my memories.

They won't get them at all. They are *mine*, and there's nothing short of a lobotomy that could suck them from my psyche.

The tube goes into my mouth, and I close my eyes. I feel it struggling against my windpipe, sense my body gagging and fighting against it, unable to even raise my chest to reposition it to allow an easier insertion.

You can't have it, I think. My lips move, but no sounds come out. *You can't have it.*

The man looks down at me, examining my eyes as I examine his. I wonder if he knows me. I wonder if he knows who I *was*, what my life *used* to be.

I wonder if he cares.

He just wants what I have inside. He just wants to do his job. I guess I can't fault him for that.

Oh wait. Yes, I can.

I chuckle once more as the blackness fades over my eyes.

CHAPTER 10
GRAHAM

SEPTEMBER 15, **2020 | local time 5:46 pm**
Siwa Oasis, Egypt

The aging professor dabbed at his forehead with a bandana, appreciating how much cooler it was in here compared to the baking sun outside. In this brief respite from the heat, Dr. Graham Lindgren took a few deep breaths. He could almost taste the dry air inside; he could almost feel his own presence disturbing the calm sanctity of this hidden place.

So many lost souls had built the walls and ceiling around him, so many artisans and craftsmen who would go nameless, forgotten for centuries. He took in the space reverently, allowing all his senses to inform him of where he stood. He saw the stone walls, hewn from giant blocks and dragged countless miles over desert to this ancient oasis. The entire site had been dug out from the ground, the temple and small city built up around it, over his head. This place had gone unnoticed for over a thousand years, no one considering what secrets might lie *beneath* the famed and fabled home of the oracle.

Covering the opposite wall from where he stood were inscriptions, many of them faded and washed away as water from above found a route down into the ground, eventually running over the original hieroglyphics here. There was no record of what used to be there, only what remained on the walls in front of him. No books or journals to compare notes with — this was pure archeology at its finest, and it was his life's work. With only a few weeks down here, he knew he and his students would be able to piece together exactly why this place had been built, and for whom. With luck, he could even piece together *when* it had been built, and who had done the building.

He had a hunch, and his hunches were often more correct than not, but without a body of evidence — or an *actual* body — it would be difficult to get his peers on board with their findings.

Graham walked forward, toward the wall. His students had been down here earlier, both carefully moving the stones from the tunnel they had excavated and offering assistance with the archeological findings. Tracings that had been completed earlier today were already en route to his university laboratory back in Sweden, where they would be photographed and stored, and his teaching assistants and peers would hopefully make some headway on having them deciphered.

But he needed no laboratory support to know exactly where he was standing. He needed no translations of the rubbings from the hieroglyphs to know what he would find in the next room over. This tunnel would lead to a tomb, or a tomb's antechamber, and while they needed far more evidence to know exactly *whose* gravesite they were standing near, Dr. Lindgren had a few hunches about that as well.

If everything went to plan — and support from both the Greek and Egyptian governments came in time — he would be able to finish his work here and declare to the world, once and for all, that he had finally found it.

It was a tall order getting more than one competing govern-ment's cooperation in a find such as this, but Graham hoped that the sheer size of the discovery — if he were indeed correct — would persuade them.

A secret like this cannot go unnoticed or ignored, he had told his graduate assistant. *They* must *allow us to reveal our findings here.*

The temple at Siwa had long been a favorite site for archeologists working to protect, uncover, and document ancient Egyptian history, and more recently had been viewed as a popular historical site for the Greeks, as well.

And that was due to the fact that many — including Dr. Lindgren himself — believed that one of the most famous Greeks of all time had been interred here. While difficult to prove under normal circumstances, Lindgren had been able to use his international clout in the archaeological community to earn a temporary investigation permit. It expired in a month, and he was, under no circumstances, allowed to use the permit to excavate any of the known buildings at the Siwa temple complex.

But Graham knew his way around governmental restrictions, and he had a knack for asking for forgiveness rather than permission, and he often got it.

Besides, he wasn't *technically* excavating one of the known buildings at Siwa.

That was because no one had known there was a building *beneath* the temple complex at Siwa.

He was standing in the tunnel whose entrance they had found under a pile of rocks, and after days of backbreaking labor, they had cleared it enough to find that the tunnel did, in fact, seem to lead to another complex — this one underneath the known existing buildings.

That alone was exciting for someone like Graham, who had spent a lifetime pursuing places just like this.

But the remains he knew had been interred here had been lost for centuries, and the world wanted badly to know where they were. He intended to find them, no matter the cost or wrist-slapping by the

Greeks or Egyptians. A discovery like this *would* change the world — and not just the stuffy archaeological and academic communities, either.

His team of students and researchers had likened a discovery such as this to one of finding King Tut's tomb — it was important enough to receive critical acclaim in mainstream news, not just in academic circles. It was important enough that it would solidify his further claims to the title of most famous archeologist in the world, but more importantly it would instantly propel his students and assistants into the world spotlight, earning them a spot at any university post they desired.

Even at camp, around the fire at night, he had allowed his students' comparison of their work here to finding King Tut's mummy because it provided them what the drudgery and mundanities of *actual* dig site work could not: the promise of excitement and a built-in motivation to push on.

There were a lot of rocks and dirt to move, and if promising his students a reward such as this gave them the willpower to continue and keep working hard, he would allow it.

As he stood in front of the wall that would hopefully tell him his next steps, Graham thought through the past weeks. Though they were only a few days into this dig, he had only been able to secure the temporary rights to this dig site after a long-fought battle that had cost him many years. He had spent countless months on grant proposals, eventually enlisting the support of universities around the world, as long as they got their requisite mention in the forthcoming articles and papers.

Graham didn't care. He had long ago grown weary of the political and bureaucratic battling that preempted the securing of an actual dig site, and he had adopted the motto *whatever it takes*. But it seemed he had forgotten just how long and strenuous that battle could be when it involved something like this, something so important to both Egyptology and Greek history — two cultures who were as cutthroat with one another as they were proud to maintain a positive image in the history books.

He also knew that at any moment, either of the two countries' governments could pull the rug out from under him, revoke his permit, and force them to leave the country with nothing to show for their hard work. Worse, if they did it *now*, he would have just cleared a path to a hidden tomb at a famous archeological site and handed it over to the Egyptian Ministry of Antiquities. If that happened, there was no chance they would give him and his team any of the credit.

He flicked off the flashlight he had been holding, then reached out to feel the glyphs to see if he could better read them with his fingertips instead of his eyes. He pulled his hand back from the wall as one of his students — a young woman named Marcia — found him in the tunnel leading toward the interior chambers.

He started to smile, until he saw the frantic look on her face.

CHAPTER 11
REGGIE

Anchorage, Alaska

Reggie looked at the front door of the small cabin with trepidation. This idyllic spot used to provide him joy, contentment. He used to stand here and imagine what it would be like to live inside a cabin of his own, to settle down with the love of his life.

That love, driving their rental car now, began stepping out of her side of the vehicle. Dr. Sarah Lindgren stretched and looked over at him.

Reggie shut the door to the car, careful to not slam it. He knew they were expected, but he wasn't sure if he was ready to enter the cabin and didn't want to be rushed.

He was doing things on his own terms these days. He was doing things the way *he* wanted them done. Sarah didn't always agree with his point of view, but then again, that was why they worked well together. She felt comfortable questioning his decisions, and he felt comfortable stubbornly persevering with his habitual ways, and somehow they both made it work. Somehow, they met in the middle and loved one another all the more for it.

They reminded him of Juliette and —

He shook his head as he crunched over the frozen dew in the grass leading to the front of the small house. He shook his head. *Don't go there,* he thought to himself. *Not yet. You're not ready yet.*

Sarah followed, slamming the door louder than Reggie would have preferred. No matter — this was a trip he was not looking forward to, so it might as well begin sooner rather than later. Better to just get it over with.

He waited for her on the doorstep, taking in the scenery once more. The cabin itself was almost perfect in a quaint, humble way, save for the stain of destruction lying next to it. One bedroom, a living room, and a kitchen, with a dining room table filling the space between them. More sofas and armchairs than a single living room should be able to fit had been crammed inside, so the whole team could relax in the tiny space.

The whole team.

The tears nearly came when he thought of the team. How it had changed over the past month.

How that team was smaller now.

Reggie took in the ruins to the front side of the cabin's newest addition to his left. Built to house the entire team, a conference room and lounge, and communications center, it was now mostly ruins. The entire front wall of the multi-room facility, top and bottom floor, had been decimated. He saw the concrete skeletons of the rooms inside, the walls ending abruptly only a few feet off the ground.

The insurance company had begun proceedings on the facility's reconstruction, but Juliette had ordered them to halt. Reggie and Sarah had argued with her, claiming that if she waited too long, the insurance company would drop the matter entirely and write it off as a scheduled loss, and they would be left holding the bag.

But Julie, almost as stubborn as Reggie himself, would not listen to her friends. For her, the only way anyone was going to remove the blocks of concrete and debris from the explosion that had rocked their world six months ago was if Mr. E himself requested it.

After all, it was his wife who had died in the blast. It was, in a sense, her grave.

While her body had long since been removed and laid to rest, a part of Reggie understood where Julie was coming from — this was the last memory they all had of the woman, and to leave the mess here reminded her and everyone else of the guilt they wore on their hearts. For better or worse, it was a way to remember the zany, badass woman herself.

He knew most of Julie's reasons were unhealthy, reasons that could prevent them all from moving on and rebuilding, but that was particularly *why* he understood. He himself wore many layers of guilt on his own heart — this was just the latest in a long line.

Even now, after more than a decade had passed, he felt the pangs of regret at the loss of a daughter.

His daughter.

She had been taken from him before he had even been able to fight for her. Before he knew he wanted to.

He wore that guilt every day, and only a few people in his life, including Sarah, knew of his past.

Still, he wondered how long Julie would be able to hold on. No one had even heard from Mr. E in months, and even though Julie — computer wizard and capable of technological feats Reggie considered akin to magic — had tried to hail him on all the channels they had previously used, the man had remained radio silent the entire time.

No one had seen or heard from him, and no one had received any information as to his whereabouts. The last communique from him had been months ago, when he was on the island of Elba, the place of Napoleon's birth, but even after calling in a favor and having a friend check around on the ground, she had found no trace of the man.

Reclusive to a fault and highly secretive anyway, Reggie wasn't entirely surprised Mr. E had gone into hiding. If anyone would be capable of holing up after the death of their beloved wife, it was Mr. E. But to Reggie and his group, it seemed as though he had simply fallen off the face of the earth.

Sarah was by his side now, her warm hand clasped around Reggie's arm. She allowed him to pull her along, two bodies slowly moving toward the cabin. It felt like a funeral dirge, as if they were here to give last rites or to deliver a eulogy. They walked side-by-side, arm in arm, their steps perfectly synced. He could sense it then — she was feeling the same trepidation as he.

"You okay?" she asked softly.

That was it. The singular time in the past few weeks she had asked him, point-blank, if he was okay. He knew she had been giving him space, he knew she had been allowing him to process everything that had happened, the shock of it all. He had appreciated that — it turned out he had longed for that space. But until this moment he had not been entirely sure she understood the depths of his depravity.

Now he knew she did. A tear finally fell from his eye, crowding his cheek and falling to intermingle with the frozen dew on the ground at his feet. He didn't bother wiping its trail away. She had already seen it, and what did it matter, anyway? Was he somehow stronger if he could convince her that he could not cry?

She squeezed his arm tighter, now, swallowing. Trying not to cry herself. She stopped him there, halting their progress toward the cabin. The person inside the house would know by now that they were here, and if Reggie and Sarah were entitled to a welcoming party of any sort, the door would have burst open by now.

That meant they were alone, momentarily in peace.

CHAPTER 12
REGGIE

SEPTEMBER 15, **2020 | local time 7:47 am**
Anchorage, Alaska

She turned to him now, pulling him around as well to face her. He felt hesitant but rolled with the motion until his eyes fell to hers and they locked together.

"It's okay to not be okay," she said. "*None* of us are. *None* of us are going to be for a really long time."

"You don't know... you *can't* know —"

He wanted to scream, to tell her not to say things like that — it was like arguing with the universe. Cathartic, perhaps, but useless. Instead, he gritted his teeth, the anger building in him. He did his best to hold it all in like he always had, to hide the rage from her. She could probably understand that he was not upset with her — she knew there was no way he *could* be upset with her — but that did not mean she deserved to see it spelled out across his face. She did not deserve to be subjected to it, no matter how close they were.

He squeezed his eyes shut and let his jaw relax, then opened his eyes again. She was waiting patiently, as she always was.

"I need you to tell me now if you're going to be okay," she said. "Not *okay* now, but eventually."

He shrugged.

"Not good enough, Reggie," she said.

He shrugged again. "What the hell am I supposed to tell you? How the hell am I supposed to know if I'm going to be okay or not?"

"You just know," she said slowly, articulating the sentence. "People just know. It hurts — but it's *supposed* to hurt. It's *supposed* to feel like someone just ripped your heart out of your throat, but you still need to know that eventually you will be — you *can* be — okay. That's the first step."

"Maybe I'm not ready to take the first step," Reggie said.

She shook her head, her eyes darkening as she frowned up at her boyfriend. He felt her ire, her own anger barely controlled behind those beautiful, soft eyes. "Reggie, if you're not ready to take the next step, then don't. Get back in the car and go back to the hotel. The next step is not just metaphorical here. I'm literally talking about the next step you take toward that cabin." She lifted her finger and pointed it to the front door.

He knew she was right. She always was, of course. Julie was inside there now, alone and afraid and scared and angry and confused. Juliette Richardson Bennett, the woman who stood in limbo between two hellish planes of existence.

She existed in the unknown, in the chasm between them. *The void.* He knew it — he had been there before. He would not have wished it upon his worst enemies, and yet she was there now, living it every day.

So Sarah was right — it would be entirely unfair for them to walk into the cabin just to add their own fears and angers and sadnesses to Julie's world. It was entirely unfair to expect her to carry their burdens as well as her own.

They had even agreed to this the night before — they were here to help carry *Julie's* burdens, not the other way around. No, he was *not* okay, nor would he be in the foreseeable future. And right now, he felt like that was the way it should be.

He nodded. "I will be."

She arched an eyebrow.

"I mean what I say," he said, his words falling out through tight lips. "I'm going to be okay. It's going to take a long-ass time, but I *will* be okay. I can promise you that."

"I don't need you to promise me that, Reggie. I already know that. I need *you* to know that, because I need you to convince Julie of that. Got it?"

Reggie looked at his brilliant, compassionate girlfriend, a woman in a league of her own. A woman who had somehow found them all, somehow become Julie's best friend over the past year. This woman Julie trusted, confided in, and leaned on for everything.

She would be leaning on her a lot more now.

Sarah was strong — much stronger than Reggie. If he had ever wondered, that was abundantly clear to him now.

He nodded again. "You're right, thank you. I'll hold it together, trust me. I'll hold it together because she needs us to." He paused, then chuckled. "Because *I* need us to hold it together."

She turned then and began walking toward the cabin on her own. She had let his arm go, but the message was clear.

Take the first step, Reggie. Right now.

CHAPTER 13
JULIE

SEPTEMBER 15, **2020 | local time 7:48 am**
Anchorage, Alaska

Julie raced forward and grabbed Reggie around the neck, pulling the tall man down toward her. His long, lanky arms consumed her, and she allowed him to sweep her up into an embrace. Her feet left the ground, and under any other circumstances, the feeling would have been exhilarating. She had always been extroverted, always appreciated being with people she loved.

Today, the sentiment fell flat. There was a tension — a fear, almost — hanging around them all. She pulled back suddenly, and Reggie stepped away, clearing his throat.

Her best friend Sarah was standing nearby, waiting her turn. They had arrived at her cabin together a moment ago, knocking and waiting on the front stoop side-by-side, smiles on their faces.

But she saw straight through the smiles. She saw through them because she had gotten very good at wearing a similar smile over the past few months. First it had been worn around her parents, who had stayed with her here for a month, then it was around her other local friends and acquaintances who had come to pay their respects or simply drop by and talk.

And after all that, after everyone had gone back to their lives, then she had worn the fake smile for herself, practicing it in the mirror every morning.

She wore it like an old t-shirt that didn't belong to her. It was comfortable, comforting even, but it was never supposed to be something she felt like herself in. It was certainly never something she was supposed to show the outside world. But, like that old t-shirt, the smile had somehow become favored. It was the thing she donned because she knew it, not because it was correct.

She nudged Reggie to the side and reached out for Sarah, who met her with open arms. She squeezed her more tightly than Reggie had, and Julie tried to pull strength from the woman. After the hug, they spread away from one another and neither of them spoke for an entire half-minute. They held hands in the open doorway.

Finally, Reggie reached out and slammed the door shut and threw her one of his characteristic huge grins. "We've got groceries in the car, Jules," he said. "They can wait for a bit, but it's not going to stay cool outside all day. We'll have to at least bring in the eggs and milk."

Julie nodded at him but ignored the groceries. *It can wait,* she thought. *It can all wait.*

They waited for a response, and she suddenly realized they were actual humans and not just figments of her imagination. She would need to put the fake smile back on, act like a grownup, and get through the next few hours.

"Right," she finally said. "Uh... what's for dinner?"

Reggie looked at Sarah. "She's the one cooking, not me."

"Chili," Sarah said quickly. "That okay with you?"

No. "Yes, of course. Always."

She paused for another awkward second until turning into the dining area and kitchen. "Come in, come in. You know this place is yours as much as mine. Reggie, feel free to pour yourself a drink. Stuff's over there."

She caught a slight nod of thanks, but the man did not move toward the standing liquor cabinet next to the kitchen cupboards.

This is too hard, she thought. *But we need to get through it.*

She waved them farther inside, nearly forcing Sarah to sit down at the dining room table. Julie walked deeper into the kitchen, her mouth already starting to water.

No matter the memories it would conjure, chili did seem like a good choice. She was grateful for that — grateful for her friends. They knew her better than she knew herself sometimes.

CHAPTER 14
GRAHAM

Siwa Oasis, Egypt

"Professor Lindgren, someone's here to see you."

He frowned, looking back at Marcia and then over her shoulder into the rectangular band of piercing light of the tunnel's entrance. "Who is it?" he asked.

"They wouldn't give me their name," Marcia answered. She shifted on her feet, and Professor Lindgren tried to read the cause of the unease he saw sprawled on her face. "But... they look like they could be government, or something..."

She trailed off, and Professor Lindgren looked back at the wall he had been touching a moment earlier. He glanced at the pile of rocks and debris that had yet to be cleared from the tunnel. It had been slow work, the kind of backbreaking stuff he had not liked even as a younger man. The tunnel walls were sturdy, still standing after so many years, but he had urged his students to proceed cautiously. It would be easy to develop a sense of complacency about the work here, since the tunnel seemed strong enough to withstand a little rearranging.

But he had heard of disasters taking excavation crews by surprise.

Here, in a place known to have more rainfall than surrounding areas, Graham knew they had to tread lightly. The temple walls were old, and he was nothing if not thorough. He had hired a nearby Libyan work crew to help with the loading. Their mining-car-like vehicles brought the larger rocks back up the gently sloping tunnel to the outside, where they were arranged in a grid-like pattern on the ground to be documented and photographed, should any of them proved to be artifacts of note.

The remainder of the stuff that had filled this tunnel shaft over time — smaller stones, bits of pottery, tons of dirt — was being removed by hand, using shovels and wheelbarrows and then sifted through under one of the large tents they had erected outside.

It was this nearest pile of pottery and debris he navigated around to reach Marcia. He stared back at her, reading in her eyes the same desire to continue on with their work unmolested. He didn't want to deal with government types; he didn't want to argue once again for their right to explore here. In his mind, places like this should be excavated as quickly and efficiently as possible, providing as much of a glimpse into their shared history as possible. These places should be public and accessible.

He knew she agreed, and he sensed those feelings might help to explain the expression he was seeing.

Or perhaps it is something else instead, he thought.

"What should I tell them?" she asked.

He cleared his throat, then looked back at his team's work. It seemed they were near the end of the tunnel shaft, or at least near a doorway of some sort. While rocks filled most of the way forward, it didn't seem like what lay in front of him was something so simple as a pile of rocks. It was dark and hard to see through the cracks, but it seemed as though...

What is that? he thought.

He leaned closer, ignoring Marcia for the moment as he examined the space between two larger fist-sized rocks. *If I could just pull these out and —*

"Sir?"

He whirled around, smiling. "Sorry — it is quite easy to get carried away down here, isn't it?" He chuckled, then answered her question. "Tell him I'll be right up. They are, after all, interrupting a sanctioned dig. They can wait their turn."

Apparently satisfied, Marcia nodded and turned to leave the tunnel.

He waited, watching his student as she ascended the tunnel shaft to inform the newcomers that the professor would see them in due time.

He hoped they would respect his wishes, but something told him these people were impatient.

He turned back to the pile of stones and began removing some of the smaller ones from the top of the stack, hastily discarding the ones that were clearly not artifacts or pieces of something important. Graham worked for ten more minutes like this, thankful for the moment that no one else had decided to disturb him. He assumed Marcia and the other students must have been keeping the government folks occupied. He knew he didn't have much time, and it was growing dark. They would get antsy before too long and send down one of the suits if he didn't hustle. Patience tended to run thin for people like that, he knew.

As he pulled larger and larger rocks from the pile, he saw that he had been correct. These rocks had not been stacked up in a pile, nor had they rolled here accidentally over the centuries.

No, they have been placed here on purpose, with a *single* purpose: These old stones were hiding something, and he was slowly revealing it.

His heart rate quickened as the pile of stones grew behind him. He felt sweat beading on his forehead but ignored the exertion. He was not that old yet. He was not going to let a young man's job get the best of him, no matter how loudly his muscles and lungs screamed for a break.

Not when I'm this close.

Finally, after another few minutes, he was able to see clearly what lay beyond the pile of stones which now littered the floor behind him.

I knew it, he thought. *I was correct.*

It was a doorway — one that very well may have gone unnoticed by his crew and students for another week as they focused on clearing out the main tunnel.

And it seemed to be well-preserved. He gently brushed along the sides of the stone frame. There was a thin, hairline crack around three of its sides, and a wider, deeper depression on the tall side to his left, indicating some sort of hinge-based system.

CHAPTER 15
MARCIA

SEPTEMBER 15, **2020 | local time 5:56 pm**
Siwa Oasis, Egypt

Marcia walked to where her fellow students and coworkers had gathered beneath one of the large tents. The three men who had arrived ten minutes prior were standing impatiently next to one of the folding tables. The table was currently covered with documents and maps of the dig site, all weighed down by stone paperweights excavated from their dig.

If the men had come to check in on their progress, it didn't show on their faces or in their actions. All of them completely ignored the contents on the table, as if it didn't even exist.

The man in the center, the smallest one, cleared his throat and stepped forward. He was wearing business attire, not a full suit but khaki pants and a crisp buttoned shirt tucked into a belt that matched his shoes. He was bald, and he looked like he could be Egyptian.

He raised his eyebrows, as if asking a question silently would save him an extra breath and a few words, his irritation evident.

"He said he'll be up in a bit," she said, doing her best to keep her voice chipper.

"A *bit*?"

The man's clipped words told Marcia that his irritation might be leaning closer to frustration. While he seemed harmless enough, there was a certain menace in his eyes, as if he enjoyed catching these Americans off-guard.

Definitely government, she thought.

The men behind him walked forward, and Marcia suddenly saw the coat the one on the right swing open, revealing a small subcompact machine gun.

She nearly stumbled backwards. *What the hell?* she thought. *That's not a government-issue handgun.* She was no expert, but if this man felt the need to travel with security for whatever reason, these weapons seemed like a bit much.

And that told her that these men might not be government at all.

"He did ask me to make you comfortable," Marcia lied. "Potentially help you with anything you might need. So, let me show you around while we wait. Over here is our documentation and Ministry of Antiquities paperwork, I'm sure you —"

The bald man held up a hand, stepping forward once more. He was close enough for her to feel his breath on her neck. "That will not be necessary," he said softly. "I do not need to see documentation of any sort. I'm merely curious as to your... progress."

It was a question, even though it had not been phrased as such. She swallowed, suddenly feeling concerned for her safety. A few students were watching the exchange and one of them, a cute graduate student named Paul she had talked to in the evenings, started walking over.

"Sir," Paul began, a frown on his face, "can I help you with something?"

Without hesitation, the lackey whose gun she had seen turned and pulled the weapon out from beneath his coat. He lifted it quickly and fired a short burst that caught Paul directly in the chest. The tall student stopped, mouth agape, then fell backwards, his hands and arms flailing as they tried desperately to gain purchase on nothing but air. He fell to the ground, blood already soaking through his T-shirt.

Marcia screamed and pulled her hand up to her mouth, backing away. Two other students shouted from somewhere behind her.

The man continued talking as if nothing had happened. "I am *very* interested in the progress here," he said. "The sooner you show me what you found, the sooner this will all be over. I hope you understand by now just how seriously I am taking this."

Her heart was beating out of her chest. Her breath was ragged, her head swimming. *What the hell is happening? Who are these people?*

She swallowed again, finally finding her voice. "Yes... yes, of course. Please — don't hurt us, we're just —"

"You are interfering with an investigation," the man said, his voice barely a whisper. "An *ancient* investigation. One that you could not even begin to understand. However, your ignorance and naivety does not excuse your actions. Now, *show us the tomb* you found."

Two other students had run to Paul's side and were trying to offer whatever medical support they could. It was futile, and Marcia could see that from where she stood ten feet away. Paul's eyes opened and closed rapidly, his mouth never moving from its shocked look of pure agony and fear.

She guessed he would be dead in less than a minute.

Two other students and a few members of the crew who had been helping with the manual labor poked out from behind one of the windbreak walls of a nearby tent, their eyes wide after hearing the gunshots. Marcia watched as one of the Egyptian workers saw the weapon, looked at Marcia, then began running the opposite way.

The second guard pulled his own weapon from his side, aimed, and calmly fired into the man's back. It seemed an impossible distance, but the worker fell, and a puff of dirt enveloped his body. He did not move again.

There were tears in her eyes now, the terror and confusion finally culminating in despair.

He said he wants to see the tomb, she thought. *Before, he just wanted me to take him to Professor Lindgren.*

She weighed her options. Would they kill him? Were they interested in the tomb, and what they might find inside? Or did they want Professor Graham Lindgren for some reason?

If the latter, had Professor Lindgren somehow been in breach of some unspoken Egyptian law? She knew superstition and legend ran high around anything related to Egyptology and these ancient sites, but they had checked the necessary boxes. They had gotten the right permissions, from the highest reaches of government.

What in the world is this all about?

The man began walking, making a line directly for the side of the ancient site where she had found the professor only ten minutes prior.

She jogged to catch up, then slowed to walk by his side. "Who — who are you? What is it you want with Professor Lindgren?"

"He is of interest to my organization." the man said.

"What organization?"

The man turned his head and peered up at her but did not offer a response.

"You *killed* that kid back there," she said, allowing the fear to creep back into her voice. "You have to answer for that."

Suddenly, the man stopped. He turned to fully face her, then spoke again. "No, young lady. I do *not* have to answer for that. His death will only prove my fortitude, my path. His death will be viewed as a sacrifice. Not now, but soon."

Marcia frowned, her mouth opening and closing as she prepared to pepper the men with more questions, but before she could form the words, he had started walking once more.

CHAPTER 16
JULIE

Anchorage, Alaska

Julie's mind raced, struggling to attempt to hold multiple conflicting ideas in her head at once. On the one hand, she was delighted to see her friends again. It had been far too long, far too many nights of sleeping alone in the quiet cabin, far too many days of listening as the workers attempted to clear rubble and repair the open wounds on the sides of her home. It was great to see their faces again, to know that they were still here, still with her.

But for what? And how long will this feeling last? They were not here for joy or fun — this was no vacation. They were here to mourn, to help her through whatever process she needed to experience, whatever cruel plan fate intended for her.

She did not want that — for herself or for them. She did not want help mourning, forgetting, remembering — any of it.

But she had a role to play, just as her friends had a role to play. She embraced Reggie and Sarah, then politely offered them a seat at the kitchen table while she began making beverages. Coffee for her, tea for Sarah, and any number of bourbon offerings for Reggie, who had not yet moved from his post. Either he had decided against drinking, or he felt awkward here, as she did.

She studied his face as he made his decision. He definitely seemed conflicted as well, and why shouldn't he be? The only times he had gone near the small cabinet of whiskey options in the cabin were the times he had been drinking with his best friend. He coughed into his fist quickly, then croaked out a few words. "I'll, uh — I'll just have tea. Thank you."

She caught a glance between Sarah and Reggie, but it didn't last long, and she returned to her duties.

As the water fell into the teapot, she waited, wondering how long it would take for the question to drop.

Apparently, only about five seconds.

"How... how are you doing?" Sarah asked, her voice quiet, exploring.

Julie wanted to throw the teapot and scream, to allow the rage to consume her once again, to break one of the newly replaced windows with the pot of water. What was one more thing broken in this world? What was one more thing lost?

Instead, she steeled her hand and continued to pour. "About as good as I imagine I could be," she said.

She silently cursed herself, knowing that she had prepared this answer, knowing that she had practiced it in front of the mirror a thousand times in order to make it sound as believable and as concise as possible.

She had failed on both accounts, and now there were bound to be follow-up questions.

"Yes," Sarah continued, her tact and mannerisms as impeccable as ever, clearly on high alert. "But I mean... really. How are you *doing*?"

Julie knew this question — the real one — would be coming as well. For what other reason were they here? Reggie's eyes slightly widened a bit, the man no doubt feeling more awkward in front of Julie than he ever had. This subject was always a hard one for him, he knew. He had been through so much in this life, so much before they had even met in Brazil.

So much pain, so much loss.

Now she had gone and dumped so much more on this man. Sure, the pain she felt was her own, but she knew him well enough to know that Reggie would be trying to carry her burden as well as his own.

She looked down, then quickly back up. It was hard to feel joy in this moment, hard to compartmentalize fear and confusion and chaos while exploring the tender intricacies of joy and love.

But she had to. It was her duty.

She owed it to him.

She glanced back up and nodded quickly. "I'm okay, thank you," she said. "I go in again next week. I'll keep you posted."

Reggie coughed again as she brought their mugs over to the table. Sarah gently stirred her teabag as it cooled, while Reggie started slurping it up while still at its near boiling temperature.

He cleared his throat now, then spoke again. "Jules, we... we wanted to see you. I mean, we came because we wanted to check in and see how you are doing and stuff, but —"

"We're glad you're doing well, considering," Sarah said, rescuing Reggie. Julie couldn't help but smile. For as confident and physically gifted as the man was, he was humorously inadept at navigating the throes of nuanced conversation.

"Right," Reggie said, regaining his composure. "It's just that, uh, there's another reason we're here as well."

This part was news to Julie. She ignored her coffee for a moment and walked over to the table to sit with her friends. "What do you mean?"

Reggie looked left and right, and then leaned in, as if about to reveal a dark secret. "We may have found something. We might have a place to start —"

Julie held her hand up and Reggie stopped talking immediately. "Do I want to know?" She asked.

Reggie's eyes flicked to the right again, to his girlfriend, then returned to settle on Julie's. "I guess... I don't know, but I figured we would present it to you and let you decide for yourself."

Julie scoffed. "I've been wondering that myself for the past few weeks. If he's *gone*, do I actually want to know about it? Or do I want to continue hoping that he's out there somewhere? Would I be better off knowing that it's over? Accept the final closure and all that?"

Sarah nodded. "Yeah, we understand. It's an impossible decision, I'm sure. But Julie, please — just hear him out. For me?"

Julie looked down once again, pushing her chair back from the table a bit. She nodded.

Reggie seemed to gain a bit of courage by her nod, and he cleared his throat and began. "I talked to Freddie a few days ago. He said he spoke with his uncle, and —"

"General Rollins?" She remembered the grizzled war veteran from their experience in Antarctica. His son, Freddie Rollins, was the newest member of the CSO team, and so far had been a wonderful asset to the group.

Reggie nodded again. "Yeah, seems like they're trying to rebuild that old uncle-son relationship, if it's not too late. Good on them, I guess."

It was Julie's turn to nod. She remembered the tension that had existed between Freddie and his uncle, and how the pair seemed to be constantly at odds. She was happy they were working to repair their relationship, but she knew it was a long shot. Both were military men, trained to push things like this aside.

"Anyway," Reggie continued, "Freddie made me swear to not ask where he got his information, but he says he found a map."

"A map?"

He and Sarah nodded.

"Of what?"

"Something of interest. That's about all I know. He won't tell me the details until you approve."

"Approve of what?" Julie asked.

"Approve of our mission."

CHAPTER 17
GRAHAM

SEPTEMBER 15, **2020 | local time 5:56 pm**
Siwa Oasis, Egypt

He heard a tapping sound from outside the temple structure. Professor Lindgren frowned, wondering what could have made a noise so loud that it could reach his ears through all the stone walls, all the way down the tunnel.

He had a few guesses, and none of them made him very comfortable.

He stopped working on the pile of debris for a moment and jogged back to the mouth of the tunnel.

Closer to the exit, he could hear a commotion from the students and work crew. There was shouting, screams. *What has them all riled up?* he wondered. *Does this have anything to do with those government people?*

As he approached the front entrance of the tunnel beneath the temple, three dark shapes came into view. A fourth — Marcia — was in tow, dragged along by one of the shapes. He frowned, his unease growing by the second as his eyes focused and the light shifted, revealing the group. The man leading the pack was well-dressed, certainly not prepared for a dig. But something about him did not seem government-like, as Marcia had suggested. There was something *too* formal, something too proper about him. Lindgren's eyes fell onto Marcia, who wore an expression of fear and confusion, and he suddenly felt more concern for her than he did his own safety.

As they continued to approach his position at the mouth of the tunnel, his eyes rose to above Marcia's head. There, back toward the tents, he saw his students gathering around something on the ground.

Is that —

His heart sank and his blood ran cold. He noticed two legs and two shoes poking out from the gaggle of students and crew members collected under the tent.

The sounds I heard...

There were two men flanking the businessman and Graham noticed one of them brushing his hand against something dangling awkwardly beneath his suit. It didn't take more than a half a second for Professor Lindgren to guess what it was.

Time's up, he told himself. He was concerned for Marcia's safety, but he knew they were here for him. *If I can put more distance between me and them...*

He turned around and ran full speed back down to his work, back to the door hidden inside the temple's substructure. He couldn't be sure they had not seen him, but he knew they were only thirty seconds away from finding the entrance to the tunnel anyway. It was likely they did not want to kill him, or they would have been running toward him already, guns drawn and waiting for a good shot.

No, this was about something else. They needed him for some reason. Alive.

He could not imagine what that might be, and as he worked his mind processed through the possibilities. Had he inadvertently stepped on sacred ground, insulting a group of people he had not been aware of? He knew accidents were common in ancient sites, and he had experienced firsthand what it was like to come to the dig site in the morning and find that looters had raided his camp the night before.

No, this was something more, something *dangerous*. They weren't here to just scare him and his students away from digging. The strange, well-dressed man and his two henchmen seemed to be on a mission to find him. Hell-bent on speaking with him or taking him somewhere for some nefarious purpose.

Professor Lindgren put the thought out of his mind. He needed to focus. He could figure this out. If anyone could, it was him. He wanted to be with his students, wanted to tell them it was going to be okay, but he did not want to lie. He had no idea what was at stake here, and if he did not finish his task now, he feared more students would end up dead.

He approached the hidden door once more and slapped his palms together, then rubbed. *Okay, focus. Let's do this.* It was not every day that he came across an ancient tomb, not every day he got to approach a site for the first time since it had been sealed thousands of years prior.

And it was not every day he got to experience opening a tomb as important as this one.

That said, he was no stranger to the games of ancient Egyptians. Tombs were often secured by more than just stone slabs. They often held clues depicting a means to opening them, meant to be deciphered only by those worthy of entrance. And since many of the pharaohs of dynastic Egypt who had been buried in tombs like this one thought themselves gods, equal to no other humans, these fanciful inscriptions and puzzles were typically just red herrings — they weren't *meant* to be deciphered, because in the pharaohs' eyes, no one was worthy.

The vast majority of the time, these tombs had been sealed and left to be untouched forever. Any clues as to how one might open them would only present harm to the opener by means of booby-traps and other security mechanisms.

And yet, some things had in fact been left with the intention of being found and opened once again. He had reason to believe this tomb was one such example. This tomb, unlike many other Egyptian tombs he had studied, did not hold within it an *Egyptian* king. And it wasn't just the person inside he and his team hoped to find — while that alone would be a groundbreaking discovery, he was interested also in what the person inside might be buried with.

But first, he had to open the door.

CHAPTER 18
GRAHAM

SEPTEMBER 15, 2020 | local time 5:57 pm
Siwa Oasis, Egypt

Graham had only about twenty seconds remaining before the men would enter the tunnel, and then perhaps another ten before they reached this seemingly dead end.

He inspected the door, quickly reading the hieroglyphs as if they were English. He saw the warnings and dangers implied if he were to open this door, but he was surprised by what he did not find.

There were no inscriptions demarcating any particular security mechanisms. No clues as to how he might bypass any of the traps that might be hidden beyond this door. There were no suggestions, no artful poems about just how he might be able to open the massive slab of stone.

That meant...

"Professor Lindgren," a voice called out, "please stop what you are doing. I need to have a word with you."

The voice echoed down through the tunnel, directly into his ears. He shifted on his feet.

That was much faster than I thought.

He had run out of time.

"Professor Lindgren," the man shouted now, louder and more intense this time.

He looked around frantically, trying to discover if his theory was correct.

There are no clues on the door about how to open it, because...

His fingers slid over the sides of the slab, finding the small hairline crack he had assumed was a hinge. He felt the dust fall out from it, widening the crack ever so slightly as it breezed back to life....

... Because it's not a door at all.

It was a clever design — ingenious, really. Not Egyptian, which further proved his theories. It was hidden in plain sight, the cleverness of the build passing a compliment down through time itself. The stone he had removed laboriously from the door had been placed here not to act as a *deterrent* — stones were easily removed, after all — but to further sell the façade of what hid *behind* them.

This door was not a door at all. It was, in fact, a dead end.

But the hinge mechanism he'd found that ran from ceiling to floor on the left-hand side of the slab was, in fact, a sort of hinge.

It was just a hinge for a different door. One that led directly to his left. One that, when he applied pressure at just the right points, points referenced in the wall of hieroglyphics on the elaborately inscribed stone slab, caused the narrow gap to open. The opening revealed itself to him, and he wasted no time. It was going to be seconds before they entered the tunnel and found him, seconds before the ruse would be up.

If he expected to get a head start, to get in front of them so he could buy more time to figure this all out, he needed to take this opportunity.

He did. He slid his body through the narrow gap in the wall to the left of the hieroglyphic-covered slab, and he disappeared deeper into the temple. In an instant, he was out of sight. He was barely through the door before he had turned and closed it behind him. He saw the low light from the sun that had found its way down the tunnel shaft disappear as the rectangular hole was once again filled by the door. He pushed it shut now, forcing it back into place so that it would be nearly impossible to spot from the tunnel, but careful that he did not make too much noise.

All sound and light was gone now. If the men were shouting for him in the tunnel on the other side of this stone wall, he heard nothing. There was a sense of depth to this place, but he was bathed in pitch darkness, as though he were floating through space. No sound or light reached his eyes or ears.

He acknowledged the initial shock of being completely alone in a subterranean tomb, once again closed off to the outside world, but he quickly pushed the fear away. He took a few quick breaths, deeper each time to calm his heart.

He steeled himself, putting a hand on the cold stone door he had just come through. He thought he heard a slight pounding sound, which meant the men were already trying to break through. They must have found the end of the tunnel and the pile of stones, and they were trying to break through the stone slab at its end. It would be a fools' errand, but they could not know that yet. They would work, decimating this ancient site, destroying its beauty and solitude with their blunt instruments.

But he needed to survive — he couldn't worry about the desecration of an ancient site right now. He needed to stay ahead of these people who would no doubt prevent him from finishing his mission. They would eventually find the real door, would eventually discover the tricks the tomb builders had played on them, but by then he needed to be long gone.

And by then, he needed to have accomplished his mission.

He hoped that mission lay just beyond, in the vast inky darkness of whatever chamber he was in now.

He took one more long, steady breath, then felt the excitement and anticipation build once again as he remembered his calling. He was in his element now; he was doing what he had been trained to do. What he had studied for many years, taught at the university level, and had made him a world-renowned expert.

He fumbled around the belt on his waist until he found the tiny flashlight. He pulled it out of its case and clicked it on.

He swept it in long, slow arcs on the floor first, checking the immediate space around him for any dangers that might present themselves.

Finding nothing to be immediately concerned about, he pulled the flashlight a bit higher and broadened the sweep of his arc. The light filled the space easily, and he swallowed as the room came into view.

And then his jaw dropped.

CHAPTER 19
JULIE

Anchorage, Alaska

"We're going to go, Julie," Reggie said.

The man's normal easygoing expression had morphed into one of empty stoicism. His amicable charisma had also seemingly disappeared, his large smile replaced by a thin, serious line.

Julie looked from him to his girlfriend and back. "What do you mean you're *going* to go?"

"I mean exactly what it sounds like it means. We want your blessing and all, but... to be honest with you, I'm not sure I *won't* be able to go. There's a chance we could actually find him, Julie. There's a chance he still —"

"I'm going to stop you right there, Reg," she said. "I love you — both of you. Reggie, I love you like a brother. And that means that if I lose you as well I will *never* forgive myself."

"Don't carry that," Reggie said. She sensed a bit of venom in his voice, but he shifted in the chair and suddenly he was unreadable once more. "I mean, I'm not asking you to carry that weight. If I go, it's because *I* chose to, okay?"

Sarah reached over and grabbed Julie's hand. "You're not going to lose him," she said softly. "Because I'm going to go with."

Julie jerked her hand out of Sarah's grasp. She pulled it back to her and piled it on top of her other, on her lap. "You — you're going to go with him? I don't understand. What is it that you think you're going to find out there? What is it do you think you know now that we didn't know before?"

"Julie this map —"

"It's just a *map*, Reggie!" Julie shouted. "Just because Freddie's old man found some satellite imagery and claims there's something there now that wasn't there before, it doesn't mean it's true. Look, I get that he's a military guy and all that, but I have access to the best satellite records around, and Mr. E's company sold data *to* the US government. So anything they've seen, *I've* seen. You think I haven't thought about that? You think I haven't spent *hours* scouring every last known place he was in, trying to make *some* sense of it all?"

She paused then, realizing that she was getting worked up far more than she had intended. She could see that Reggie wanted to yell back at her, to argue with her and take her to task. She could also sense that he was just as conflicted as she was — that he didn't want to hurt one of his closest friends. It was a testament to the man's character, and she hoped she could remember it long enough to thank him for it one day.

"I just don't see how finding some island off the coast of Turkey means anything," she said. "And why couldn't the general himself send a team out there to see what it was?"

Reggie swallowed, glancing at Sarah for a moment before he responded. "When Freddie called, there was a lot of hesitation in his voice. I sensed... something that wasn't being said."

"Something 'not being said?'" Julie asked.

Reggie nodded. "Look, I've been out of the service for a long time, but I vividly remember these sorts of intelligence discussions. The reason a lot of missions go awry is not due to lack of planning or training, but due to a lack of written clarity. There's only so much these guys feel comfortable writing down. There's only so much they know they can get away with, and they don't want the record to show it. Still, it's a requirement that they write up a brief and mission parameters, if only for posterity. But so much of what actually takes place is expressed verbally, from one coordinator to the next, and on down the line."

"Sorry, Reggie, I don't think I follow where you're going with this."

He shook his head once and started over. "Sorry, let's say it this way: it wasn't what Freddie said. It was what he *didn't* say. I assume it was the same with the conversation he had with his uncle. The reason his uncle can't act on this is a moot point. Call it politics, bureaucracy, call it whatever you want, but the old man's hands are tied. Still, he has enough of the intelligence gathered and enough of the information around whatever this place is that he's suspicious, to say the least. To turn it over to his nephew — who is no longer active duty, no longer in the military at all — says a lot. He didn't want to be anywhere *near* on the record with this, so he simply dropped it as a hint to Freddie, who he knew would do the same for us."

Julie nodded, finally starting to understand. "So you're saying that whatever this place is, it's not just a good target to investigate — it's a *really* good one. Enough of a good target that a career military man is staking his career on the fact that his nephew and his ragtag group of civilians won't screw it up. And you're also saying that it must be a dangerous target to investigate, since the US military itself won't even officially touch it."

Reggie's stoic face fell into one even more grim. There was no smile, no twinkle in his eyes. This was not a mission that excited him. This was not a mission that would rekindle his spark for adventure and danger.

This was a mission he would take on with purpose, drive. Not because he wanted to, but because he *had* to.

"Yeah, that's about where I'm at with it."

Julie accepted this with a quick knock on the underside of the table, then looked up at her friends. "You know I can't go."

There was a long pause. She wasn't sure what she expected — would they fight her? Would they accept it? Had they even been planning to ask her to accompany them in the first place?

Sarah leaned forward, her hands not having anything to grab now that Julie's were still tucked beneath the table. "We do understand," she said. "We would never ask you for something like that." She leaned even closer to Julie. "But Julie, please — allow us to go. Let us figure this out. Let us bring him back to you."

Julie wiped a tear from her eye. "Do you think it will work?"

Another pause, and then Reggie leaned forward as well, clearing his throat. "Does it even matter?"

CHAPTER 20
GRAHAM

SEPTEMBER 15, 2020 | local time 5:57 pm
Siwa Oasis, Egypt

The pounding grew in volume, and Professor Lindgren knew it was only a matter of minutes before the three men hounding him would break through and find this inner sanctum he was hiding in. He needed to be long gone by then, but the inherent fascination about this place was pulling him to explore it further.

No time for that, Professor, he told himself. *With any luck, I can get out of this alive and come back later.*

...Assuming they don't destroy this place as well.

The regret was building inside of him — he hated feeling rushed, and he hated knowing that the men outside did not have the best interests of this beautiful, miraculous place in mind. They wanted something, clearly — something they thought Professor Lindgren had — and they would stop at nothing to get it.

The challenge he was facing now was whether or not to succumb to their desires in order to save himself and his students, or to push on and try to figure a way out of this mess and stop whatever larger purpose they were working toward.

His flashlight examined all the nooks and crannies of the space, his mind building a picture of what it would look like fully illuminated. He had no doubt this was the tomb he and his students had been looking for. The one the Egyptian government had consistently denied the existence of for decades. Whether they knew of this place or not, no one had been in this space for ages.

Graham had never fully understood Egyptologists' hatred for archaeological advancement, their disdain for outsiders looking around and researching their history. Sure, most of these ancient sites of interest to people like Professor Lindgren sat on Egyptian soil, but the history and stories they contained were humanity's, not the sole property of a single country.

Whatever.

He had finally found it, the tomb of the Great One himself — and although there were DNA tests and samplings to be taken and performed later, it was undeniable this vault — a tomb within a tomb within a temple — should not exist. And by all official accounts, it did not.

And yet here it was, right in front of his face. Here it sat, contradicting everything historians claimed about the ancient site of the Oracle.

He approached the dais on which the sarcophagus sat. He would not be able to completely lift and remove the stone cover of course, as the slab was nearly three inches thick. But in the darkness he had felt around and knew there was just enough of a lip to get his fingers underneath it, or possibly even his palms.

Perhaps he could slide it just a bit off-kilter, enough to get a hand inside and...

Ground shook beneath his feet suddenly, and debris and dust fell into his hair and face from somewhere up above him. The entire room seemed to quake, groaning with movement after centuries of stillness.

They're using explosives? *Seriously? They'll bring the whole place down on our heads. Me, them, my students.* He was furious at their sheer audacity, but he was also growing fearful — if they were willing to go to these lengths to apprehend him...

This area of the country was not particularly geologically active, though it had been at one point. He knew that while the builders of these temples had taken pains to construct their sites with as much architectural fortitude as possible, and the results spoke for themselves. Buildings constructed thousands of years ago were outperforming buildings constructed less than a hundred years ago.

Places like this had already made it many millennia and would likely continue on.

...Unless some idiot decided to blow one up.

He hoped that the stones holding up the walls and ceiling around him could withstand the blasts of a few small grenades. He knew that was all these men could have been carrying on their person. Sure, they could go and find something a bit stronger, plastic explosives or C4 or something of that sort — but neither of them had been carrying a satchel or bag of any sort. That might allow him just enough time to finish his task.

With a practiced reverence that no longer felt forced, he braced his feet against the side of the dais and pushed his palms up beneath the lip. He gritted his teeth but was surprised to feel the slab give way almost easily. It was heavy, but it seemed there was graphite, or some other lubricant had been applied to the underside of the container's top to ease in its ability to slide off later.

Another interesting feature of this sarcophagus, he thought. The Egyptians and Greeks would have opted to seal it completely. There would be no reason for anyone to enter this place in the future, and certainly no reason for anyone to uncover these remains later.

Which told Graham that there *was* something in here worth retrieving. Something the ancient world wanted him to find.

His hand crawled into the space inside the sarcophagus, his mind ignoring the imaginative horror movies he had seen that implied thousands of creepy crawlies or venomous snakes would be lying in wait inside. There were no scarabs, no poisonous beetles, nothing of the sort.

In fact, he was even more surprised to find that the tomb was completely empty.

No bones, no remains, no dust that implied they had disintegrated over time. There were no mummified wrappings of any sort, just a gentle breath of air as the previously enclosed box was once again opened to the world.

This was not what Professor Lindgren had expected to find at all. In one sense, he was glad his students weren't here. Glad to not have to endure their fanfare and expectations being deflated. Finding out their sarcophagus contained nothing but empty space was a blow to anyone's ego, especially for students for whom this would be one of the most important digs of their careers.

Another explosion from outside rocked the surrounding walls, and more dust and bits of stone dropped from the ceiling once again, some landing on his hand inside the sarcophagus. *Fools,* he thought. *Cretinous wretches, interested only in profit.*

He still had no idea what they wanted with him, but he was not naive — everyone like this ultimately wanted money. Somehow, some way, he must know something that they could trade for profit.

He returned to his exploration of the interior of the sarcophagus. He raked his fingers alongside its bottom, trying to draw even lines so as to inspect the entirety of the space. He used his shoulder and a free hand to push the lid farther off the opening, then brought his flashlight back up and pointed it into the space.

The interior of the box was immediately cast in a yellow glow, and he saw that he had been wrong.

The sarcophagus was *not* completely empty. Sure, there was no *body* inside, no skeletal remains of the man the entire world have been looking for a thousand years.

That was a disappointment, but this exploration and dig was not going to end in *complete* failure.

Sitting inside the sarcophagus, almost dead-center in the space, was a mint-condition ceramic container. It looked as though it had never been handled, the hieroglyphs and decorations on the sides gleaming as though the object had been placed inside only yesterday.

He frowned, not quite understanding its purpose. He recognized the craftsmanship — Egyptian — even making an educated guess which dynastic era it might belong to. It was certainly old — or if it were a forgery, it had been crafted with exquisite attention to detail — and he almost did not want to reach for it. He almost wanted to just replace the stone lid and walk away from this place, to let the dead lie.

But then again, there were no dead in this room. There were no other humans at all, and it seemed as though there hadn't been in quite some time.

He had come here not just to find a body, the remains of one of the world's greatest historical figures of all time, but to find what that man had been buried with.

A secret that man had brought to his grave. A secret apparently worth keeping even after death. Rumors of it had existed in some academic circles, but to see evidence of it here — to actually have found something beyond just the remains of a man — it was nearly unbelievable.

His heart skipped a beat, his hand hesitated, then he tentatively reached out and stroked the outside of the small piece of pottery. It was a simple two-piece construction — a bowl and a lid that fit perfectly on top, only the slightest hint of a line running around its circumference to imply that it came off. He reached it and pulled it closer, lifting it from its station in the center of the sarcophagus' interior.

Suddenly, the question he had asked himself thousands upon thousands of times over the course of his career — even as a young man, long before his proper career had begun — returned to him in full force. The question he knew career archaeologists like himself, those interested only in the truth, interested in recovering the secrets of the past — constantly asked themselves.

It was an exalted question he felt pushed beyond politics, beyond bureaucracy, beyond geopolitical infighting and economics. It was a question as simple as it was profound, as it was the reason he and every other archaeologist he knew had gotten into the field:

What the hell is inside this thing?

CHAPTER 21
PRISONER 348

Imrali Island, Turkey

I'm weak. More tired than I've ever been. I never thought exhaustion was a disease; now it feels as though it's the one that will kill me.

I had read once that starvation leads to exhaustion, but scientists aren't sure which actually causes the real damage. It doesn't matter, the organs shut down one at a time anyway, like some domino effect with each domino growing larger than the last.

It won't be long now. Days? Perhaps a week? Impossible to know.

The force-feeding has continued, but it seems even the guards themselves aren't as interested in my torture as they once were. They're going through the motions. As if I have finally won. Whatever they think is inside me, whatever they want from me, I will take to my grave. I was steadfast in that decision, and it seems as though my captors finally agree.

They go through the motions now, putting the tube in my mouth, my hands and legs strapped to the metal table, frail and weak. They feed me, but it is hardly enough nutrients to truly rejuvenate. Just enough to keep me alive, to string me along.

I'm in bed now, in the bottom bunk just as I had predicted. The Poet switched with me two or three weeks ago. I was too weak for my own good, or something like that. I can't remember his reason. Something poetic, I'm sure.

After they feed me they let me lay there for an hour, likely to make sure I digest the food and don't just spit it up when I get back to my cell. Not sure where I would hide the sick anyway if it came to that, but I assume their rules are more for their benefit — their desire to feel in charge of something — than in actually keeping the order.

My mind is surprisingly clear — I guess removing all distractions, including sustenance and life itself — is a motivator for staying sane, or at least lucid. Not sure why, but I suppose it makes evolutionary sense.

Of course, who knows if I'm staying sane at all? Perhaps I went mad only one week into this stint and I've just been trapped in my own head ever since. Perhaps I'm really eating steak and shrimp every night, thick pads of butter dripping over the sides of the pile of mashed potatoes, guzzling Cabernet to wash it down...

The thought of food makes my sides hurt, and I groan and shift a bit in the bed as I hear motion outside the cell.

It's The Poet; he's being dragged along by two of the guards. His arms and feet are manacled — not something they do here very often. In fact, I didn't even know they had those. Why shackle us at all when we can't leave, anyway? Not many of the prisoners have shown any proclivity to violence, and any violent reactions are treated with uncommonly egregious punishment.

I see throngs of prisoners behind The Poet and the two guards, all watching, all eager to chase after him. They want to know where he is going, where he is being taken. None of us have really seen much of the outside since we've been here. I certainly haven't, besides the prescribed exercise they allow us every other day. I carefully swing my legs over the side of the bunk. It hurts worse than I could imagine, but the fear of missing out is even greater. Who knew I was so starved for entertainment, for something out of the ordinary, that I would torture my own body to find it?

I smile grimly. This is my life, or what's left of it. It won't be long now, might as well see what The Poet did to deserve so much attention.

He was always a calm man, still is. I go in and out when he talks, as usual, but I suppose he's been nothing but kind to me. Said something about a wife and a small child. A daughter? Not sure where she is, or if they are even still in the picture. He spoke of them as if they were already gone.

Perhaps it was The Poet himself who was already gone. Just like me. I wonder how I'll talk about those I remember who are, as far as I know, still around somewhere.

The Poet is dragged out the front doors, and I'm surprised to see the door left open. I've never been out this door, and I feel my heart race as it begs my body to pick up the pace. I realize how badly I want to be outside suddenly. To see the sun, to feel its warmth on my skin.

At this point, after so much malnourishment and mistreatment, I wonder if the bright rays will simply crack my skin and turn my bones to dust.

I trudge into the line forming. It becomes a blob as we are all — for whatever reason — allowed access outside.

I suddenly see why. More guards, far more than I've seen before, line a field just outside. As I step out, the life-giving sunlight reaches down and caresses my skin. It's wonderful. One of the best feelings I've ever experienced.

And yet it somehow does little to assuage my fears. Each of the men standing in formed rows is holding a sick-looking assault rifle. I recognize the guns, though not from where. Have I fired one before? Was I someone who used to fire those? Has someone used something like it to shoot at me before?

There are vague recollections, memories like single puzzle pieces, floating through my mind. I'm lost, and yet I have a spark of recognition. A faint glimmer of remembrance. I don't recall completely who I was, but I know now what I am.

I'm broken, perhaps permanently. Yet I get the sense that I *was* something once. *Someone.*

I try to recall, to understand why my mind suddenly went there after seeing these weapons, but I'm distracted.

The Poet is pulled forward still, to the edge of the field. Beyond it, I see only blue. Water? I've forgotten what the ocean looks like. I assume it must be what's all around, otherwise we must be in the clouds, and I'm looking at endless blue sky.

The light is too bright for my eyes, and I lift my hand a little to shield it. As soon as I do, my eyes adjust, and I am allowed to see our surroundings more clearly. I'm shocked. We are completely surrounded by the sea. Small gauntlets of white lap upward out in the distance, forming peaks and troughs as waves fight with one another. They're not large, but the sea is not glass, either. I focus my attention back to The Poet and the others gathered around. A few of the guards — it doesn't take many of them — come forward and wiggle their rifles at other prisoners. The emasculated walking corpses comply immediately, their terror existing on their faces long before they react. Any hope they might find salvation out here is lost as they shift and settle in like cattle.

I understand now how futile any escape attempt would be. How far is it to the water down below? A hundred feet? More? It has to be two hundred at least in some places, now that my eyes have begun to measure properly. What lies below? Surely jagged rocks. Even if it were sand, beautiful idyllic beaches, an impact from that height would end with my being nothing but a splat on the earth.

The guns and all the men are completely unnecessary. A show of force, of power.

Then I realize: this isn't for us. They're not worried about our escape, because there is no escape.

This is a demonstration. A show of power.

My blood runs cold. Colder than it has been, and I shake with fear. What has The Poet done? Is it something he said? Will they come after me next, afraid that he lured me into his secrets?

He stands there, eyes locked on mine. So far away, and yet right in front of me. His face simple yet questioning. It's a face I've seen before. He's trying to pass on while still alive, to force his mind and soul to move from this plane of existence to another. He called it something once, said it was something ancient monks used to do. I didn't believe him at the time, still don't. But I don't know anything about monks, and while I'm sure he doesn't either, it was an interesting tidbit. Even more interesting to see it in real life, now. We'll see if it works.

To pass peacefully, with eyes open.

Something like that. I can't remember. That was the gist of it, though it was at the end of one of his longer ramblings.

There are no voices. Not even the prisoners whisper amongst themselves. We are all riveted to the scene, all looking for answers to the question that bemoans us: what is going to happen? What did he do to deserve this attention?

The answer comes seconds later. The guards who brought The Poet out here pull back and join their counterparts in the rows of men. Another guard, this one dressed far better than any of the others, appears from a spot behind the prison building. No one notices him at first, and suddenly he is in the middle of the field.

He's holding something in his hands as he walks toward The Poet. It's small, almost completely hidden inside his palm. I recognize the slight bulge of it and decide that it is round in shape, about the same size as —

My mind suddenly reverts back to a state I wasn't aware was still with me. A memory I thought had faded and died, but it hits me suddenly.

I know what this device is, and I know what it does.

I know what they are about to do to The Poet.

CHAPTER 22
REGGIE

Anchorage, Alaska

Reggie leaned back and let the back legs of the chair balance his weight until he felt the rear of it resting against the front wall of the cabin. He gripped the table with two hands — one biological, one mechanical. His artificial left arm and hand was the most advanced tech available, and thanks to Mr. E's connections, he had been able to select a few additional features for the limb that were technically still in the prototyping and testing phase.

After the accident in Peru — which had not been an 'accident' at all — Reggie had been left to bleed out on the torturous pedestal, the guillotine that had threatened to chop off the hands of him and his girlfriend laying close, his arm and hand on one side of it, the rest of his body on the other.

The man who had built that machine and affixed Reggie and Sarah to it was now *very* dead, and yet Reggie found himself still wishing there was a way to seek vengeance.

Not to say he did not enjoy the artificial appendage — it was far stronger and more capable than any muscular human limb, and he had found no shortage of incidents where having it on his person proved to be beneficial. Holding up heavy steel doors, hanging from ledges yet not worrying about his grip failing, and more.

But with the attacks on the cabin and the deaths of their team-mates, Reggie was feeling particularly vengeful. He wanted a target, wanted someone to take out his frustrations and angers on.

He *needed* to seek justice, and he needed to do it in his character-istic vigilante way.

He looked at Julie, trying to measure her reaction. He had never been one for trying to read people, never had a desire to be a closet shrink. But he had spent a lot of time operating with and around people, forced to make educated guesses about what their next move might be based on their mannerisms and facial expressions. He figured he had as good a knack for it as anyone at this point.

But for the life of him, right now he could not figure out what Julie was thinking. Was she upset? Concerned for their safety? Disap-pointed she couldn't go along and help? All the above?

He shook away these half-baked psychological theories and instead focused on the facts.

"This island off the coast of Turkey — Imrali — we've been surveilling it using the old satellite array Mr. E put up, the one whose data he lends to the US government."

"I thought the contract was that the government would funnel all of the data through their servers first, then back to Mr. E's company, to keep anything his satellites shouldn't see, or something like that. Maintain purity of data, or whatever the hell they used to call it."

Reggie nodded quickly, forcing a smile. "Yes, that was part of Mr. E's genius — and no doubt his wife's as well — he wanted to be fair to the US government about what his promise to them was. They needed to be sure they could trust the integrity of the data, and they could. The way he explained it to me was that whatever images the satellite captured would be downloaded first to cold storage servers owned by the government, essentially a long-term storage vault for anything and everything Mr. E's satellites saw while in operation. But that first stream was also funneled through US military intelligence depots around the world, meant to be seen by human eyeballs. Military personnel, checking and crosschecking that if there was anything they needed to see, the US government got to it first."

"Is that not how it works?" Julie asked.

"It does, and that's why Mr. E could claim he had never lied to them. He was contractually obligated to give them the one and only download stream from the satellites. If a particular satellite took an image or video of anything, the only place allowed to *store* that footage was the US government's servers. If and when they saw fit, they could turn that data over again to Mr. E's company, which we know he used for his commercial endeavors."

Reggie saw Julie's eyes widened and a bit of a smile appear on her lips. She was the most brilliant computer scientist he had ever met, even though he had barely seen the depth of her abilities. On the most recent assignments, she and Mrs. E had typically provided the bulk of the computing support, eventually working from the brand-new facility located right here at the cabin.

He couldn't help but feel his heart sink once again at the remembrance of the loss of that state-of-the-art facility when it had been bombed, killing Mrs. E with it.

He saw in his mind the white panel truck pulling up to the cabin, the dark eyes of the brooding man inside behind the driver's seat. He remembered killing him outside the cabin later...

Julie's voice broke in. "The US Government had the only download of *that* stream," she said quickly. "But it wasn't the only stream — the one being sent to cold storage could have been split off and sent somewhere else. No one would be the wiser."

"Precisely," Reggie said. "As long as he adhered the letter of the contract, he could tap into the stream headed to cold storage and split it again, sending one of the streams to *his* cold storage. Or somewhere else."

"Meaning he had full access to the satellite imagery and data his satellites collected," Julie said. "The government was happy because they thought they were controlling the stream of information, when in fact Mr. E could access all of it — *before* they could even parse through it."

"Right," Reggie said. "My understanding of it is that it's not really uncommon, either. I mean there are a bunch of satellites floating around up there, all owned by different governments and corporations. Every government with even a halfway decent defense budget is making all sorts of deals to get the best satellite data, first. Mr. E just had good lawyers, I suppose."

Julie was nodding. "Okay, I get that part. But Freddie got this information from his uncle — a military guy — and *I* missed it. I didn't think to consider this island, but why would I?"

"That's the point," Sarah said. "You missed it because you had no reason to look for it. It's not that it wasn't on the map, it's that there was no reason to suspect that he might be there."

"Freddie's uncle thinks there is a reason?"

"He does," Reggie answered. "He basically wrapped it up and put in on a silver platter for us. He can't do anything about it, but we can."

"And you're going to."

Reggie paused. He knew she wanted him to ask her permission again, to make sure she was fully on board with their plan.

But he also knew that the little she knew of their plan — which was still being formed, he had to admit — the better.

"Yes," he said. "We are. There's a chance we can get him back, and I'm not going to pass up the opportunity."

He watched Julie as she moved her head slowly side to side, examining each of their faces. He could not imagine the trauma that had been reignited in her mind, the wound that had only just started to heal being ripped wide open once again.

Finally, she reached forward and put a hand on both of theirs.

Sarah's right wrist and the back of Reggie's left palm. She swallowed, then wiped a tear away.

"Listen to me," she said softly. "You go find him. You bring him back to me."

Reggie started to nod, but he felt her hand squeezing his. He saw her eyeing him coldly. "And Reggie: once you've found him — *only* after you've found him…"

"Yes?"

"I want you to take them out. Destroy them. Once and for all. Whoever they are — wipe them from the face of the earth."

CHAPTER 23
GRAHAM

SEPTEMBER 15, **2020 | local time 6:03 pm**

Siwa Oasis, Egypt

Professor Lindgren held the small object in his hands, tightly gripping it close to his chest. The pounding outside had grown in volume, indicating that the men were now working feverishly to break through the stone door. He knew how they had found it — the door would have sounded hollow compared to the stone walls around it, indicating open space behind.

So they've finally found the inner sanctum, he thought.

He knew what would happen next. He had disobeyed their direct order, and since they were armed and clearly not afraid to use explosives, they were probably not going to take his insubordination lightly. He would pay for their trouble in pain.

He was surprised at his overall sense of calm about the situation. Over the course of his long and distinguished career, Professor Graham Lindgren had been faced with plenty of challenges. There had been no shortage of people who wanted to stop his work, to ban him from expeditions and dig sites and even entire countries in some cases. They wanted to prevent him from doing his job, from uncovering the truth of ancient history. They did not share his philanthropic views: that all human history should be freely available to all, unfettered by politics or narratively rewritten by those with power.

He had even been kidnapped once, back in Sweden. Yet he had never faced a situation quite like this — where those threats to his work were physical and direct. He had never been on the business end of a gun, nor did he ever want to be. The games of coercion he often found himself embroiled in were typically just that: nothing but games, played at the highest levels.

This, however, was no game. He felt his life was on the line. He needed a solution, a way out.

A way out. That's it, he thought. His mind raced with possibilities. He knew the temple complex above his head was far larger than just this single room, no matter how large this room seemed. While the person for whom this tomb had been constructed was a larger-than-life figure, they had wanted to keep their tomb a secret from the outside world, which was why it had been sealed and hidden beneath the temple's floor. They had chosen to forego the garish luxuries and elaborate decorations and opt instead for a simple, quaint space in a sacred site.

But Professor Lindgren knew something else about this space — something he was positive the men chasing him did not know.

He recalled the line from one of his all-time favorite throwaway movies. *"The first thing the builders would have done after getting down here was cut a secondary shaft back out for air..."*

Or, in other words, a second exit.

Professor Lindgren was positive there would be another way out of this tomb. He was not content with having to try to figure out how to open the door he had come through, as that would allow himself to be captured by the strange men currently pounding on it.

But he was also running out of time. How long before they were through the door? How long before they —

His heart caught in his throat again as he heard the sounds of metal impacting stone, then clattering as pieces of rubble and rock fell to the floor.

He heard voices now, even saw a faint sliver of light peeking into the tomb.

They've done it.

A massive sledgehammer was being used on the door, and the stone was already starting to give way. *How long now? Mere seconds?*

He flicked the light up and looked around at the simple hieroglyphs and writings around him. Most were invocations — prayers and recollections of this man's great life and untimely death. There were symbols that mentioned the great plagues that had befallen this area, famines that had cursed these lands, and even something he thought mentioned a disease this great leader must have struggled with.

Strange. These were Egyptian writings, but the man for whom this tomb had been constructed was not Egyptian. Many believed this was the place he had longed for, wanting to be buried here, but it still did not explain why Egyptian characters would be decorating the space.

His eyes danced over them without pause, finding them beautiful yet unhelpful to his current campaign. How he would have loved to spend all day down here, reading the ancient ritualistic writings. But there was nothing here that told him where to find another exit.

Nothing here that might give him a path to follow.

The sledgehammer struck two more times, the final round opening a six-inch-wide hole in the stone door. He didn't dare turn the flashlight back toward it, for fear that it might give away his location and give the men on the other side a clear shot. He did not want to see them push the barrel of a gun through it and cut him down.

Think. You can figure this out. If anyone can, it's you. He tried to force himself to come up with a solution. He tried to remember how the typical Egyptian tomb was constructed.

No, that's not right. There was nothing 'typical Egyptian' about this place. This was not the burial tomb of a Pharaoh.

The clues would be around him, not in his deep knowledge of Egyptian history. They would have to speak to him, and he would have to pay attention.

And he was running out of time.

CHAPTER 24
GRAHAM

Siwa Oasis, Egypt

His heart continued to race, beating faster by the second. It had been coinciding with the bouncing noise from the sledgehammer, now it was winning the battle of tempos. Lindgren looked back at the opening — in the door leading into this chamber. He needed to find a solution, and quickly. He guessed he had less than two minutes before the hole was big enough for the men to fit through.

Suddenly, his mind supplied him with a potential answer.

He jogged back over to the center of the room, daring to remain in sight by anyone who might peek through the hole. It was worth the risk, especially if he were correct. He had scoured every inch of the room so far, and while it had not been an incredibly thorough search, it was the best he could do with the tiny flashlight he had brought along.

That meant there was only one remaining option, and the idea had snuck up on him in the midst of his building trepidation.

He eyed the sarcophagus in the center of the room with new eyes.

This isn't a tomb, he realized. *Tombs have bodies in them. Remains.*

He and his team had originally thought that this place could be the final resting place of Alexander the Great, but during his examination of the inside of the sarcophagus, all he had found was the tiny object he still held clutched in one hand. No Alexander the Great — no human remains of any kind.

He had yet to open the small ceramic jar to see what was inside — that could wait until he had reached relative safety. His escape from these men would not be through the opening of a tiny jar.

But he had a feeling the location he had found the jar in might hold an additional clue. He remembered feeling the uneven floor of the sarcophagus, wondering why it was so shallow. Barely deep enough to have held a body, now that he thought about it. He ran the flashlight over the exterior of the rectangular box once more, seeing the upper cavity that he had found the object inside sitting atop a stone pedestal about waist high. It was a strange design, as if it were not a singular sarcophagus but rather two rectangles stacked on top of one another.

And that's exactly what he hoped would be the case. He brought his light up and through the open gap between the lid and the upper rectangle he had made earlier, feeling the dust at its bottom slide around as his fingers ran over it. The uneven base of the sarcophagus' interior was the thing that had piqued his interest previously, although he had not consciously realized it at the time.

If this had been a typical stone sarcophagus — or even any other artifact of antiquity — he would have expected the base of this upper rectangle to be smooth to the touch, aside from the dust. It would have been hewn from a single block of stone, its edges weathered or smoothed down by hand. Certainly not the uneven, multifaceted floor inside the sarcophagus he found now.

And now that he was focused on it, he realized it did not feel like stone at all.

In fact...

The sledgehammer swung again, its thundering impact helping

to reveal six more inches of the tunnel outside. There were now dark shadows joining him in the room, the light from the tunnel hallway finding the interior of the sanctum.

His hands brushed some of the dust away and he felt the splintered, worn tops of long planks of wood.

I knew it, he thought. *Wood was not a typical building material for Egyptian temples and artifacts meant to stand the test of time.* The ancient civilizations seemed to know that while wood made a perfectly acceptable building material for their contemporary architecture, cheap to acquire and bend to the will of the architects. It was a great material for construction of buildings meant to last dozens, potentially hundreds, of years.

But it was not the greatest material to use when it needed to hold up or stay in place for *thousands* of years.

It meant that whoever had placed these planks in here, whomever had fashioned them together in a perfectly sized floor for the stone box, had placed them here for a *temporary* purpose.

They intended for the wood to be removed.

His fingers worked around the edges of the planks, pulling up splintered, decaying fibers of wood. The thing might be thousands of years old, but the craftsmanship was evident — there was no space between the edges of the wood and stone walls. It had been perfectly shaped to exactly fit the floor of the sarcophagus.

Then, just at the opposite corner from where he had started, he found what he was looking for: a small, finger-sized hole. He stuck an index finger into it, clamped around the base of the boards, and pulled upward. Dust flew upward into his eyes, but he ignored the stinging and continued to pull, careful to also hold the ceramic artifact still in his hands. The wooden floor was heavier than he had expected, almost as heavy as fresh wood would have been.

The wood, like any human remains that may have been interred here, would have been kept in relatively good condition, thanks to the still, airless environment it had been in all these years. He pulled the floor up diagonally toward him, his flashlight in his mouth as he worked. He moved his head and pointed the beam in the space that the floor revealed, and he felt his heartbeat increase even more.

Though this time, it was not from fear.

He saw down beneath the wooden floor, expecting the *real* floor of the sarcophagus to reveal itself.

Instead, there *was* no floor.

The bottom of the sarcophagus was lost beneath a steep, square shaft that disappeared into the depths of the temple.

He gasped audibly.

Graham worked quickly now, juggling the flashlight and the ceramic artifact as he pulled the floor completely up, then rested it against the inside of the sarcophagus itself. He knew what he would have to do, though it pained him to do it.

But there was no other way. There was no one else to help him.

He set the ceramic artifact on the floor and placed the flashlight back into his pocket. This part he could do in the dark, and it would help him stay out of sight from those wanting to get in and catch him.

With two hands, bracing his feet once again on the floor, he pushed the lid the rest of the way off the sarcophagus. The heavy rectangle of stone reached a tipping point and then fell behind the sarcophagus and leaned against its rectangular base. It cracked, now two pieces. Professor Lindgren winced quietly in the darkness. *This is not the way I wanted to have to do it,* he told himself. *If anyone's watching me here, know that.*

He hoped future explorers and archaeologists could forgive his missteps, or at least understand why he had desecrated this place. He was not robbing a grave.

He was going *inside* it.

With the cover completely off and space now to climb inside, Professor Lindgren did just that. He felt around for the artifact on the floor and then held it close, tucking it under his outer shirt for extra protection. It was too large to fit into a pocket, but thankfully small enough that he could carry it with one hand. He swung his leg over the edge of the tomb, then the other.

There were stair-like rungs poking out from the wall on one side about every foot, but the shaft descended straight down into complete darkness. *What am I doing*, he thought. *This is insane.*

He didn't know what he might find below, and there was no *way* to know. According to all evidence of geology in this area — admittedly a minuscule amount of data — this entire plateau was on solid or near-solid bedrock. For a shaft like this to have been carved, it would have taken decades, an incredible feat considering it would have been done with hand tools.

This was not the secondary exit he would have expected, but it was his only saving grace at the moment. He had no choice but to continue. When he got low enough to hide his head, he grabbed the wooden floor again and lowered it over the hole, careful to ensure it lined up perfectly once again. Now that the dust had been disturbed, it was likely the men would eventually find his hiding spot and escape route, and the ruse would be up. But he would take this tunnel all the way to the bottom, no matter what.

He thought it likely he would run into a dead-end or end up in a well that had filled with brackish water over centuries of flooding and leaking, but it would potentially buy him more time for his students to get to safety — or for the authorities to arrive.

Now safely inside the shaft, he heard another crack as the sledge-hammer tore through another massive bit of stone above. He heard voices now, the men conversing in a tongue he didn't understand. It sounded like Greek, but more antiquated, more guttural than conso-nant-laden.

He frowned and pondered the sounds for only a moment before returning to his task. He climbed down, brick rung over brick rung, using two feet and one hand while he held the priceless artifact with his other. He expected the bottom to be ten feet away, and then twenty.

After thirty rungs straight down, he stopped and listened again. The men were still discussing something up above, but their voices down here were a mere whisper. They had not yet found his hiding spot.

He climbed another dozen feet, then dared turning on the flashlight once again. He needed to know where he was headed — he needed to know where this shaft would end.

The light flicked on, and to his horror and amazement the blackness down below simply consumed the light's beam. It was not strong enough to penetrate more than another twenty or thirty feet, though he was appalled that this shaft could even *be* that deep.

Whatever this place is, it's no tomb. And it's far more than a simple resting place for an ancient artifact.

Graham felt his insides twirl. This was a secret the world would want to know. Whatever was down here, he was going to be the first to find it, and the first to bring it to light.

And now he knew without a doubt that this place was a secret the men upstairs would *kill* to keep. Whether they knew it was here or not, they would certainly not allow him to escape unscathed, armed with a discovery like this.

The question for him was, was this all worth it?

Was it worth his life?

CHAPTER 25
FREDDIE

SEPTEMBER 15, **2020 | local time 9:00 pm**

Chicago, Illinois

"Thanks for coming, especially on such short notice. And especially at this hour. For most of you, I know it's well past your bedtimes."

Freddie looked around, flicking his eyes from one snickering man to the next down the line, until all four ex-soldiers seated in front of him and Reggie had made eye contact.

"We're not that old, yet," one of the men said. "Except for Jason. I'm surprised he ain't dead already, to be honest."

Another round of snickers erupted, but it was cut short.

Only one of the ex-soldiers gave any sign of emotion after the quick round of jokes and pleasantries, which Freddie had expected. Jason Roth sat with disheveled, unkempt hair, wearing a smirk on his face, and seemed to be the one soldier around the table completely uninterested in the mission. But Freddie knew better — he had served with Jason longer than with anyone else in the room now, though he trusted the other three men as much as he trusted Jason. He had called on these men in the past, been assigned to fight alongside them on black ops missions around the globe. Most of the time, those missions had been sanctioned by the US military — at least indirectly. Now, however, *he* would be calling the shots.

This was his mission. Or rather, his and Reggie's.

Reggie had been happy to cede command of the small operation to Freddie, on account that Freddie would be providing the bulk of the personnel and had already provided the intel they had used for the plan.

Freddie appreciated that about his new friend — he was not in this for glory, and there were no medals or leadership awards he was after. Sure, he knew Reggie was capable of leading far more men than a small unit like this, but he didn't need a patch on his arm or a badge on his shirt to signify who he was and what he had done.

He didn't need fame or recognition — he needed answers, and they had a problem to solve.

Both men had left military service completely, reaching the same conclusion through opposite routes. While Freddie had willingly resigned, Reggie had been discharged for insubordination. But his heart matched Freddie's: he felt more comfortable fighting for himself and for his own idea of what was right and wrong than just trusting those decisions to the faceless entities who ran the country.

And it meant far more autonomy.

Since the Civilian Special Operations had been sanctioned by their benefactor, a man known only as Mr. E, the group had faced no shortage of militaristic threats around the world. The US government required a bare-bones cadre of military staff to keep tabs on their operations, though there was no formal arrangement between the two organizations. Freddie's understanding of the situation was that the US government had given the CSO nearly full authority to operate on and off United States soil, so long as they didn't get into too much trouble and didn't pull the US down with them.

He was sure the group had dodged more than a few bullets in the past, literally and figuratively, but he respected their approach.

Their job now was to fight injustice, no matter what it looked like. No matter where it was coming from.

In that sense, he and his new friends got to play judge, jury, and sometimes executioner.

Seated around a table in a room inside of a discreet office building now were six men hoping to fight injustice once again. Two worked for the CSO, and four were old friends — there was a hefty stipend for each of them upon completion of the mission, but Freddie knew they would have jumped at the chance to be useful once again, with or without pay. They would technically be operating illegally, using questionable sources for weaponry and equipment. It was not their first choice, but they needed to move quickly, and this was not the CSO's first time dipping a toe into the international arms dealing market.

Reggie had assured Freddie and the others that it would be no problem to acquire just about whatever tools for the job they would need, and the United States itself would turn a blind eye — especially if they never knew the mission had taken place.

The challenge now was for Freddie and his crack team to actually pull it off.

CHAPTER 26
FREDDIE

SEPTEMBER 15, 2020 | local time 9:03 pm

Chicago, Illinois

"So, where we headed?" Chuck, the only group member who was as large as Freddie himself, spoke with a gravelly, deep voice, that was almost soothing. "Surely somewhere exotic, right? Hawaii, maybe?"

"Maybe the Caribbean," another man said.

Freddie watched this soldier — Curtis — as he spoke, unable to smile at his drooping, sad-looking eyes. People always assumed he was upset about something, but Freddie had known him long enough to know that his face had simply given up many years ago, a look of permanent annoyance forever fixed upon it. He didn't smile when he asked the question.

"You two aren't married," Jason said, "so yeah, I could see why you *would* like a little romp in paradise. No one to have to call home and explain it to."

"Right, J-man," Chuck shot back, "like you're *so* loyal to the missus."

Freddie was about to jump in and join the fray when Reggie's expression made his blood run cold. He was all business, and he wanted these men to know it. Instead, Freddie looked at each of them again, slowly, trying to set the tone. "You know things are never *that* easy," he said. "All the good jobs go to the softies, the ones who wouldn't know the difference between a Glock and a glockenspiel."

"The hell's a glockenspiel?" Curtis asked, his eyebrows never moving.

"Man, I *knew* it," Curtis said. "I should've retired from this shit a long time ago."

"You did, asshole."

He laughed. "So that's it, then?" Curtis asked. "You can't tell us? 'Wheels up, boots down, eyes shut till the sun goes down?'"

Reggie shook his head, forcing a half-smile, and Freddie felt a bit of relief. *This is good*, he thought. *We needed rapport, and I think we're getting there.*

He knew Reggie's presence in the room was almost enough to convince these men to do just about anything, sight unseen. Gareth Red was as close to a legend as it came in circles like this one — these men were soldiers' soldiers, and Red had been the best one, with the credentials and medals to prove it. What really sold the legend, however, was that Reggie had made even more of a name for himself *after* his discharge. His unsanctioned, unofficial missions had grown to epic proportions, and rumors of his experiences had reached just about every career grunt in and out of the military.

No one he knew — Freddie's uncle included — agreed with the terms of Reggie's dishonorable discharge, but Freddie also knew of no one who would disagree that Reggie was a better soldier *now* than he had been in the Army.

"This one's personal," Reggie said, obviously sensing that the men needed him to speak, to rally them. "Close to home. It's not top-secret, because it's not even anywhere on paper. Not sanctioned from above. This one's for me and Freddie, yeah?"

There were nods all around, Freddie's included.

"We can tell you where we're going because by the time we get there, it won't be a secret, anyway. The organization that's been tracking the group we work for has been hounding us since last year, and we're relying on the fact that they're going to know our every move — somehow. So get used to a little bit of extra scrutiny."

Reggie stopped, and Freddie waited for a few more seconds before nodding. "We're going to Turkey. Specifically Imrali, an island off the coast. We've got some surveillance capabilities in place that we trust, and we think it's where he's being held."

Eyebrows rose around the table.

"He?"

Freddie nodded again. "This is quite literally a smash-and-grab. In, out, no extra baggage. No extra weight, but the subject we hope is there. The pay is good, but we're hoping you won't do it for the money."

Freddie watched as Reggie leaned out over the table, his long, lanky sleeveless arms nearly able to reach all the way across. He stared at his friend's prosthetic as the fingers on it tapped in a quick, dance-like motion on the table's surface. "As I said, it's personal. I'm hoping you'll do it for me, for him. Freddie's in charge because I know he can make the right call when the shit hits the fan. And boys, *do not* misunderstand me: the shit is *absolutely* going to hit the fan."

"At least it's an island, even though it ain't Hawaii," Curtis said. "And I can use a little more action, anyway."

Reggie gave Curtis a solemn nod, then sat back, waiting for the three other hired guns to toss in their thoughts.

"For obvious reasons, we can't give you a lot more details until you commit," Freddie said. "This one's off the books, much like they all are, but there's no backup this time. No airstrikes to call in or drones to provide surveillance. It's just us. No man's a coward for wanting out. No hard feelings, nothing like that."

Jason leaned forward and spoke, his eyes darting to Curtis and Chuck first. "If Curtis is in, so am I. I've never seen his eyes flutter around so quickly — he's either horny for Turkish chicks or just needs to shoot something. Seems like a mission he can get this excited about is one I can get excited about as well."

Curtis' face had not moved, and his eyes expressed to Freddie everything *but* excitement.

At the end of the table, Chuck giggled. He was short, barely up to Curtis' shoulder. His voice was high-pitched, and if Freddie had not experienced firsthand how ruthless a killer and whip-smart an operative he was, it would've been humorous.

He whistled. "So you actually *found* him? You think he's —"

"I'm gonna stop you there," Reggie snapped, "not because I believe he's alive, but because I don't even want to *wonder*. I don't want to think about it. Call me emotional, or superstitious, or whatever the hell you want, but this is our only chance at finding out. He's either there or he's not. Alive or dead. No way of knowing 'til we get there, and I don't want to get my hopes up or anyone else's."

"Fair enough," Chuck said, his hands out in front of him. "I'm in too, so I want to hear those details. Yeah, I'd love to kill the sorry souls who took him, but I mostly just want to get him back. For you two."

Freddie swallowed. "I was passed some intel. And no, I won't tell you who it's from even if I could. But it's good intelligence, vetted and even verified by a secondary source. But we still don't know if he's there or not — we really don't know damn near anything, but Reggie and I have been sitting on our butts for close to nine months, waiting for anything useful to fall into our laps. We've turned over every rock we can find, except this one."

Next to Freddie, Reggie shifted in his chair. "And this one's a big rock, so it could be promising. The place were going is known as the Alcatraz of the East. Except where Alcatraz has been hyped up over the years as some larger-than-life Supermax federal prison, this place was every bit as impenetrable as Alcatraz *should* have been. It would have made Ed Harris and Nic Cage cry."

"Was?"

Freddie nodded, taking over the thread from Reggie. "Yeah. Only rumors of this place exist, but it's likely the Turkish government just didn't want outsiders checking in on where they were keeping their most dangerous prisoners. However, it seems like the prison complex itself, as well as the land it's on, was sold off to a private company after the prison was closed down in the '90s. Since no record of its location exists, when we saw evidence that there was at least one building on this tiny, supposedly uninhabited island about eleven miles off the coast of the main continent, we got suspicious. Everything we found suggests that this might be the location of what used to be the Imrali Prison."

"And you think he's there? You think it's still a prison?"

"There's only one way to find out. Our best guess is that, yes, he was brought there about nine months ago — that's our hope, anyway. We were investigating the theft of an antique sword and the kidnapping of a mutual friend, and that brought us to Europe. We ran around like idiots, eventually ending up on the island of Elba."

"That's the island where Napoleon was?" Curtis asked.

"So you do know a little history," Freddie acknowledged. "Yes, he was exiled there. Afterward, we split up. Reggie, me, and the others headed back to the states, but he went a separate way. He wanted to check in with someone and get some more information about this group that's been following us. Last we heard from him he was on his way to Corsica, the birthplace of Napoleon."

"How do you know he's not still there?" Jason asked.

"As I said — we've turned over a *lot* of rocks looking for him. We were able to hack into an airport server and check with the towers that interacted with any flight that left the island over the next weeks. Obviously, most were commercial flights that had routes logged through official channels. Those were the easiest to track, and all of them ended up where they were supposed to be. Private jets were a bit trickier, but there weren't as many. We were able to nail down the destination points of every single one of them."

"Except for one," Reggie added.

This got everyone's interest. Even Curtis' left eyebrow wiggled slightly.

Freddie continued. "A Learjet took off from Corsica three days after he would have arrived. Surprisingly, it actually filed navigation instructions and a flight plan with the European equivalent of ATC. But it seems the plane made an unscheduled, mid-flight adjustment, and never updated the regional tower. Last data we can glean from the server was that radar had the plane heading almost due east, over the Mediterranean."

"Heading for Turkey, I presume?" Curtis asked, now with a fully raised eyebrow.

Freddie smiled. "Not just Turkey. Heading *directly* toward Imrali island."

"I see," Chuck said. "But you said it was a Learjet. Is this tiny little island big enough for an airport?"

"No, certainly not in the traditional sense. But we have seen some satellite imagery that suggests a large enough clearing on the northern half of the island, which might support a single runway."

"And so the mystery is solved," Chuck said, following it up with another whistle. "And whoever's behind this must have some serious clout if they're able to erase actual map data from worldwide servers."

"And you gentlemen must have some friends in high places if you're able to commandeer military satellites to prove otherwise," Curtis added.

"No one said anything about commandeering anything," Freddie said with a sly grin. "But as I said, our sources *are* trustworthy. That island *is* out there, and that plane landed on it — I can feel it. Either way, we have no other likely candidates, so we're going with this. We *are* going to find him."

"Damn right we are, man." Jason said. "But you haven't told us the best part: how *exactly* are we supposed to get to this Alcatraz of the East, sight unseen, and then get out with a high-value prisoner?"

At this, Reggie leaned forward once again and smiled. "You're right — that *is* the best part."

CHAPTER 27
SARAH

Anchorage, Alaska

Sarah pulled the phone out of her pocket and checked the number on the screen. Dr. Lindgren frowned. She didn't recognize the number, and it was not a US-based phone line.

She pulled the phone up to her ear as she pressed talk. "Hello, this is Sarah."

There was a pause for a few seconds, as if the person on the other hand was deciding whether or not to actually speak. Finally, a soft woman's voice rang out through the digital connection. *"Hello? This is Dr. Sarah Lindgren?"*

Sarah swallowed. Reggie and Freddie had left four hours ago, and though she had expected to hear from Reggie once they had checked in, she knew the men would be busy planning. She hoped this wasn't someone calling on his behalf, as that could only mean bad news.

"Yes, this is Sarah Lindgren. Can I help you?"

"I hope so," the woman's voice said. *"Sorry, I hate to intrude. I don't even know what time it is where you are. I'm — I'm in Egypt, it's morning here. I looked up your number at the university, but I wasn't sure if it was an office line or —"*

"Slow down, it's okay," Sarah said. "This is my cell. I never bother with the office phone. You're in Egypt, you said?"

Perhaps this had nothing to do with her boyfriend after all, but someone calling out of the blue from a completely different country still did not bode well.

"Yes, I got here as fast as I could. I was at Siwa, almost in Libya. I had to steal a jeep from the camp, then drive across — "

Sarah shook her head. "I'm sorry, can you slow down a bit? I'm trying to track with you. You stole a jeep? And what do you mean, you were at Siwa?"

Her heart had begun beating faster, and she felt a subconscious realization donning on her slowly. The woman on the other end of the line answered her premonitions before she could herself.

"Sorry again. My name is Marcia Rosenthal. I'm a student, from Penn State, but I've been working with your father for the past two years."

Of course. Now things were starting to pull together. She vaguely remembered an email from her father alerting her that he was going to be traveling to Africa for another expedition. At this point in their careers, that was about as much of an update as one needed to give to the other — professional anthropologist and professional archaeologist, father and daughter, working separately toward a similar goal: to reveal humanity's shared past and weave an interconnected series of stories into the tapestry of knowledge.

She and her father got along very well, yet it was an irony that the more successful each got, the more they drifted apart. She missed him, but that seemed to be a constant in her life these days.

"Yes, I remember now. He was going to Africa for a dig. You can give me the details later, though. Marcia, what happened?"

There was another pause, and Sarah heard voices in the background behind Marcia.

"We found it," she began. *"The tomb, I mean."*

Sarah frowned, trying to understand.

"The reason we were excavating — it was his latest pet project, and he was right. It's beneath the temple at Siwa, and we excavated a section of tunnel that descended under the southern structure complex."

"A tomb? At Siwa?" Sarah asked. She needed to brush up on her ancient Egyptian history, but she knew Siwa to be an oasis in Egypt, just across the border from Libya. Inhabited only by a relatively small group of people, and to the Egyptians, the ancient site was considered to be one of the most sacred sites on Earth.

She had a hunch as to the nature of the dig her father's team was working on, but she hoped her hunch was wrong.

If it's that, we've got far bigger problems, she thought.

And she knew that if her hunch was correct, it meant her father could be in danger.

They could *all* be in danger.

"Marcia, can you tell me more about what you and my father were working on out there? What *exactly* you were doing?"

Sarah knew her father better than anyone. He was a true modern-day Indiana Jones — brash, driven to success, and more than a bit swashbuckling. He was not lacking in experience or training — the man had not become a world-renowned archaeologist because of a lucky break or a celebrity endorsement. He had earned each of his proverbial stripes. His publications — countless papers and more than a few books — tended to get quite deep into the academic side of his profession, which solidified his expertise with his colleagues and contemporaries.

But he also seemed to enjoy bucking the trend of towing the line in the archaeological community, a fact which often put him at odds with most of the hive-mind-like professional researchers. But over the years, his peers in the outside world had come to understand that Professor Graham Lindgren was going to do things his way, no matter what. If his opinion differed from that of the accepted norm, it wasn't out of a sense of contrarianism. Rather, it was usually due to a unique perspective he had stumbled upon after hard work and careful study.

The difference between him and the established archeological norms was that he was not afraid to further explore — and publicize — his findings.

"He believed that the actual tomb and resting place of Alexander the Great was in Siwa," Marcia said quickly.

"Alexander the Great?" Sarah asked. Once again, she found herself at a loss for recalling this particular section of history.

"I can send you the brief he wrote," Marcia said. "I know it sounds strange, but since his tomb was never found..."

Sarah nodded along. "Yes, that does sound like my father. Always turning over rocks, looking for lost pieces of the past."

And what a piece it would be to find Alexander the Great's tomb... While she didn't know much about the currently accepted ideas as to the whereabouts of the ancient leader's tomb, she did know that it had never been officially found. She had heard reports, usually one or two every decade, that some archaeologist had new thoughts as to where the man's tomb may be, but it was either due to a lack of funding or government intervention that had prevented most of these digs and excavations from even breaking ground.

The fact that her father's search was an exception was not surprising to Sarah. He was well-connected, and it would not even be surprising if her father's team actually found something.

"Did he find it? Did you actually discover the tomb?"

There was a pause on the other end of the line. *"In a sense, yes. The temple complex at Siwa was never built to be a* tomb, *so the fact that we found a tunnel no one knew existed, which then led to a subcomplex beneath the temple, was quite thrilling."*

Sarah understood the slight shift in the woman's tone, even over the phone. "Let me guess," she said, "he rushed in before the rest of you, wanting to make sure it was safe for the rest of you, but just ignoring safety protocols altogether because he was too excited to wait."

Marcia chuckled. *"You do know him well. However, that's not exactly what happened. Everything was in place to remove a pile of rocks from the end of the tunnel, one that we believe had been placed there in order to block the doorway that led into the tomb's antechamber. But..."* she trailed off. *"But someone came to the site. Three men, actually."*

Sarah immediately felt adrenaline begin to pump through her. She felt dread, even without knowing what Marcia would say next. She could not predict the words, but she had a feeling they were going to spell bad news.

"These men were hostile," Marcia continued choking back tears. *"They — they* shot *one of the students. One of my friends."*

Sarah heard the rise in Marcia's voice, a swallow and a struggle to force her vocal cords to engage.

"I'm so sorry," Sarah said, already moving toward the counter where she had placed her keys in the Anchorage hotel room. "I'm coming over there."

"Wait, you're coming? Here?"

Sarah nodded. "I already have a bag packed. I can be there by tomorrow."

"That's — well, I appreciate it, but that's not why I was calling," Marcia said. *"Your father disappeared into the tunnel complex, but I left when the men were walking toward the entrance we had excavated. I didn't see them enter, but two of the men were holding guns. I don't want you to come all the way out here for no reason, Sarah. I hate to be the one to call, but I know you would want to hear it from one of his students. You know, instead of... on the news."*

Sarah swallowed, finding it was now her turn to hold back tears. "Yes, thank you. I understand."

"Not that it would be a waste of time," Marcia said. *"I just mean you shouldn't rush. If your father —"*

"If they killed my father, I want to know who they are. I want to find them."

Sarah felt a sense of resolve, of determination, starting to replace the dread. It seemed that hanging around the CSO and her boyfriend — a well-trained, well-practiced sniper — had taught her more than just how to handle a weapon and how to survive in the real world. It seemed it had taught her to see clearly in terrifying situations.

She was not going to simply accept the fact that her father might be dead until she saw his corpse. *Either way, I want to know who these men are and what they want with my father.*

"But if he's not dead — if he somehow found a way out — they're going to be looking for him, right?"

There was a long pause, and when Marcia's voice came back on the line, it was barely a whisper. *"Yes. I believe so. They wanted to speak with him. They were determined."*

"Then I'm on my way. Figure out what you can, if you're able, but stay in the shadows. I don't want you to get hurt, Marcia. I'll pick you up at the embassy tomorrow morning."

They exchanged contact information, and Sarah hung up the phone as she walked through the hotel's spacious room and grabbed her duffel bag on the bed. She had planned to stay in Anchorage for the week, to be nearer to Julie as well as to offer remote support for whatever Freddie and Reggie might need for their own journey.

But now a new element had entered the game, and this element was personal.

She was not going to simply lie in wait and hope for the best — whatever her father had gotten himself into, she was going to find a way to get him out.

ACT III

"Like the generations of leaves, the lives of mortal men. Now the wind scatters the old leaves across the earth, now the living timber bursts with the new buds and spring comes round again. And so with men: as one generation comes to life, another dies away."

— Homer, *The Iliad*

CHAPTER 28
ALEXANDER

JUNE 2, **326 | local time 9:05 am**
Siwa Oasis, Egypt

Alexander looked around the room. It was small — smaller than he would have imagined — but size was nothing. In his world — the world he had created, the one he had *earned* — size was measured by control, by power. Not by the measure of physical form. He wasn't large in stature himself, and yet he had toppled empires, he had *earned* control of most of the known world. He had built armies from vanquished enemies, stolen the hearts and minds of the young and old alike.

So no, this room did not need to be of any particular size. It needed to please him, that was all.

And it did please him. The room was not lavishly appointed, no garish decorative elements that had consumed lesser men. Those sorts of trivialities were just what he intended to avoid. None of that could accompany him where he was going.

None of it had any value in death — therefore it had no value to him in life.

"Will this do, sir?" his aide asked from behind him.

Alexander gave a curt nod but sensed his aide was not satisfied.

He sighed, then turned to address him. "A man shall not be measured by what follows him to death, but by what follows him in life. Pleasantries are but a distraction. A means with which a man might busy himself while others do his dirty work."

His aide stammered. "Is — so, is the room up to your expectation, my liege?"

"Yes. It shall not even offer a remembrance of me, of what I have done. It shall not remind of the things I have stolen. Instead, it shall represent that which comes with me — nothing but the memories I have made. Those in my mind, and those in the minds of others."

"There is one more thing, sir," his aide said. The young man was but twenty years old, a decade younger than Alexander, yet a lifetime less experienced. He was not incompetent, but of late Alexander had felt the growing realization of just how far he had been set apart from his fellow man.

If the man standing in front of him should be considered average, Alexander was a God.

The rumor was that Alexander's father was none other than Zeus himself. Some days, Alexander even believed it.

He cleared his throat, waiting for the boy to speak again. When he did, Alexander watched him with intense, curious eyes. He read men like this as though they were a book, their pages open to their most intimate parts, the thoughts and feelings and secret fantasies spilling out. Whereas at one time, Alexander used to have to pull at the threads of these words to fully understand them, to coax them to life, now they simply spilled out of people as if begging to be understood by him.

And this boy's face and mannerisms and words told Alexander that he did not want to be here. He was afraid, though not of Alexander himself. He knew this boy revered him, even before he had earned this prestigious role in Alexander's inner circle.

He was afraid of something else. Could it be Alexander's bold refusal to adhere to the traditions of this place? This boy seemed as though he could be partly of Egyptian descent. Perhaps that was the issue? Perhaps Alexander was not showing enough honor to the young man's heritage?

The boy tried to continue. "There — there will be a statue, I believe it is currently —"

"No," Alexander said softly.

"Sir?"

"No statue. That is all."

The boy hesitated, no doubt to try to persuade Alexander that he should accept the gift as it was intended — an honor to his character, to his leadership. That to spurn a gift such as this would speak powerfully to others that Alexander was not a gracious host.

To spurn such a gift, in a place like this, meant he had no respect for these people. Sure, he had conquered, but there was still an expectation of honor, and this would be crossing the line.

He didn't care. There was no more time for that sort of petty maneuvering. This place was not going to house his treasures. It was meant for something else.

With any luck, this place would not be seen again by the outside world for ages to come. By then, hopefully, there would be a way to stop it.

Suddenly, he understood the young aide's fear.

"You are afraid to be here," Alexander said. It was not inflected as a question, but he saw it register on the boy's face, nonetheless.

The kid swallowed, then nodded once. "Yes."

"For what reason should you be afraid? Even now, as our armies march on, the battle tomorrow will be won decidedly. It is but a formality."

"Yes — yes, sir," the boy stammered. "No, it is not for the battle or for our army. It is..."

"Say no more," Alexander said, turning to face the other direction. He understood what the boy would say, and therefore there was no need to hear the words aloud.

He felt similar, in fact. This place itself was not a place that could invoke fear — it was just a *place*. It was just an empty chamber.

It was what this place *represented*. His aide surely knew it, too — he knew of the disease, of the fear of plague or the gods meddling in the lives of their people. He knew of the blackness that was consuming Alexander, and he knew — or at least he thought he knew — of the reason why.

Alexander had been fearful of this as well. It was why he had built this place. Why he had chosen a spot hidden away from the world, beneath a temple that would commandeer and hold the attention of the populace.

No one would think to check here. No one would imagine what is buried beneath their feet. What would rise *from the ashes of death here.*

And *that* was what this boy feared. That was the reason for his aide's foul attitude.

This young man, like the rest of the world, did not understand. This place was not a tomb, not a resting place for Alexander's body after he had perished.

It was a *resurrection* chamber — for that reason, it had been constructed for secrecy and utility, not garishness and symbolism. If Alexander's closest associates did their jobs well, this place would hardly register in history as an interesting location.

What would *happen* here, however, would change the world.

Alexander smiled at the young man, hoping to reassure him. It would not work, but it was the least he could do.

The boy had every right to be fearful, every right to be terrified. For he was not standing in the presence of a man.

He was standing next to a *god*.

CHAPTER 29
GRAHAM

Siwa Oasis, Egypt

Professor Graham Lindgren walked along the dark, cavernous corridor that was one of the many that made up the complex beneath Siwa. The air smelled damp and musty. It was pitch black in the space, save for the small light he held tightly in one hand. In the other, he gripped the strange urn-like object.

It had been hours — perhaps even half a day — since he had been trapped down here. Not one prone to panic, and certainly not a man uncomfortable navigating ancient sites and undiscovered tombs, it was still surreal to have been here for so long, without so much as even hearing a noise from the outside world.

He had spent the first hour at the bottom of the shaft waiting, tense, for the men above to find this place. He knew they would — it was only a matter of time.

And then another hour had passed, and nearly another. At some point, he had fallen asleep. Sleeping on rock was not his idea of a great night's sleep, but he had to admit the cool, dark conditions had allowed him to rest well, even if he had not intended to fall asleep.

He had awoken frightfully, at first unsure of where he was. The recollection came quickly, and he shook off the fear and got back to work, surprised that the men from the chamber above had given up the search — or had decided to come back later, perhaps with more help.

Graham had chosen then to continue working through the myriad puzzles in his mind. The first, and most important, was the puzzle of where, exactly, he was — and whether or not he could find an exit from it.

He knew the Siwa temples well, at least those aboveground. While this was his first actual dig onsite, he had visited the location of the fabled oracle numerous times, even lecturing for a semester on the oracles and their crucial role in the conquering civilizations of old.

But he didn't know *this* temple well. It was not situated like a traditional Egyptian tomb, and yet he had found a sarcophagus inside its hidden room. But that sarcophagus had not held the body of the tomb's supposed namesake, which left even more puzzles.

He had spent the next two hours analyzing the walls by touch. He did not want to waste the battery on his flashlight, which was already at around a half charge. He had a charging device in his pack capable of bringing the USB light back to life three or four times, but he had left the pack back at camp.

After determining that the only way through this new maze was forward, through the only hallway leading away from the shaft, he had decided to move slowly up the hall toward whatever this place wanted to show him. He moved methodically, the years of excavations and experience allowing him to work without needing his eyes. He wanted to capture as much of this space as possible, converting it from his fingers' touch to a semi-three-dimensional map in his mind. If there were any glyphs that might clue him in on what he was about to walk into, or the purpose for this whole place, he wanted to know.

And until he started to hear noises from above, he had time. There was no sense in rushing forward, running through an unknown temple site in pitch-black darkness, especially if he were running *from* something. That's how accidents happened. One misstep, one wrong turn, and he might successfully get away from his pursuers, only to end up dying from thirst lost in an ancient building.

So he moved slowly, working up the hall until his mind switched over to the puzzle that really wanted his attention: *what is inside the ceramic container?*

His mind raced with the possibilities. Whatever was inside the object would be likely valuable to his escape from this place — a key, or a map, or something similar.

However, it could also be a trap. Something inside could act as a last booby trap to deter grave robbers. Some arcane torture device that would grasp a hand when thrust inside, or something far simpler — poison.

There was a chance that if it were poison, it would be inert anyway after all these years, but he had learned to not question the ingenuity of the ancients. In addition, he had learned from his studies that the ancient societies were capable of being as cruel as they were advanced — often far more so.

Of course, there was also a chance that it was, simply, a funerary urn.

He walked to the end of the long hallway he had found after descending the tomb's shaft. He guessed he was underneath the southern temple, a location long believed to be a sort of decoy temple, meant to attract attention away from the real temple.

It was a ploy which had worked for over 2,000 years, he knew, as his own team had been the first outsiders to find the complex and southern wing since it had been built.

However, they had not had time or the necessary equipment to do a proper scan of the subterranean features and cavities as a way to determine the shape and layout of this newly discovered area, so Graham was completely lost.

The hallway he jogged down finally ended about a hundred feet to the north, where it dumped him out into a small stone room. Cracks lanced upward from the floor, and he could see a pile of rubble and dust in one corner where the shifting ground around the place had already begun reclaiming this building.

He hoped the men's banging to get into the chamber above his head had not caused much permanent damage. Best-case scenario was that it would lead to the unreconcilable loss of this ancient site — worst case, it meant the whole place could come crashing down on his head. While he was comfortable in small, tight underground spaces such as this one, he did not want to make one his grave.

As if hearing his thoughts, the universe decided to remind him then of the reason for his haste. He heard another crash, the echo reaching his ears from the hallway.

They're here, he thought. *They found the shaft.* Apparently they were unhappy, too — they were now clanging around and making as much noise as possible, likely to get down it quickly.

He needed to make a decision, and fast. If the urn, or whatever it was, held the answer to how to get out of this place, he needed to open it.

He ran to the corner of the room nearest the entrance, knowing that if all else failed he might be able to use the urn as a weapon — blunt objects did a number on human skulls. He crouched down, pulling the lid off the ceramic pot.

Inside was, surprisingly, another pot. This one smaller, wrapped in a cloth.

There was a moment of hesitation. He had never seen anything like this. It was not Egyptian, and it clearly was not Macedonian — or if it was, it had been crafted uniquely to stand apart from the civilization that had produced it.

But he could not hesitate any longer. If he wanted to survive here, he would have to move quickly and without regret. In one swift motion, he reached into his pocket and pulled out a small knife. The flashlight he sat on the floor in front of him, but its light was too direct to be useful. Thankfully, the knife was just large enough for him to detect by touch alone, even in the dark room. He slid it between the cloth wrapping around the object and the cylinder itself, slowly making an incision around its circumference while placing his ear against its surface to hear if there was any sound emitted from within — a ticking sound that might indicate some sort of weapon about to strike at him or some other such diabolical device designed by those who had placed it there thousands of years ago.

He paused for a final second before slicing through the final layer of cloth wrapping around it. With one quick motion he slashed through all layers beneath it until nothing stood between him and whatever secrets lay inside — with one exception: the object inside was affixed to what felt like rusting metal protrusions on either end of its length. Whatever was in this thing had been secured in place by something beyond even time itself — likely corroded metal spikes driven into wood long since crumbled away into dust. Whatever had been lodged inside the double-walled ceramic container must have been incredibly secured.

Graham's mind raced at the possibilities.

It's not a key. Not a map. It was not an object of any sort that would help him escape. It was a third container, about the size of a tennis ball but shaped like a miniature football. Made of some sort of smoothed stone, it seemed to be hollow as well, judging by the weight of it. He held it in a palm, letting the age and the beauty and simplicity of its creation carry his mind away.

"Get up," a gruff voice said.

Graham nearly dropped the object. He shot up, surprised at the ruse.

The men were here. He had not realized that they might try to purposely make noise in order to sneak up on him, and he saw that the flashlight's beam had illuminated a section of the wall in front of him, visible from the hallway. He had lit a beacon for them, and they had arrived before he had time to make a plan.

Not like there would be a good enough plan, anyway, he thought. There were no exits from this room, either. His best bet would be, unfortunately, to cooperate.

He looked up, sniffing at the dust that had risen in the room. He saw the large hulking frame of the first man who had entered, knowing that the tiny ceramic container likely would not have done much damage on the ape's thick skull.

That's it, he suddenly realized. *My only shot.* He traced the man's eyes and followed his gaze down. *He hasn't seen it yet.*

The man was only looking at the ceramic pot the smaller object had been in. Graham was still holding the tiny orb in his palm, keeping it out of sight.

Professor Lindgren smiled, then stood. "Oh, hello," he said nonchalantly, slipping the football-like piece of stone into a pocket, careful to keep it out of sight from the man in the doorway. He cleared his throat as the second man peered inside. "I wasn't sure if you would find me. I was told you wanted to see me?"

CHAPTER 30
GRAHAM

Siwa Oasis, Egypt

Professor Lindgren had watched, helpless, as the two huskier men dragged him through his now-empty dig site at Siwa. None of the students or contracted laborers remained, but a quick glance over a shoulder to the tent showed something akin to blood stains marking the ground. He seethed, hoping none of his team had been injured.

For now, there was no way to find out. The men shoved him into a black sedan, then they had shown him his own cellphone, retrieved from the camp. Any hope he might have had for reaching out to someone, of calling for help, had died then and there.

Only the shorter, clean-cut man had spoken to him during the hour-long journey across the border to Libya, and even then he had asked only about the dig site. Graham had told him what he knew — that it was a temple, and that they were in the beginning stages of its excavation, and that his men had ruined priceless historical artifacts — but the man had not seemed impressed.

However, he had not pushed further. Whatever questions he

wanted answered would be waiting for later, waiting for when they reached wherever it was they were going.

It was another hour after that — after boarding a helicopter that had appeared like a surreal mirage in the desert — when the man had started asking questions once more.

"What did you find in the tomb?" the man asked through the chopper's intercom system. Graham had been shoved into a headset that fit completely over his ears and blocked out enough sound to almost make it seem as though he were not flying over the desert floor in a loud machine. Unfortunately, his eyes gave up the illusion. He swallowed and squeezed his eyes shut, trying to ignore the coming motion sickness.

"I — I don't know what you're talking about," Graham stuttered.

"Of course you do." The man smiled sadly. *"You found him, didn't you?"* He held up the ceramic container his men had taken from him. If he wondered what may have been inside, he did not say anything.

"Found *who*? It's not really a tomb," Lindgren said. "It's a temple. An old temple."

He was playing dumb — surely a ruse this man would see through, but Graham had no better options in front of him.

The man sighed as his voice crackled into his headset. *"Please, we are running out of time."*

"Do tell," Graham said. "What is it you have planned? And how, exactly, does an old temple —"

"Tomb," the man interrupted.

"Sure, tomb. Whatever. What's so important about this tomb?"

"You tell me," the man said. *"You used all the political and academic clout you could muster — not to mention more than a little of your own money — to get this dig approved. To what end? I understand you are a historian, but what —"*

"Siwa is an incredibly important temple to history. And it's falling apart. If we don't excavate and protect it now, it may be —"

152

The man held up a hand, and Graham immediately went silent.

"Professor, you of all people should know that there are ways of making you talk."

"You — you're going to torture me?"

"Will it make you talk?"

"I *am* talking. You don't seem to like my answers. You believe that torturing me is going to get me to, what? Make something up so you'll stop?"

The man examined Graham for a moment across the cabin, as if eyeing a gerbil on a wheel. Graham felt a sudden sense of trepidation, but before he could speak again, the chopper broke its line and turned sharply.

He felt his stomach rise to his throat before settling again.

"No, professor — to answer your question, we are not going to torture you. Those arcane methods produce arcane results. I was hoping for more from you, however. A man of science — a man of history — surely you can imagine a more fitting solution to our dilemma?"

Graham frowned. He genuinely had no idea what this man was referring to, though the implication that he *should* know something was not lost on him. *Who are these people?* he thought once again. *What do they want from me, and what do they think I know?*

He suddenly felt the pressure of the football-shaped object pushing against his inside pocket. Designed to keep pickpockets from perusing wallets and personal items stored on one's person, Graham had often made use of the sewn interior pockets of his work clothes to sneak objects through places he knew could not appreciate their value.

Thankfully, he had been wearing just such a pocket, and it was into this pocket he had shoved the small... whatever it was.

Now, staring at the three men staring back at him, trying to rack his mind for what they could *possibly* want from him, he realized the little object, Alexander the Great, *and* these men were somehow probably related.

These were more than treasure hunters, judging by their clothing, equipment, and the expensive ride they were currently in. But what more could they be? What else besides invaluable treasure could justify such an expense?

He felt the object in his pocket once more and imagined it throbbing, as if begging for attention. He focused on it, imagining the shape and design of the trinket. How it fit snugly inside the carefully crafted ceramic pot, the style of which was unknown to him. It lacked many artistic details, as if it had been designed for a simple task, not something intended to be displayed publicly.

But what was its intended use, then? To his knowledge so far, there was no way to open the small stone. It had not seemed hollow, and there did not appear to be any surface marks or lines denoting a way to crack two halves of it apart.

However, Graham got the distinct impression that this device or artifact or treasure — whatever it might *actually* be — had more than a little to do with the reason he had been captured. Perhaps it was the sole reason they had taken him, and perhaps it was the reason they had been inclined to violence toward his students and team.

And perhaps it had something to do with Alexander the Great himself. After all, *he* was the reason Graham had come to Siwa. The great leader had been the entire goal of their dig at the oasis, and his corpse had been the sole driver of Graham's interest.

And yet he had not found a body, mummified or otherwise, in the tomb. There had been a sarcophagus, sure, but it had not contained human remains of any sort. Instead, it had held a purpose-built container, tucked away inside the folds of shadows in the subterranean temple.

Someone had buried it there, over a thousand years prior, and allowed the future world to believe it was related, somehow, to Alexander the Great.

Professor Lindgren had not had time to analyze the object, nor the ceramic pot he had found it in. He had not had time to cross-reference its style with anything else from this time period, nor had he had the ability to research when and why Alexander the Great might have commissioned something like this.

But he *did* know plenty about the deceased conqueror. He knew as much as any modern researcher and historian, and he had spent countless hours brushing up on the latest knowledge related to the man.

As such, he had only a single idea as to how the man and the object might be connected. It was not a surefire bet, but it was as good a lead as any.

The problem was that the implication of that idea — and the fact that he was now in the hands of known killers — was absolutely terrifying.

CHAPTER 31
SARAH

SEPTEMBER 17, 2020 | local time 9:45 am

Cairo, Egypt

Sarah Lindgren walked through the grand entrance of the US Embassy in Cairo. She had sent Marcia a text message informing her of her arrival and confirming the time, and she had found the woman seated on one of the long benches along the marble walls of the foyer. As Sarah approached, Marcia stood, a strained smile on her face.

She was young and pretty, but she looked tired, haggard even. She was worried, and for good reason.

Sarah didn't waste any time. She walked over and embraced Marcia, eliciting a change of expression on the young woman's face to one of mild shock.

Sarah pulled back, apologetic. "I'm sorry, I just thought —"

The hug was more for her than for Marcia, and she hoped she hadn't crossed the line with this new acquaintance.

"No, it's not that," Marcia said. "I'm sorry... it's just — this is going to sound weird, but your dad is a hero to me. You're a close second."

Sarah scoffed. "Me? A hero?"

Marcia shrugged. "I told you it would sound goofy. But it's true

— I read your father's books when I was a kid. I knew from eight years old that I wanted to do exactly what he did. I wanted to be an explorer, to lead expeditions and find answers to the questions we all have. I *never* thought I would get the opportunity to actually *work* with him"

Sarah smiled and nodded as Marcia recounted. That was certainly the father she knew and loved. It was also no accident that Marcia had twice now mentioned working *with* her father instead of *for* him, which would have technically been more accurate. Professor Graham Lindgren was known not just for his brilliant mind and archaeological experience, but for his ability to engage the attention of his students and earn an almost revered status. He made them feel welcome, made him feel equal. To him, no one worked *for* Graham Lindgren. They worked *with* him, and it was one of the traits unique to him Sarah was most fond of. He had no superiority complex among those interested even slightly in his line of work.

"Well, that doesn't sound strange at all," Sarah said. "I'm glad you called. No matter what happens out there, I'm glad it was someone close to my father who brought me here."

Marcia nodded, her face once again solemn and distant. "So, what — what do we do now?" she asked.

"I've got a rental car, parked in the visitor lot outside," Sarah said. "Full tank of gas too, which should get us most of the way to Siwa."

"We're going back out there?"

"Is this your first time in Egypt, Marcia?"

"I visited as a kid once, but yeah — first time as an adult. First time working here."

Sarah pulled Marcia toward the lobby entrance. She was parked to the left of the building once they exited, and she didn't want to waste any time, so she wanted to walk and talk. "Look, this isn't America. Sure, Egypt is much more modern now than it's ever been, but there are still... ways of doing things. If we call the authorities, the police or Interpol or anything like that, we can't be sure that whoever comes to help us *actually* has our best interests in mind."

Marcia nodded as they walked along, swallowing a lump in her throat. "Your father told us basically the same thing," she said. "He said even though we're not doing anything wrong out there, some of the locals will always refuse to see it that way. Any exploration into their past is considered a desecration of ancient idols, or something like that."

"That's the tame way of putting it," Sarah said. "And of course the truth is always more complicated. But yeah — for every officer who might lend us a hand, there are probably three who would jump at the opportunity to just make us disappear."

Sarah stopped suddenly, then turned to the younger woman. "Marcia, you've been at the embassy for a couple of days now. I'm sure you've talked to *someone*, because you had to check in to get a room. What did you tell them?"

Marcia's eyes danced upward. "I tried to be discreet, of course, but I also needed them to know that I was in dire straits, since I did not have a credit card or any way of paying for a hotel. I've tried reaching out to other students that were on the dig with us, but..."

Sarah nodded. No need for her to recount her worst fears. "Did you talk to any embassy staff? Any government officials? Did anyone come to question you?"

Marcia thought for a moment, then nodded. "They gave me a room without much trouble, but yesterday, shortly after I talked to you, a man and a woman who said they were from the Ministry of Antiquities came and knocked on my door. They asked what university I was with, asked to see our grant and paperwork from the Ministry — I didn't have any of that on me, of course — and finally asked about your father. They wanted to know where I thought he was."

"What did you tell them?"

"I told him what I knew — that I hadn't seen him since I left. I didn't know if he was still at Siwa or not."

Sarah squeezed her eyes shut, then opened them quickly. She didn't want to startle Marcia, but this was *not* good news. "Okay, so they knew to look for him out at the oasis."

"Yes, but *who*? They're not from the Ministry of Antiquities? You think they're the same people who showed up and shot Paul? You think they're working together?"

"First of all, I don't think the guys out at your camp were government at all," Sarah said quickly, trying to de-escalate to help with Marcia's anxiety. "If those had been real government employees who had come out there, they would have at least pretended to play by the rules. They would have just strongly insisted you all stop the research and come to their office in Cairo, or something like that. Whoever came out there to look for my father was working for a different group."

"Then, what's the problem?" Marcia asked. "You think these people who came to see me from the Ministry are like some of the corrupt police you were talking about?"

"If they really were Ministry officers, then yes. Or they also weren't who they said they were, and they were working with the guys from your camp. If I've learned anything about this place, it's that secrets don't stay secret for long. They'll know I'm here," she said. "And because of that, they'll know *you're* here. They'll know someone from my father's team made a call to me."

They reached the parking spot where Sarah had parked the rental car not ten minutes prior, and both women got in. Sarah started the car and backed it out of the space. The hot Egyptian sun had already baked the steering wheel and center console, even in the few minutes the car had been idle.

She turned on the air conditioning full-blast and turned to Marcia as she pointed the car out of the lot. "I hope I'm not scaring you, but the group I work with now has been under heavy scrutiny from some nasty players. I can't be naïve and think I'm not in their sights as well."

Marcia looked shocked once again, and Sarah hoped it was not also a look of betrayal.

"I didn't mention it on the phone because I wasn't sure it was worth potentially frightening you away. If you weren't visited by any government types, I would have less reason to think you were in any danger. But there's no doubt in my mind they know I'm here now. They know my name, so they know I'll be looking for my father."

Marcia swallowed again, and Sarah thought she could see tears in the young woman's eyes.

"Marcia, I can't ask you to run around the country with me when there are bad people trying to find me. Bad people trying to find my old man. If you want to leave, now's the —"

Before she could finish the sentence, the rear half of the sedan completely exploded.

A fury of metal and glass rained over Sarah's body as the sound of crunching steel and aluminum tore through her ears.

Next to her, Marcia was jolted sideways, violently. Her head hit the side window and her eyes shut as the smacking sound of skull on glass reached Sarah's strained ears.

CHAPTER 32
FREDDIE

Sea of Marmara | Near Armutlu, Turkey.

The plan was simple. The group would attempt a water-based approach, aiming for the only side of the cliff-ringed island that appeared to have any shoreline whatsoever. Upon landing ashore, they would then unstrap climbing gear and scale a two-hundred-foot rock wall on the northwestern side of the island, which — conveniently enough — also seemed to be the side of the island that was farthest from the building complex on its surface. The decision had been made that this approach would provide the easiest way to breach the main compound.

They expected resistance in the form of prison guards at least, and potentially hired security as well, which meant that their best shot of winning a gun fight was to get onto solid, flat land as soon as possible.

Simple enough, Freddie thought.

The trouble nagging at him was that plans that were simple never ended up actually *being* simple.

No plan survives first contact with the enemy.

His uncle — and scores of military strategists before him — had regurgitated the quote so often it had become lodged in his mind as objective fact. Freddie used to be annoyed by the saying, as it was one of those things that sounded so obvious as to be unhelpful. But then he had joined the military and served with special operations teams, and he had quickly realized how deeply nuanced the phrase could be.

'Making a plan' wasn't just about creating backup plans upon backup plans — that was an exercise in futility more often than not. Instead, the designed plan was usually the only plan that needed to be made, as it was widely considered that the most efficient use of time and resources to achieve an objective was the 'best' plan.

But he had learned the hard way that every single plan, no matter how efficient, would need to be adapted in the field — sometimes subtly, sometimes in more drastic ways. In order to pull off something incredible, a plan's success came down not to its inherent quality as an efficient *plan*, but in its efficient *execution*.

And *that* efficiency often came down to the quality of that plan's executors. Freddie trusted his own experience, and he trusted Reggie's like a brother's.

He trusted the three men he had hired for the job as well, though he had not worked with them in years. They all seemed to be fit and ready for the job, and as the small five-man team raced out toward the tiny pinprick of a rock off the northern coast of Turkey, he could almost feel the camaraderie between them building once again. He imagined their soaked, tired bodies, hours after completing the mission, waltzing into a local Turkish pub for a beer and the quiet confidence of finishing a hard day's work. He could picture the back-slapping, the jokes, the recounting of the myriad ways the mission could have gone wrong, and how they had overcome and prevailed.

It almost felt like the good old days, back when the missions were not personal but professional, back when something like this could be pulled off in the morning and they would all be drinking beers on the beach by the afternoon, just in time for sunset.

But as with all missions, Freddie knew they had to *finish* the mission first. There was no celebrating until the job was done, until their objective — the ultimate prize — had been retrieved successfully.

And even knowing the stakes, this mission felt somehow different. Sure, this one was personal, especially for Reggie. But there was something else — there was something about this whole endeavor that seemed... menacing to him. Was it the team? Was one of his teammates not actually as capable anymore as he was letting on? They had all aged by a decade since they had worked together last, so that was probable.

But he had laid all the cards on the table, he had explained what they would be required to do, physically and mentally. Each of them had given him their word that they were capable, and he trusted them. They did not need to prove their worth by passing some sort of PT test.

And physical fitness was one of the aspects of their plan that could be overcome — if someone couldn't cut it, they could still serve a purpose elsewhere.

No, he was sensing something else, something he couldn't quite put into words.

If Reggie was feeling the tension as well, he didn't show it. The man's face was stoic, unmoving as it had been the past nine months.

Since the disappearance of their friend — the suspected kidnapping, more accurately — Freddie had seen Reggie change from an exuberant, extremely charismatic individual into a soulless man bent on finding answers — and revenge.

He had seen it before in soldiers, and he worried that Reggie might be too far past the point of recovery, even if they were able to accomplish their mission here today.

Lesser things had broken men before, and he hoped to God Reggie was stronger than that.

They had a mission to accomplish, and it would not do for their leader to express worry he could hardly put into words. They all knew the risks. Freddie shook away the strange sensation and spoke over the in-ear headset they all wore. "Approaching drop point. Scuba gear?"

"*Scuba, check,*" Chuck said. The man's high-pitched voice was not helped any by the low-quality vocal transmission that reached Freddie's ear.

Comical or not, however, the man was coldly efficient. He ran a third check on all the scuba gear and nodded as he worked.

Curtis was driving their lithe speedboat, standing in the cockpit while two massive outboard engines pummeled them forward over the choppy waters of the Sea of Marmara. They had been riding up on plane for nearly an hour, none of the five men complaining about the bumpy ride, none of them hardly speaking at all. Rather than making a direct approach, the group had started from the southwest, making a semi-circle around the western side of Imrali to stay out of sight as long as possible. There were other boats in the water, so Freddie was not worried that they would look suspicious to anyone on the island checking them out, but he knew as they got closer and closer, they might start raising red flags to the security team.

CHAPTER 33
SARAH

SEPTEMBER 17, **2020 | local time 9:52 am**

Cairo, Egypt

She had seen the oncoming truck only a split-second prior, her eyes not able to register it as a threat until it was far too late.

Marcia screamed, and Sarah felt the steering wheel wrench free from her hands as it spun wildly. The sedan twisted sideways, hitting a curb and then spinning through the air. They were rolling now, airborne and upside down. Mercifully, the small car completed the spin and landed on the two passenger side tires, bending them inward and causing the floorboard beneath the rear seats to rupture, otherwise leaving the interior cabin intact.

They had both buckled their seatbelts out of habit upon entering the vehicle, and that safety precaution was the only thing that had kept them both from flying out one of the smashed windows.

Sarah felt the throbbing in her head begin as the car came to a halt, steam and smoke and a hissing sound now filling her senses to replace the twisted confusion from before. Her head had struck the window, though she wasn't sure if it was her head or the impact with the pavement that had smashed it in. Tiny shards of safety glass splashed onto her lap and legs. She looked over at Marcia, which caused her headache to complain in force. Marcia looked dazed, her eyes darting left and right frantically as she worked at something with one of her hands.

Sarah was about to ask if she were okay when she saw the shadow creeping toward them.

She gulped as panic set in. She fumbled with her seatbelt, still looking over through the window at the approaching form. "Marcia, now."

"Now?"

"Yes, now. It's time to go. *Now.* Unbuckle your seatbelt and crawl out my side." Sarah already had her door open, and Marcia did as she was told. Sarah fell sideways out of the destroyed sedan into a puddle of antifreeze now pooling beneath the smashed wheel well. She pulled herself up onto her knees, feeling the liquid wetting her jeans, and reached out for Marcia. She saw what it was Marcia had been fiddling with — her hand had twisted into the seatbelt in an awkward way.

Broken wrist, perhaps. Sarah knew the woman wouldn't be able to feel the pain as much through the adrenaline, but it was going to hurt like hell later, even if it was not broken. Sarah assessed the rest of the young woman's body quickly and saw that Marcia was otherwise free of injury.

Good, she thought. *That means we can run.*

And it's time to run.

"Into those trees, get as far away as you can," Sarah said, breathless. "I'll be right behind you. Go!"

Marcia darted outward on command, reaching the trees just as Sarah heard the sound of gunfire. Two shots — barely even pops, meaning they were rounds fired from a small caliber pistol — whizzed by her ear. The shooter was close, just on the other side of the car. No doubt one of the shadows that had crept up on them, likely someone from the truck that had rammed them.

Their attackers had apparently survived the car crash and were out hunting for them now.

Sarah did the only thing she could do. She ran the opposite direction as Marcia. She pulled up from her wet knees and darted forward, out into the middle of the street. She had expected the accident to have caused at least someone who had not been involved to stop, to check in with the people and see if they were okay. Instead, it seemed the drivers in this part of Egypt had far better things to do.

There were cars everywhere, speeding around the wrecked and smoking truck as if it were not even there. Traffic in both directions began honking as soon as she stepped onto the road. She knew from personal experience that drivers in Egypt — especially in Cairo — were as reckless as they were impatient, but she had not considered that they would completely ignore a seconds-old car accident.

She played the dangerous game of risking her life — again — as she ran through the street. As she ran, dodging angry commuters, she wondered if one of the drivers inside of the vehicles might decide that getting to their appointment on time was worth ramming a woman.

She didn't care. She would either get hit by a car or be shot. Both outcomes would end with her severely injured, but at least she could assume that most of the commuters did not *want* to run her over, whereas with the shooter, she knew exactly what they wanted from her. She hoped Marcia had gotten away; she needed to double-back and eventually join her in the small copse of trees next to the embassy. From here, the area Marcia had disappeared into looked to be some sort of public park, and Sarah hoped it was big enough to conceal Marcia inside until Sarah could get around and find her.

So far Sarah had noticed only one man shooting at them, which meant he would have to choose his target: would he go after the younger woman who had run into the trees, or would he also risk playing leapfrog through traffic to chase after Sarah? Sarah assumed that she was the man's primary target, but she could not know for sure.

She reached the opposite side of the road as three more cars whizzed past, each honking at her as if they were the first drivers to alert her that she was in the wrong place.

As her foot hit the curb on the opposite side of the busy street, she whirled around and immediately got the answer to her question.

The gunman was standing across from her, staring at her from near her crashed rental car, gun in-hand, raised and pointing directly at her.

And he was smiling.

CHAPTER 34
FREDDIE

Sea of Marmara | Near Armutlu, Turkey.

"Propulsion gear?" Freddie said, looking toward Jason at the bow.

Jason turned around and gave a thumbs up. *"Looking good here. I'll run a better check once we're in the water, but everything is brand-new. Should be just fine."*

Jason Roth was a soldier but had spent a good portion of his early days as a rescue swimmer and dive instructor. Best of all, he was a huge gear head, addicted to new and shiny objects, and when Freddie had explained their goal — particularly how they would be reaching the island — Jason's eyes had lit up. Having him in charge of their underwater propulsion devices was as good a decision as Freddie had ever made.

Curtis cut the motor at the drop point, and Freddie watched Reggie reach under the seat and grab the anchor, which he then tossed overboard. The water out here was about two-hundred feet deep, and with the wind picking up, Freddie didn't want to take the chance of their boat floating out of range of their propulsion equipment. They were going to need every last joule of energy, especially if things went well, since they would have an extra human-sized weight with them on the return trip.

Two of his men, Jason and Chuck, were in the water before the boat had even stopped moving. Freddie waited until the anchor was set and everything on the surface was good to go, then he and Jason pushed the two massive propulsion devices over the edge and into the water, followed by the scuba gear. Their tanks had already been strapped on to their backs, so they each swam forward and grabbed flippers and masks from the floating bag. They passed them around, then each man did verbal and visual checks on every other man's equipment and gear.

Finally, Freddie reached into the inflatable buoy bag and pulled out three floating cases. Since each case weighed about thirty pounds, this chore was actually easier to accomplish in the water. He passed a case to each man by pushing it over the surface of the water, allowing the gentle waves to bring them to each of his soldiers. The men opened two of the cases and assembled six rifles carefully — one for each of them and one extra — using the open cases as water-supported folding tables. While the cases could almost double as life rafts on account of how buoyant they were, the guns were another story altogether. The first thing each weapon mandated when it was assembled was to snap it to the dual carabiner apparatus they had each donned before putting on their scuba tanks.

The rifles would ride on their backs next to their scuba tanks until they reached shore, at which point they would snap off the scuba gear, leave it on shore, and start their ascent. Their ammunition was in two more waterproof bags, these already strapped to Reggie's and Freddie's belts.

From the third case, Reggie put two large pieces of pipe together to form the harpoon gun. It was a final measure of precaution. They did not want to fire their rifles underwater if they could help it, so the harpoon was a relatively inexpensive, lightweight way to provide some peace-of-mind. It was not a perfect insurance policy, but the harpoon offered at least a bit of security in case anything larger than them swam up and decided to interfere with their ocean crossing.

"Ready to roll out, boss," Curtis said. Freddie sensed enthusiasm in the older man's voice, probably excitement for getting to rush into battle once more. It was the soldier's blessing and curse, Freddie knew: none of them *wanted* to die out here, but none of them had ever expected to die warm in their beds — this was the life, and potentially the death — they had signed up for.

As Freddie ran through his own mental checklist, he once again hoped he had brought enough gear and enough men. None of them knew what they were going to find on the island — was it an abandoned prison, or was it a fully functional military installation?

Reggie activated one of the propulsion systems. The top-of-the line SubCart EL-3000, not yet available to the consumer market, allowed three men to fly through the water at nearly 20MPH. It was a simple, powerful device. The engine was housed in the same horizontal rod that had six handles affixed to it, and this whole apparatus was attached to a front 'windshield.' The wide, bubbled plexiglass shield was both bulletproof and completely transparent, and underwater it would act as a viewport to the world around them. The backs and legs of its riders hung freely behind the device, flippers and bodies acting as a unified rudder to turn and steer the submersible.

The SubCarts had been designed for military use, and the company producing them had outfitted each of the units with a mount for the exact make and model of the harpoon gun Reggie was carrying — another reason they had chosen it. However, Reggie had opted to strap it to his back like the rifles on the other men's backs. He argued that the ability to have both hands free to help control the submersible was more important but having the harpoon with them as an option that could still be reached in a second or two gave Freddie some security.

In all, the SubCart was an ingenious system that combined the best parts of stealth and speed without unnecessary weight. He heard the whir of the submersibles' motors sing to life as each of the five men found their designated spots on the crafts.

Freddie took the middle handles of his machine, Reggie to his immediate right and Chuck to his left. Curtis grabbed the leftmost controls of the second device, leaving the central spot open on the second SubCart for Jason, who seemed to be more than ready to put this new machine to the test.

Freddie understood the man's excitement — Jason lived for this sort of thing, and the younger man's face seemed absolutely giddy before slipping under the water and testing the controls. Freddie tried to adopt some of Jason's excitement, hoping he could use it to offset the trepidation he was still feeling.

It didn't work. Freddie's face and mask slipped beneath the surface and an entirely new world came to life. Dark, shadowy streaks darted left and right, and he felt his way around the controls, working to nudge the craft a few inches forward and backward.

Here goes nothing, he thought.

CHAPTER 35
SARAH

SEPTEMBER 17, 2020 | local time 9:57 am
Cairo, Egypt

Sarah ran behind a small restaurant, dodging an aproned man hauling out a bag of trash. He shouted something at her as she soared past, ducking under a low overhang that cut across the back patio of a similarly sized shop. The air behind this restaurant smelled delicious, and she was almost tempted to run inside and get the name, so she could return later.

Instead, she continued bouncing up and around the back stoops populating the alley that ran parallel to the street, hurtling over banisters and refuse bins until the alley cut to the left once more. This turn led her back to the road she had started on, and the park Marcia had disappeared into was across the street from that.

She heard shouts from behind her and assumed it was the gunman arguing loudly with the shopkeeper who had been taking out the trash. She hoped that was the case — it meant she still had a good lead on whoever was pursuing her.

She ducked around a raised outdoor patio, surprised diners watching her with wide eyes as she raced past. While seeing someone emerge from an alleyway should not arouse any suspicion, seeing someone in Cairo with Sarah's light complexion and springy, reddish hair — running at full-tilt — would. A product of her Jamaican mother and Scottish father, Sarah looked to be a mix of a thousand different ethnicities.

She knew the frantic look in her eyes only added to her distraught and hyper-vigilant expression.

One older woman even audibly gasped as she sprang up on her lithe, long legs and over an entire dumpster, landing neatly on the other side like a modern-day Catwoman.

For a moment, the road was clear. She didn't waste the opportunity. She sprinted forward, crossing the street in five long lunges. Without slowing, she dove into the thick wall of trees adjacent to the embassy. She didn't know if the embassy would have erected fences back here that would block her progress, but this was where Marcia had entered, so this was where Sarah would follow.

She caught sight of the restaurant she had just rushed past and saw the gun-wielding man about to jump into the street as well. A taxi driver leaned on his horn and the man jumped back just as it roared past, accelerating rather than slowing down, as if asserting its dominance over the feeble human.

She didn't wait for the man to recover before starting to move across the street again. She continued running, moving serpentine through the trees. The ground was soft, impeding her progress a bit, and she wished she had put on boots or tennis shoes rather than the sock-less flats she had chosen for comfort. It did not matter to her now — she had a lead, and she intended to keep it.

The wall of trees opened to a field with an old rickety playscape and a single, weathered soccer goal with rusted posts and crossbar. There were no children playing, and the only person in sight was a man running around a muddy track on the far side of the field.

She paused there for a moment, catching her breath.

In a flash, she saw her.

Marcia was across the field from her, waving as she stood between two large tree trunks.

Sarah's legs jolted forward before she was ready, pulling her body along with it. She was getting tired, the physical exhaustion finally catching up to the mental fatigue she had earned from the days' worth of travel.

It took her fifteen seconds to cross the field, where she pulled Marcia deeper into the woods on the opposite side. They were still in downtown Cairo, so there was no reason to expect that this forested area would continue for long. Even now, she thought she could hear the roar of traffic a few hundred feet ahead. She guessed that this park was no larger than a single square city block, though she had not seen any signs or maps indicating such.

"Who was that?" Marcia asked, her voice frantic.

Sarah saw the sheer terror in the young woman's eyes, felt her heart beating out of her chest even from feet away.

"First, try to calm down," Sarah said. "Panicking is not going to help either of us, and I know you can get through this. Just breathe for now."

Marcia closed her eyes and nodded. She forced a few long steady breaths, each one making her more and more calm.

"I think they're with the same group that's been trying to find me," she said. "I'm sorry again. I should not have dragged you into this."

Marcia paused, and Sarah thought she was about to burst into tears. To her credit, the woman instead straightened her back and looked behind them at the field. "No, *I* dragged *you* into this. It was the least I could do for Professor Lindgren, though. I want to find him as much as you do."

"It's not going to get easier," Sarah warned. "They've got the taste of blood on their lips. They know I'm here. They know I'm close. And I stick out like a sore thumb in this country, as do you."

Marcia nodded again. "Then we have to keep moving. We have to figure out what they want, and why."

"I'm not sure about the men who came to your camp," Sarah started. "But I know *exactly* what this other group wants from me."

"You do?"

Sarah sighed. "Yes. They've been hounding us — the group I work with — for almost a year now. It's a long story, but apparently we've stifled their plans in more than one way. It's an organization called The Faction, and they are far bigger and better organized than we could ever have imagined. We've already had a few run-ins with them, and we've barely escaped with our lives."

And some of us didn't even make it that far, she thought, recalling the events at Ben and Julie's cabin. The explosion, the man in the white truck, the horrifying reality that a team member had perished.

"So yeah, I know what they want," she continued.

"What?"

"Well, it's pretty simple, actually. They want to kill me."

CHAPTER 36
SARAH

SEPTEMBER 17, **2020 | local time 10:00 am**
Cairo, Egypt

"Are you okay?" Sarah asked.

She didn't look to her side as she spoke and walked. She kept her eyes locked on the target — the tree line opposite the field. They were heading back in the same direction they had come from, although they had pushed through the woods for another few minutes, continuing to move around to try to stay ahead of the man who had been chasing after them while keeping hidden in the trees.

Next to her, Marcia nodded. Sarah caught the movement in her peripheral vision and smiled. "You can be honest — it's just me."

There was a slight pause, followed by a deep sigh. "Okay, fine. I'm terrified. I'm not okay. I feel like I've had to wear a stoic expression ever since we got into the field, mostly for the younger students. And then... all of this happened."

"It's a lot," Sarah confirmed.

"I mean, I don't think I've ever been run off the road, almost killed in a car accident, then been shot at. Certainly not all in the same day."

Sarah looked to the younger woman and chuckled. *Good, at least she's working to process this.* The last thing she needed was for Marcia to turn into a zombie and completely shut down. She could not blame the girl for wanting to, but it would only make their progress toward finding her father that much more difficult.

"To be fair, he was sort of aiming at you. So I guess you could say *I* wasn't the one being shot at."

Marcia laughed now, both women moving in tandem toward the trees. Sarah hoped that the man looking for them would assume they had simply continued in the same direction — making their way through the woods encircling the park and then out the other side onto the busy intersection behind the embassy complex.

With any luck, Sarah and Marcia could get back to their wrecked sedan without much fuss. Bystanders and police were likely to be descending on the area any moment now, if they were not already there.

"So you think that was that group you mentioned? The Faction?" Marcia asked. "Who are they, anyway?"

Sarah shook her head slightly. "Honestly, I don't know. They're a new threat, one we didn't even know existed before about a year ago. We're not sure what they want, which makes them even more dangerous."

"Terrorists can be like that."

"You know, I don't think they're terrorists. I mean, sure, they do things terrorists do. That attack in that Roman plaza about a year ago? That was the same group. But I think there's a deeper thread; I think that all these events are connected because they — The Faction — want something. It's not just about terrorizing the populace; it's about accomplishing some mission."

"That makes sense, even if it is terrifying. But you're implying there were other events? I remember that horrific thing in Italy, but you're saying there were more attacks?"

"Unfortunately, yes. Rome, Cozumel, that mining incident, and all those planes that went down simultaneously."

Marcia suddenly stopped, pulling her hand up and over her mouth. Sarah wanted to pull her along, to keep moving, but she knew the woman was dealing with a lot. And now this...

"Oh... oh my *God*," she said. "That — that was all the same group? That was all The Faction? These people organized each of those things?"

"Yes, and perhaps more, but those are the ones we know about, because we were able to chain them together and figure out the similarities between the attacks. We were even able to stop them for the most part, but that was only right at the end — *after* they had pulled off the other attacks. We never knew they were related until we figured out the thread connecting them. All that, and consider the fact that they did not claim responsibility, which is almost a requirement for terrorist attacks these days."

Marcia nodded.

"So yeah — we think they are far more organized and resourced than we ever imagined, and we're really the only group that knows about them."

"Have you tried talking to the government?"

Sarah smirked, then scoffed. "Which one? The Egyptian government? The U.S.? We can't be sure they're not in The Faction's own pocket. And besides, how could we prove it?"

"You said you stopped one of the attacks, right?"

"Sure," Sarah said, recalling the incident from earlier that year. "But the man behind it — the CSO member who figured it out — is missing. So we can't exactly put him on the stand to testify against The Faction."

CHAPTER 37
MARCIA

Cairo, Egypt

Marcia could see the concern in Sarah's eyes. When she swallowed, it almost seemed as though Sarah was about to cry. Marcia wanted to keep her talking — any information they could share would potentially help them find Professor Lindgren.

"So what was the thread?" Marcia asked. "The reason you think those events were interconnected and related to The Faction?"

"Good question," Sarah said. "Well, since we don't know any of the *actual* perpetrators, and no one we've come across had a t-shirt that says, 'I'm part of The Faction,' it was really a stroke of luck that we figured it out at all. Basically, one of my team members with the CSO discovered a thread that led to a manifesto that we believe was a Faction document, one that invoked all sorts of strange puzzle pieces we aren't quite sure what to do with yet."

"A thread that led to a manifesto that you believe was Faction-related?" Marcia did not intend for the restatement to come across accusatory or skeptical, but Sarah nodded as if she too agreed it was far-fetched.

"Look, without giving you a complete history of the CSO and

our adventures — or, I should say, *mis*adventures — over the past year, it's kind of hard to lay things down in a way that makes sense. Trust me, I *want* to tell you everything. But we don't have enough time."

"Fair enough," Marcia said.

"But you are correct in that I'm being vague. My apologies. Basically, we tracked down someone who has been studying The Faction's movements — who they are, what they might be planning, where they could be operating from, and more."

"Great!" Marcia blurted out. "So we take *that* person to the authorities and —"

"That person's dead," Sarah said. "He was killed by the same group he was trying to track down. They found him first."

Marcia let out a deep sigh.

"But as I said, *he* had information that was helpful to us. Namely, this manifesto of sorts. We're still picking it apart, to be honest, since it's very cryptic. Almost like it's written in code. But one thing it contained was an incantation of Earth, Fire, Water, and Air."

"I recognize that," Marcia said. "Aristotle?"

"He popularized it, but it was introduced some time before him; we don't know exactly when or by whom. But yes, that's the same concept. Earth, Fire, Water, Air — the four elements the Greeks believed governed the world. So when these events transpired, the final one — all the planes' autopilot systems getting hacked, and their pilots locked out — we realized what it meant. It was a message: *that* event happened in the air. The events with the flamethrowers in the plaza in Rome represented, obviously, fire. Cozumel, water."

"And that mining collapse that killed all those men," Marcia said quietly. "Earth."

Sarah nodded. Her tone solemn. "We started to realize that these weren't just singular, isolated events, just mere terrorist attacks happening randomly around the world. These were events that were happening by design — on purpose. And if that were true, they were events that would have to have been planned *long* before the actual date of the attacks. The organizational and planning requirements alone are staggering but think about the manpower it took to pull it off. It wasn't the work of three or four people."

"So why are you — and the CSO — being targeted now?"

"Well," Sarah answered, "at first, we figured that we just made them angry when we stopped their attack on the planes. We saved a lot of people that otherwise would have been murdered that day, so we assumed they took our intervention as a personal attack on their goals and beliefs."

"It's more than that now, though?"

"It is. We're sure of that, unfortunately. We've been targeted by The Faction not just because we were meddling in their business, and not just because we are a threat to their organization. It's deeper than that. As it turns out, The Faction — at least what we have been able to guess — was a secretive organization that existed in Napoleon's time, possibly even before that, if the Earth, Fire, Water, Air credence has any historical importance to them. Whether or not Aristotle started the organization or if it was later we can't know, but we do think some of his closest aides were in on it as well."

"Napoleon's aides? As in, *the* Napoleon?"

"Napoleon Bonaparte, yes," Sarah said. "And The Faction's purpose and mission has probably morphed over the years, but we do believe it was Napoleon's original spy network during his war years. Similar to the network George Washington used during the Revolutionary War in America."

"That's incredible," Marcia said, her eyes wide. She could not help but feel the excitement learning of another breadcrumb of history that had been previously hidden from view.

Sarah continued as they walked. "It's clear now that The Faction is far more than just some ancient spy network, and so it's clear that their mission and purpose has changed to something more sinister. That they're interested in more than just trading secrets and passing them up the chain. We think they are planning something *far* larger — world-spanning, even — than what has already happened, so they want us and everyone else out of their way. If I had to guess, even though we're a pretty small group, the CSO is the single largest threat to their power simply because we've interacted with them the most. Because we know about them and we've lived to tell about it, and we are starting to put the pieces together that will unveil who they really are and what they want."

"Yeah, I imagine they don't want that at all."

They came to the edge of the copse of trees, and Marcia saw that indeed some bystanders had come out from the embassy to gawk at the wreck. A security guard was examining the wreckage as well, and Marcia realized they were going to have to develop some sort of plan to get closer.

Sarah's duffel bag was in the back seat, and she would want to retrieve it before they moved on. Thankfully, it had not been in the trunk, which was almost sure to be wedged shut now.

They needed that bag, but if they got close enough to nab it from the backseat, it would signal that they had been the victims and people might start asking questions. Already she could see phones out as Egyptian locals and tourists alike streamed footage of the wreckage to their social accounts.

"How do you know all of this?" Marcia asked. "I mean, I get that you've been privy to their movements and their attack, but it almost seems like you have insider information somehow. Why is The Faction *so* hell-bent on not just *stopping* you, but in *finding* you? They're not playing defense, Sarah. They're playing offense. So it's not just about the information you have on them, is it?"

"Not entirely, no," Sarah said, smiling. "That's an astute guess, I might add. I can tell my father must really like you. You think like he does."

Marcia beamed. "So what is it, then?"

"You know Harvey Bennett, right?"

Marcia's eyes widened. "Not personally. But yeah, I've heard of him, of course. Everyone in our field knows the name." She frowned. "Though not lately. Seems he fell off the face of the earth."

Marcia could almost see Sarah's heart sink. "He disappeared," Sarah said. "About nine months ago, after he visited Corsica. We had just figured out that last piece of intel on The Faction, so we split up while he went to talk to the man who originally put together the Civilian Special Operations."

"He was in Corsica?"

Sarah nodded. "Yeah. Harvey — Ben, as we call him — went to go meet with this guy, but he never returned. No one's been able to get in contact with him or the man he visited since. They both might as well have fallen off the face of the earth."

"Do you think he — this person he went to meet with — *did* something?"

Sarah's head fell sideways and back. "It's not outside the realm of possibility, but we suspect that nothing happened to our benefactor. His lack of communication is frustrating, but it does fit his character, and his wife died suddenly, also nine months ago. So we think Ben's visit with him was harmless. We think that The Faction grabbed Ben at some point before he left Corsica."

"That's pretty specific — 'before he left Corsica.' Why do you think that?"

Sarah nodded again. "He was able to get a text message out to Julie, his wife, just before he left. So most likely it was at the airport in Corsica, right before it actually happened."

"Before it happened?"

"Yeah. All it said was, *'Something's happening. Need you to get me.'*"

CHAPTER 38
FREDDIE

SEPTEMBER 17, **2020 | local time 11:19 am**
Sea of Marmara | Near Imrali Island, Turkey.

As the SubCart EL-3000 submersible surged to life, Freddie felt his arms strain as the acceleration tried to rip them from his body. He felt his hands almost slip off the control handles but wrenched them tighter as the machine picked up speed.

The submersible had a heads-up display of sorts, an inverted reflection from a tiny projection module that flashed their navigational heading and speed onto the plexiglass wall in front of them. It was distorted to a concave shape to match the bubbled contour of the plexiglass itself, so that when it was projected in front of them, it appeared to be a flat screen, hovering in front of his eyes.

It was a pretty cool piece of tech, and Freddie had been excited when Jason had tracked down the dealer — a friend of a friend — and the man had agreed to allow them to borrow two of the high-dollar units for what Jason had told him would be 'testing purposes.' The dealer had winked back at him, and the deal was done.

Freddie was not naïve — the man who had lent these devices to them would have known full-well that there was no testing going on, but he also knew that this particular dealer had not exactly come across these propulsion systems in the traditional sense. As long as they did not somehow find their way back to the company that had created them, neither the dealer nor the team using them now would be in any trouble.

Of course, that did not include any trouble they might find once they hit the surface again. They were going to try breaking into a prison complex in a foreign country — not exactly an easy task. Intel had shown that the prison complex was quite small, which Freddie hoped would work in their favor. A single rectangular building, with a couple of small outposts scattered around the top plateau of the island, and from their GPS-based measurements, it appeared the main complex itself was only a couple hundred feet long and about half that wide.

Sure, Freddie knew there was always a chance the entire place could be packed with soldiers, but if it truly were a prison, it was more likely they would find many unarmed prisoners in a detention center with a few armed guards milling about on duty.

By their estimate, they expected anywhere from five to ten armed personnel, with perhaps double or triple that hidden within the confines of the prison performing off-duty chores.

And these men would most likely not be military. Ex-police perhaps, or simply professional security guards. They would have minimal training with firearms, hand-to-hand combat, and mission logistics.

At least, that was the idea. In truth, none of Freddie's team knew what to expect up above.

But that was a future Freddie problem. Right now, they needed to get to the island. Then scale the cliffs, then get the prison complex in their sights and figure out the best way inside.

He pushed any thoughts of failure away. Of course, it was possible that Harvey Bennett was not even here, that they had been chasing a dead end. He knew that it was not only possible, but it could be probable. They may have been duped from when Harvey went missing in Corsica all along, following the thread of a plane that had never had him on board — or it could have stopped off at any number of unregistered locations before heading to this island.

At least that part of this mission had checked out. Their surveillance had shown a narrow strip that could only be a runway, and GPS data implied that the plane they had tracked from Corsica was about the largest model that could safely land on the runway. Anything bigger would find the runway far too short, and thus severely cripple their theory.

Freddie brought his mind back to the present, once again focusing on the task at hand. He curled his body to the left, the other two men copying his motions, and he felt the machine banking easily, the plexiglass-fronted device falling to the southeast. The other craft was traveling by Freddie's left side, a little in front of them. Curtis and Jason had a lighter load, so they slowed the motor to keep pace with Freddie's three-manned vessel.

His eyes shifted as tiny shadows flitted past them. Fish and other unknown sea creatures swam up to greet them as they were pulled through the water. He didn't see anything larger than the length of his arm, and while shark attacks were far less common than the movies would have people believe, he knew they did roam these waters.

That's all we need, he thought. *We've got enough to worry about — all we need now is a shark taking a bite off my leg.*

Curtis and Jason drifted farther to the southeast, beginning to outpace Freddie. He kept his bearings straight — he wanted to conserve as much battery as possible, so there was no reason to drift out and around and attack the beach from a different angle, arcing in from farther north of their target landing spot. Still, he couldn't fault the two men for making that call — approaching their rendezvous point from multiple vectors would only increase their chance of success. He watched them grow smaller through the plexiglass viewport, when he suddenly saw a flash of light.

What the hell?

His eyes flicked over the console quickly, trying to glean any information from it. It told him the same two data points it always had, and neither number had moved much.

When his eyes glanced back upward, the world in front of him exploded.

CHAPTER 39
FREDDIE

SEPTEMBER 17, 2020 | local time 11:21 am
Sea of Marmara | Near Imrali Island, Turkey.

Water smashed against him. A bubble grew from the outward pressure and swelled outward, enveloping him and his teammates, smashing them all against the plexiglass control unit. If not for their own small shield, Freddie knew the blast would have completely decimated them. There were no cracks in the shield, and Freddie hoped the propulsion system's electronic components had not been fried.

But he was not focused on the propulsion unit, or Reggie and the man next to him. He was looking out the glass as the blast dissipated, trying to piece together what the hell had just happened. A pinprick of light had grown into a massive orb and then all in the same second, vanished. With it, his second team and propulsion unit.

Debris and detritus was everywhere, pieces of man and machine floating around the area where his second propulsion system and its two operators previously existed.

What the hell caused that? Freddie wondered. He swam forward, then pushed to the right, his primary control module sending subtle signals to the other two operators, and all three men bent sideways in unison and veered to the right. He wanted to get away from whatever had just detonated underwater. Some sort of semi-buoyant mine, he guessed. Something tethered to the sea floor, but floating high enough to catch any submerged traffic, like an underwater proximity bomb. He had never seen anything like it, outside of movies about naval warfare. *Were these people that paranoid about keeping boats away from their shores?*

No, that couldn't be it. He knew that those sorts of charges, at this depth, would have to be far larger to take out a ship hull if it was large enough to maneuver this far beneath the surface. He assumed there were not massive naval ships and submarines operating in these shallow waters of the Sea of Marmara.

He felt Reggie pulling back against his silent orders. He frowned, then realized what his friend was implying.

Whatever blew them up has already exploded, Freddie understood. *That means we're actually safer going through the middle of the blast zone.*

Freddie nodded and reversed direction, and within moments they were floating amidst the wreckage and carnage. Freddie stuck his thumb up, then all three men pulled back on their controls, allowing the submersible to push toward the surface.

Once Freddie's head broke through the water, he pulled off his dive mask regulator and looked at the others. "Anyone want to tell me what the *hell* that was?"

Reggie and Chuck looked solemn, crestfallen.

"No idea there were military installations out here," Reggie mumbled.

Freddie shook his head. "I don't think there are. It's too shallow for submarine naval activity, and we're too close to the Turkish border for any other surface vessels. They would start a war just by being out here."

"Whatever it was though, that was a hell of a blow. Whoever's bomb it was is probably going to know we're here."

Freddie felt his stomach drop. "I trust the intel we got," he said. "I can vouch for it. And the intel suggests that this place is nothing more than a prison."

"Hell of a prison, in that case," Reggie said. "What kind of prisoners are they harboring here that they need defense systems like that?"

"Shit," Freddie said. "Maybe's it's not for defense."

Reggie frowned, then nodded slowly. "You think they're mining the waters around the island in case of a prison break? Rather than chase down somebody who escapes, they just blow them up?"

Chuck nodded. "That's my guess, yeah. Not sure whose idea it was, and it is rather macabre, but it would be effective."

"This is a shitshow," Reggie said. "Who the hell do they have in the place, that they're so worried about a prison break?" He turned to Freddie, floating beside him. "So what's the call?"

Freddie squeezed his eyes shut, knowing he didn't have much time. Reggie was right — whoever had bombed their teammates was sure to know that their perimeter had been breached. He couldn't understand why a prison would spend so much effort and money on creating an explosive moat around its property, but he figured they had good reason.

It didn't matter to him, though. They had a job to do. "We have to push forward," Freddie said. "At least for them." He motioned to the chunks of metals and organic material floating in the water.

"Poor bastards," Reggie muttered.

Freddie shivered in the cool water as he pictured the pieces of bone fragments and flesh he had seen floating by their plexiglass shield.

Chuck nodded. "Wouldn't have it any other way, if you ask me. Let's get to shore asap. The one that exploded didn't cause a chain reaction, which ruled out the possibility that there are tons of mines in a relatively small area. The closer we get to those rocks, the less likely there's a bomb waiting for us. Anything that explodes too close to the rocks would put the entire island at risk."

Freddie nodded and pulled the regulator back into his mouth. He looked at the two other men, their faces unreadable behind their own scuba goggles. He waited for them to ready up, then sank his head beneath the surface once more and grabbed at the controls of the propulsion system. They pointed directly toward the underwater cliff that loomed about a hundred yards away. Freddie flicked the motor's speed to its highest setting, and they darted through the water once more, the acceleration nearly yanking his arms off.

All three men held tight to the controls, none daring anything but a ramrod-straight line behind the plexiglass.

Freddie hoped Reggie was right. He hoped the builders of this island prison had put only a single row of mines around the island rather than an entire mine*field*. The waters were too dark to see clearly, and the rocks beneath them that sloped upward to meet the cliff of the island itself made spotting anything out of the ordinary down below impossible.

They reached an outcropping of underwater boulders a minute later. Fish darted back-and-forth around their propulsion unit, either checking them out as potential predators or prey. Freddie pulled back slightly and allowed the propulsion system to glide upward again, following the angle and contour of the rocks. There was about twenty feet of sloping cliff beneath the waves, angling upward, and he headed for the base of it. With luck, the cliff would continue to rise until it was vertical, and they could just ascend straight up to the edge of the island's base and resurface.

He began to see more detail as light from above the water reached their shallower depth. He saw brightly colored fish and anemones, as well as large starfish, barnacles, and urchins clinging to every surface they passed. He slowed the propulsion system to nearly a crawl, hoping the quieter drone of the motor would help them reach the cliffs with more stealth. A modern nuclear submarine could hear two rocks bumping together on the surface of the ocean over a mile away, so he prayed that there was no listening station in the prison above with similar capabilities.

Still, an explosion like the one that had taken out his teammates would have been obvious to a curious bystander, and while he fully expected someone to eventually come out and examine the wreckage, Freddie hoped they would reach the island long before anyone realized they had gotten this close.

They reached the crease where the vertical cliffs shot upward from the base. Huge, barnacle-encrusted boulders and rocks pockmarked the surface of the underwater mountain, and he reached a hand out underneath the plexiglass bubble to prevent it from cracking against the cliff wall. Once there, he again signaled upward, and the men started to float upward. Chuck held one hand out as well, guiding the propulsion system upward manually.

Suddenly Freddie's hand lost touch with the surface of the rocks. An indentation in the cliff's side caused the propulsion system's bubble shield to disappear into the side of the mountain.

He expected a hollowed-out cave, one that could be ignored as they rose from the water. Instead, his hand found the surface once again about six inches into the concave formation.

...Except it wasn't *rocks* his hand hit. Now the cliff's surface was smooth, almost like...

Oh, shit, he thought. *Oh, this is* not *good.*

He saw Chuck's hand making the same motion, feeling the surface of this new feature they had found hidden away in the cliffs inside. He rubbed in a wide circle, feeling the algae and grime slide away easily, confirming his fears.

The surface of this wall was slick, smooth. *Perfectly* smooth.

It was glass.

He yanked the controls backward and pulled the propulsion unit with him. The hydraulic motor reacted immediately, switching from forward motion to backward motion with ease. He backed away from the glass and turned on the flashlight attached to his wrist. The bright yellow light immediately illuminated the space in the cave-like indentation in the cliff.

Freddie nearly spit out his mouthpiece.

It wasn't just glass they had found. It was a *window*.

CHAPTER 40
SARAH

Cairo, Egypt

Sarah and Marcia had reached the edge of the forested section of the park behind the embassy and turned east, heading toward a large, open-air marketplace hinted at by signs on both sides of the road. They had not seen anyone resembling their pursuer, so for a moment Sarah felt safe. She knew they needed to keep moving, however — The Faction was well-resourced, and they would stop at nothing to track her down. Now that they had been spotted here, she knew it would be all-hands in the search to bring them in.

Or worse.

She pushed the thought out of her mind, instead focusing on lightening the tension. Marcia was a student, and she had never been in a situation anywhere close to something like this. She was not prepared to handle being chased by trained killers, and while Sarah was hardly trained herself, she had at least been through situations like this.

From being kidnapped from her office to getting into some *very* tight spots with the CSO group, she was no stranger to being pursued for nefarious purposes. So far she had proven herself worthy, but that luck could change at any time. As the CSO's resident military and operations expert Reggie — and more recently Freddie — had drilled into all of their minds, getting out of hairy situations required a solid amount of luck, no matter how well-trained you were.

She hoped there was a bit more of that luck to go around, both for her and for her new friend.

They stopped at a traffic light, then continued across the street onto an avenue that seemed to be bustling with activity. Neither woman was familiar with the area, but it was a busy thoroughfare, and street vendors lined both sides of the avenue, tourists and locals alike congregating and mingling.

Marcia stopped them at one vendor's stand and within moments had purchased two bright-colored, dyed handkerchiefs, each large enough to wrap around their hair and lower half of their faces. Covering faces, at least partially, by way of the niqab, was not an unpopular thing for women to do here, and Sarah nodded to Marcia as she put hers on.

"Good thinking," she said.

"I figured it's better than nothing," Marcia said from behind her own cloth wrap. "They're not traditional hajibs or niqabs, but I think we can get away with it without offending anyone. Unless you see someplace selling the real thing... it'll have to do for now." She smiled. "Or a full-on costume shop."

Sarah's eyes lit up. "Ooh! I would be a pilot. Old school-style, like Amelia Earhart. Leather bomber jacket and glasses, a cute hat, the works."

Marcia laughed. "Okay, okay. I think I would go with... archeologist."

Sarah's head fell backwards, and she snorted in laughter. She held a hand over her mouth. "That's hilarious — you *are* an archeologist."

"I'm *training* to be one," Marcia corrected. "I've studied and I've traveled and written and read and everything that's required of me, but none of that matters. I don't want to be what a *real* archeologist is. Deep down, if you force an answer out of me, I want to be Indiana Jones."

Sarah felt a pang of regret, a flash of grief. *He's not dead,* she told herself. "You know, I wanted that too. My dad *is* one of those real archeologists, and — arguably — the best at it. Everyone knows his name."

Marcia's eyes lit up. "He's as famous as it gets."

"But you're right — he's not Indiana Jones." She laughed again. "I think early on he thought he could be. Sometimes I feel like he's as close as someone can get to the fictional Indy. But if you were to force an answer out of him too, he would say he got close but not close enough."

"Why is that?"

"I guess he hasn't found the Holy Grail yet," Sarah answered.

"And no giant, perfectly round boulder on a hand-carved, cleared and maintained stone path has chased him."

Sarah chuckled. "Yet."

"Yet," Marcia parroted. "Of course, there's still time."

Sarah stopped. "You think he's still alive?"

Marcia seemed stunned by the question, but she frowned, pondering it before answering. "You *do* know him, right? I mean, your old man is going to outlive us all! He may *actually* be old enough to be my grandpa — no offense — but sometimes I think he's younger than all of us."

Sarah nodded. "Yeah, I can't argue with that. He's always been that way. Active, nonstop, like adult ADHD or something. But still — you think he's out there somewhere? Alive and well?"

"I wouldn't say he's doing *well*, as he's probably hoping for some help," Marcia said. "But yeah, sure. I'd bet he found some secret corridor lost to time, and he's just exploring it, getting his jollies before coming back up to earth."

"Yeah, I can't argue with that, either. That would be him — who the hell cares he's being harassed by some killer mobsters? He's just living the dream."

Marcia burst out laughing at that image, and the two started walking once more.

"So," Sarah said. "What exactly were you guys looking for?"

"The tomb of Alexander the —"

"Alexander the Great, yeah, you told me that. But I looked up your articles and addendums with the Ministry of Antiquities here in Cairo."

Marcia's eyes widened.

"You have to remember, I'm not new to this game. And I'm not new to the 'pseudo-illegal-digging-at-ancient-sites-game,' either."

"So you know..."

"I know you guys *said* you were just exploring the ruins of the temple there. But my dad wouldn't have invested that much of his own money on exploring something that's been that well-documented already. He has access to plenty of grants, plenty of backers. The fact that he was out there, under the guise of 'just poking around,' even if it *did* mention Alexander's final resting place, tells me there's more to it. He wanted to keep this as quiet as possible, while still ensuring the government wouldn't step in the way."

Marcia nodded. "That's... that's all correct, as far as I know. I was probably his closest confidant, but I'm sure I don't know everything."

"But it's more than just the tomb?"

"Well, not really — the tomb really *is* what we've been looking for. He made us all experts in Alexander the Great before we even lifted a shovel. But I think it was something *in* the tomb he wanted."

"In the tomb?"

"Not the body, if that's what you're asking. I don't think he cared much for Alex's remains, honestly. I mean, what's he supposed to do with them? He can't sell them to make back his investment."

"He wouldn't do that, anyway," Sarah said.

"Exactly. So there was a hunch — or at least, *I* have a hunch — that there was something in the tomb. Either in the room with Alexander, or inside the sarcophagus itself."

Sarah stopped once more, right in the middle of the sidewalk. She had suddenly remembered something — something that had almost not registered in her mind.

"What about the sarcophagus?"

CHAPTER 41

REGGIE

SEPTEMBER 17, 2020 | **local time 11:25 am**
Sea of Marmara | Near Imrali Island, Turkey.

"Move up, *now!*" Reggie yelled. Unfortunately, he yelled directly into the mouthpiece regulator attached to his scuba hose, and the command only fell out as a series of frantic syllables that did nothing but add more bubbles to the immediate area.

Fortunately, the others knew what to do. Freddie, Reggie, and Chuck moved as one, pulling back on the SubCart controls to send the thing flying toward the surface. They narrowly missed driving the plexiglass shield into the top of the concave rock structure, but Reggie was able to use his hand to push off the ceiling of the small cavern and get them righted before impact.

They were just about free of the area, traveling backwards rapidly, when the entire area around them — bubbles, men, propulsion system and all — was suddenly bathed in bright yellow.

It only took a half-second for Reggie to realize what had happened. The window they had bumped into had revealed to them a dark, empty room, only now the room was no longer dark. Someone inside had turned the lights on.

And that someone was staring directly at them from inside the room.

A man, average height and build, wearing a suit. His eyes were fixed on them, steady, as if both unbelieving and somehow accepting of what he was seeing. As if he had been *expecting* them.

As if he were *prepared* for them.

His dark hair did not quite match his brownish eyebrows, and his straight-lined, chiseled face offset the calculated rage in the man's eyes as he watched the group outside.

Shit, Reggie thought. *If they didn't know we were here before, they* certainly *do now.* It didn't bode well for their progress so far that half of their team had been destroyed by a proximity mine and the other half discovered before even getting up the cliff.

He swallowed, mouth still on the regulator, and forced a few breaths of air through his lungs. He needed to calm down, to work the plan they had agreed upon. It would do no good to any of them if they panicked now.

They continued to rise, the yellow light of the room leaching out into the darker waters and illuminating their ascent toward the surface. Within a few more seconds, they were once again completely out of sight to the glass-walled room below, but the damage had been done.

They had been spotted. Whatever security the man had amassed here that allowed him the comfort to barely react was about to be alerted to their arrival. Whatever security force they might have been able to surprise was now going to be working hard to surprise *them*.

They needed a new plan. Something this man and his army would not expect. They had failed to bring their entire team to the cliffs, which meant their already underwhelming force would be that much more desperate in a face-to-face battle. It meant they were going to be outnumbered if they went head-to-head with the prison guards up above.

And something told Reggie that it was not just guards they

needed to be worried about — the look on the man's face was so cold and empty it simply seemed sinister. They were playing into his trap, apparently, and that could only mean one thing: their plan needed to be scrapped. Completely.

Reggie and the others sailed upward another twenty feet, careful to watch their depth meters and diving controls, as well as the propulsion system's front end, which was uncomfortably close to the sharp rocks of the cliff wall. He and the two other men worked their controls as Freddie led their ascent, his massive arms persuading the powerful propulsion craft upward with the gentle and practiced ease of a Navy SEAL. He knew the drill — Freddie was making sure they all had time to rest and prepare for the next phase of their mission, even though they would have to adapt it on the fly. He wanted to give them every bit of peace and solace as possible before heading once more into the fray, and Reggie was glad for it.

He breathed in and out, the breaths timed with his internal count, both to steady his nerves and to prepare his heart for what would surely be a breakneck pace as they began scaling the cliffs after exiting the water.

Finally, after a minute of slower ascension, Reggie's head breached the surface. His teammates' heads slid upward out of the water and together they pushed the propulsion up and over a boulder, all of their combined strength required to get the heavy machine out of the water against the crashing waves. More than once, Reggie felt his body pushed heavily into a boulder on the opposite side of the narrow divot they had found in the cliff, and he knew that a wave any stronger than this would send him into the razor-sharp barnacles hiding just beneath the surface.

After they had finished, they took turns pulling each other up and out of the water, balancing on the large boulder until they were all clear. Reggie removed the regulator from his mouth and whistled.

"Phase one, complete," he said. "I guess."

"Yeah," Freddie added. "Barely."

The three men stood silently for a moment, each of them recalling their fallen comrades. Each had found a watery grave, and Reggie only hoped they were going to be the only members of their crew who met the same fate today.

"All right, listen up," Freddie said. "We need to change plans. Our little sneak attack ain't gonna be so sneaky anymore."

"Right," Reggie added. "You see that guy? He was staring daggers through us."

"I imagine he's got his goons coming over to this side of the island as we speak," Chuck said. "And they're probably as pissed-off to see us as he was."

"Yeah, you're right," Freddie said. "But consider this: we're on a *very* remote, otherwise deserted island. Airspace is restricted, and the only way in is mined and patrolled. We made it this far, which is lucky. Remember, I think we can expect to see only a small force up there — a few men, maybe half a dozen, max — and that's it. It wouldn't take much to keep the prisoners in line, and I'm sure they don't have a ton of break-ins like this. We need to start getting up that cliff before that guy's security team gets to the edge and starts taking potshots at us. We'll be sitting ducks."

"Still, it would be a bit easier if we hadn't lost the element of surprise," Chuck said. "I *hate* going in hot."

"About that," Reggie said, running his prosthetic hand through his wet hair. "I think I might have a solution to that problem."

Freddie and Chuck stared at him.

Reggie grinned, holding up the combat knife he had retrieved from its ankle sheath with his left hand, attached to the prosthetic arm. He waved it around in the air in front of his teammates. "How do you boys feel about having a bit of fun?"

CHAPTER 42
REQUIN

SEPTEMBER 17, 2020 | local time 11:30 am
Sea of Marmara | Imrali Island, Turkey.

Requin's mind raced with the possibilities. *Could they be here by accident? Lost? No, that is nonsense.* He knew they were here for a reason. The three men he had startled a moment ago were prepared. They had a propulsion machine; some sort of new design Requin had not seen before. They had scuba equipment on their backs and in their mouths, and on one of the men he thought he had seen climbing gear. Ropes, carabiners.

It meant they had come prepared to scale the cliffs of Imrali and attempt to break into the prison. *His* prison. Head of *La Guerre International,* Requin had purchased the prison from the Turkish government years ago, slowly turning it into the company's head-quarters and laboratory.

And, of course, he had kept the prison active. While the number of men — and they were all men — imprisoned at Imrali had shrunk considerably since the sale, Requin found that his work for The Faction was far easier when he had the ability to simply lock up Faction enemies for a time.

Or, in certain cases, to use those enemies to further The Faction's cause.

Requin assumed he was near the top of the organization, considering his bountiful wealth and information, as well as near-infinite resources from a lifetime of business success, but then again there was no way to really know. The Faction operated in cells, each almost completely cut off from one another, only existing on paper for individualized missions. The logistical coordination of such an operation was immense, but Requin knew of a few companies whose sole purpose was to manage and maintain these supply chains and communications for The Faction.

At the helm of his own large operation, Requin assumed he was one of the power players, one of the men in line to take the throne if and when the need arose — and if there were in fact a throne to take. But to actually come out and ask someone, to broach the subject of human leadership in the forward-thinking organization, was taboo. The Faction prided itself on sovereignty. No one knew who exactly was in charge of it all, but the assumption down to the lowest ranks of foot soldiers was that no one person controlled the organization. Rumor had it that a new form of governance had been drafted and put into place, combining the best features of modern rule with hierarchical progression and meritocratic principles.

In essence, the company line was, 'do your job, and get rewarded,' and Requin needed no further motivation to do that job.

Today the job had been more challenging — he had gotten the report back that his men sent to Egypt had failed their mission. Or, rather, they had not yet checked in after its completion. He had no information to pass up the chain of command, no knowledge of what had transpired.

They had been so close to finally discovering the secret they knew would be found within the tomb of the great leader, and yet Requin had to wrestle with the possibility that his men had somehow been subverted.

The men above him in the organization would not be happy to hear this. Sure, there was still time before he would have to report in, but the fact that his men had already missed their scheduled communication gave him pause.

Added to that this new pressure from outside — three men, likely well-trained for these types of scenarios, trying to gain access to his company's property. He had a team of guards on the island, of course, but the skeleton crew was kept light to better manage resources. The Faction did not approve of waste and keeping a large team of guards fed and sated on a remote island from which there was no escape anyway would be seen as a gratuitous waste.

Still, he had radioed his head of security, a man by the name of Phillips, to be ready up on the grounds for a potential breach. Only one of the underwater mines around the island had detonated, and he had seen with his own eyes that three intruders had crossed the submerged moat. There were no other automated defenses on the cliffs, and judging by the climbing gear, these men were planning to reach the summit and then breach the grounds.

Phillips, as always, was ready. He corralled all but one of the guards, whom he had ordered to watch the prisoners and provide backup only if needed. Two of the four guards in Phillips' unit would be meeting together at the northwest quadrant of the island, nearest the location of the window Requin had seen the intruders gather. His best guess was that the men would climb directly up from the window once they breached the surface of the water, but just in case he ordered Phillips to have his men patrol the entire quadrant. The other two would wait by the prisoners up on the plateau, watching the building for the attackers.

Requin flicked the light off, then left the room and hustled back upstairs to his office, where there was a private elevator that would take him to the surface. He wanted to see Phillips in person, to gauge the man's confidence and hear from his own mouth his plan of attack. If at all possible, he wanted Phillips' men to take these intruders alive, but they also needed to be prepared for anything. It could very well be that these three intruders would soon be joined by more men, or that they were only here to offer a distraction for a much larger force that would arrive soon.

Neither option was acceptable, and Requin needed Phillips to be prepared. Most of the guards had been trained by the Israeli army, but he knew they had not seen much action. Guards like Requin's men were soft after years of not seeing combat, and the bit of frustration they took out on the prisoners was hardly enough to retain their edge.

No, Requin needed to be there for Phillips in case his small team proved unworthy of defending his prison. He wanted to watch the battle unfold before his own eyes, rather than wait for Phillips' updates.

Not because he wanted to lead the men himself, and not because he wished to be the last line of defense in case these intruders somehow overtook his guards.

He needed to ensure the secrets here *stayed* secret. There was not much to find in the laboratory — at least nothing that would make sense to anyone outside of The Faction. There was a chance the intruders could capture and interrogate the scientists he employed here, but he doubted this could happen before The Faction would be able to retaliate and completely wipe the island of human life.

Besides that, The Faction was almost ready to take action on the massive project they had been working toward for years. This intrusion was unwelcome, but could perhaps be serendipitous, an action that may force The Faction into action. Requin believed The Faction *needed* to act now. They had been dragging their feet, waiting for every little piece to fall into place. Requin knew better — no plan was ever perfect and waiting for everything to line up perfectly was a recipe for frustration.

But he could not allow so much as a chance that these intruders might find the object he kept locked in his office. There was always a

chance that these intruders had stumbled upon this place by accident, that they had no idea who these prisoners were and who
employed their guards. There was a chance they would not care
about this object, and what it portended.

But he had not succeeded in this life by *chance*. He preferred
planning to luck, assuredness to chance. He would not allow the
object to fall into enemy hands, no matter the cost.

So he planned to retrieve the object, connect with Phillips, and
continue past the prison complex. He had no interest in staying
behind to watch the battle unfold, if these intruders somehow were
able to scale the cliffs and reach the grounds. Surely Phillips and his
men could handle them then.

Requin instead planned to be far away from the action — he
intended to take his most prized possession with him, to ensure his
further usefulness to The Faction.

CHAPTER 43
MARCIA

SEPTEMBER 17, **2020 | local time 10:30 am**

Cairo, Egypt

The pair of women had circled back to the car by taking the longest route possible — through the park and open space, across a busy thoroughfare, around three commercial complexes, and finally back to the southwest, where Marcia could see the wrecked vehicle still in place where they had left it.

They slowed to a halt as Marcia considered Sarah's question. *What about the sarcophagus?*

"Why? Do you know something about where we might find it?" she asked.

Sarah shook her head. "No, I wish I did. It's been lost for centuries, right?"

Marcia frowned, not sure if Sarah was genuinely curious or simply testing Marcia's knowledge of the subject. Thankfully, it was a subject she considered herself an expert in, thanks to Sarah's father's urging.

"Correct. We don't even know where the tomb of Alexander is, at least officially. That's the main reason we were studying and digging at Siwa — no one had ever definitively crossed it off the list of options."

"Options that also include Babylon, Memphis, and Alexandria."

Marcia smiled. *She may not be testing me, but she isn't ignorant, either.* "Right again. He died in Babylon, but his death was not immediate. There would have been days, perhaps weeks, Alexander was on his deathbed, conversing with and planning his funeral and burial."

"Didn't he ask to be buried in Siwa?" Sarah asked.

"Yes, he did. That was his request — to be buried beneath the temple of Zeus Ammon at the Oracle at Siwa. This was a big deal since his father was buried in Aegae, and Alexander thought himself the son of Zeus incarnate. However, he was never brought to Siwa. On the way back to Macedonia, his funerary procession was hijacked by one of Alexander's generals — a guy named Ptolemy of Lagos — who brought him to Memphis instead."

Sarah laughed. "And he didn't stay there, either."

"Nope. He was brought to Alexandria, where the Ptolemaic Cult of Alexander the Great began shortly after."

"Hmm."

Marcia watched Sarah's face for her response, but none came. Instead, her face was pointed toward the wreck. They walked on, approaching a small group of people gathered around it, seemingly more interested in their own cellphones than the wreckage.

There was no sign of the man who had shot at them, though Marcia was not about to let her guard down. He could be anywhere, hiding in the shadows in an alleyway or behind a tree. Or in the group of people milling about.

"I think we got lucky," Sarah said.

Marcia followed her gaze and saw Sarah's bag next to the vehicle. A police squad car sat nearby, and the officer was on the phone near his open driver's-side door. He was listening intently, and — more importantly — he was not facing the bag on the ground.

"I'm going to grab it," Sarah said.

"Wait, what? Sarah, don't —"

But her new friend was already gone. Marcia pulled the handkerchief farther over her eyes and ducked down, working her way toward the crowd of people. Thankfully, no one seemed to care about the newcomer, but she noticed a few sets of eyes looking up and noticing Sarah's movements.

Sarah deftly pranced around the vehicle without showing her face, then lifted the duffel bag and threw it over a shoulder. She started walking across the parking lot toward the embassy building where they had first met, all without breaking stride.

Brilliant, Marcia thought. The woman had not stopped, turned, or looked at the crowd, and she had not been there long enough for anyone to realize she was not supposed to be.

Most importantly, she had not started to sprint away, as if trying to get away with something she should not have done. She had calmly, confidently, waltzed up and snatched the bag, then continued onward into the embassy's front doors.

If anyone was going to accost her now, they would have to do it in on United States soil.

Marcia smiled and left the safety of the group of bystanders, looping wide around the area and approaching the embassy's lobby entrance from the south. She did not dare a look around, but no one shouted or hailed her as she crossed the threshold.

Inside, Sarah whistled. Marcia saw the woman in the corner of the lobby, hiding in a cluster of comfortable-looking lounge chairs. The duffel bag sat in one of them.

"Check it out," she said as Marcia approached. She motioned for her to look into the bag, and Marcia obliged.

She gasped as she looked down into the open duffle bag. She now understood what the Cairo police officer was so interested in besides the wreck itself, and why he had been on the phone.

"These are... these are yours?" she asked.

Sarah smiled. "I'm a relatively new member of this Civilian Special Operations crew. But I've been part of it long enough to know how to travel."

Marcia stared at the items inside, suddenly feeling very vulnerable. There were two sets of metal detectors about twenty paces away, deeper into the lobby, for visitors who had business farther inside the building. She hoped the guards standing beside each unit were preoccupied enough to not pay the two women any attention.

"I borrowed them," Sarah said, pointing at each of the guns in turn. "Two rifles and four handguns, and enough NATO rounds to keep each one of them happy for a while."

"And... you knew we would need them?" Marcia asked.

"Not really," Sarah said. "But as I said — I refuse to be caught unprepared. I've seen too much by now, and with The Faction actively searching for us and hunting me down..."

Marcia nodded. She was no pacifist, but her comfortable upbringing in the northeast corner of the United States had kept her well clear of firearms. She had never even held one.

"It looks heavy," she said.

"It's damned heavy. But not too heavy. It'll slow us down, but I'm hoping that if we have a repeat of what we hit before, these will slow *them* down even more."

"If we have a repeat of before, I'm hoping you'll give me the crash course in how to use them."

Sarah's smile shifted to a smirk. "That's why I picked these particular weapons. They're dead-simple to operate. Just point and shoot."

Marcia studied Sarah's face. *Just point and shoot. Like in the movies, right?* She did not ask the question aloud. It wouldn't matter now. Her plan was far from trying to learn how to use a rifle in the next five minutes.

Instead, her plan was what it had always been: *try not to get shot.*

CHAPTER 44
REGGIE

SEPTEMBER 17, **2020 | local time 11:32 am**
Sea of Marmara | Imrali Island, Turkey.
You're insane.

Freddie's last words to him resonated through Reggie's head, reverberating through his skull. He hadn't argued with his friend at the time because he hadn't *disagreed* with him at the time.

But Freddie hadn't argued, either, which told Reggie he was just as insane as he, and just as desperate.

They simply *had* to get inside the base. Going up and over the cliff's edge, as they had previously planned, had all but been ruled out, on account of their surprising discovery of the window and the sinister-looking man within. Their element of surprise had been wiped away, and they needed a new plan.

Reggie had that plan — it wasn't pretty, but it was certainly not something the man and his guards in the prison would expect.

It also had a high probability of getting them all killed. At best, he could expect to destroy his *very* expensive prosthetic arm in the process.

Reggie had pulled the harpoon gun from the holster latch on his dive suit next to the scuba tanks and had placed it on the submersible's mount just beneath the plexiglass shield. The sharp tip of the harpoon itself reached forward about a foot from the front of the plexiglass. Reggie had played with the mount and gun to tilt the harpoon up a bit, then extended the lance forward a few more inches until satisfied.

He had smiled at that thought. *Satisfied,* as if this were not a half-baked, terribly ill-thought-out plan.

Random shot felt more accurate. And yet, he had smiled the entire time, as if maniacally excited about the opportunity to kill himself and his teammates in an even more elaborate, crazed way than he had ever imagined.

But none of the men had offered a better idea. They had all nodded along like it truly was their best shot, and that told Reggie everything he needed to know.

They were going to do this.

Freddie, this crack team's leader, had even blessed with a verbal, *you're insane,* before smacking him on the back and pulling the googles back down over his eyes.

A few minutes earlier they had reentered the water, checked their propulsion system's readouts for anything that may have gone awry, then drove the submersible bubble shield out in a wide arc, back toward their boat somewhere over the horizon.

As they finished their turn, their faces and harpoon gun pointed once more at the side of the cliff, Freddie motioned for them to begin their acceleration.

They had discussed it at length — for as long as they had decided was safe. After about five minutes of going through potentialities and figuring out the logistics, they had all agreed on two things: it could work, and they *really* needed to hire an engineer next time they tried something like this.

Reggie watched Freddie's hands as his fingers counted down the numbers. *Three, two...*

One.

The propulsion system darted forward, eased into acceleration by Freddie's control. He watched their speed climb. *10 MPH, 12 MPH, 15 MPH...*

They were now traveling toward the cliffs faster than Reggie had gone before. 20 MPH in a car, saved by glass all around, felt *nothing* like traveling in the open air — or in the open water. He had been waterskiing dozens of times as a kid, and every time he got up for more than a minute, feeling the wind through his hair and drying the beads of lake water on his face, he had been shocked to find out that his top speed was only barely crossing the 15MPH mark.

As far as he could figure, the human body simply wasn't meant to travel without outside protection faster than about 10 miles per hour.

Now he was going twice that and barreling toward a cliff. Not a good combination.

As the rocks — dark, shadowy shapes twisting just out of sight — slowly appeared in his vision, he and the other men worked their controls swiftly and gently. A nudge left, one down, trying to ensure they were on target. They had had to guess at the proper depth, and at this speed, getting it wrong by more than a few yards either direction would not allow them enough time to course correct.

His heart rate rose as the rocks below began to crawl up toward his belly, quickly. He swallowed; his eyes widened. He could hear nothing but his own heartbeat in his chest.

This would be a great *time to be right,* he thought. *But if I'm wrong, it won't really matter to us anymore.*

But there was nothing guiding their progress now. They had planned on seeing the bright yellow lights of the room, spreading outward at least fifty or a hundred feet from the glass, but now there was nothing.

No.

The man inside had turned off the light, turned off their only beacon.

Now it was a crapshoot where they were headed, but Reggie figured the odds were likely they were drifting toward the side of the cliff — *not* the window. They had been shot from a cannon, aiming for a bullseye, but now it was a bullseye they couldn't even see.

There would be no correcting, not if they couldn't tell what to correct *toward*.

He swallowed again, the bile rising quickly in his throat. He tried to push it down, feeling his hands growing warm, sweating even against the cool waters.

Then he saw it. A glint, a small reflection. The window they had accidentally found earlier, hidden in the shallow cave. Freddie's light must have caught just the corner of it.

But it was enough, and thankfully his two teammates had seemed to notice it as well. The three men worked in tandem, following Freddie's lead, and they eased the craft and their bodies down and to the right a bit, putting them — hopefully — dead-center of the window.

And it was just in time, too. Reggie hadn't realized how fast they were moving. Their sleek bodies, combined with the constant thrum of the motor, had pushed the needle on their speed to about 23 MPH.

Everything inside his mind told him to slow down.

And yet, at the same time, Reggie wondered if it was going to be fast enough.

He removed his hands from the controls, as they had planned. He placed his prosthetic into the nook between the harpoon mount and the SubCart, the metal alloy fingers around the harpoon, feeling the trigger slide into place beneath his finger.

He counted down a silent counter. *3, 2, 1...*

And then he fired.

CHAPTER 45
REQUIN

SEPTEMBER 17, 2020 | local time 11:32 am
Sea of Marmara | *Imrali Island, Turkey.*

He reached his office and walked straight to his desk, where he kept the one thing he knew the intruders would not expect. It was the sole item in his possession that could give him an edge, the item that had been discovered on accident, honed by forward-thinking geniuses thousands — potentially tens of thousands — of years ago, and finally perfected by the small team of scientists and researchers he had hired. These scientists worked just on the other side of the glass wall from his office, down below in the *La Guerre* laboratory, where he could keep a close eye on their progress.

It was the item that had solidified his membership in The Faction. The item that had started the organization down their most recent trail, exploring new avenues toward controlling populations and shaping the future of the planet.

Many of his subordinates — the brilliant men and women working for him — had shared their hesitations and pessimisms regarding those ends. They thought his goals too lofty, too far-fetched. And they expressed concern that though they had discovered an incredible use for this ancient chemical technology — and had even found a way to create a synthetic version of it for mass-production — they still needed the *antidote.*

That antidote was the very thing the team in Egypt was supposed to find, the assumption being that the antidote to the amazing chemical compound that they were studying here in the laboratory was buried in the tomb at Siwa. It had long been postulated that Siwa was the possible location of the tomb of Alexander the Great, though no one had been able to secure enough funding and the proper permissions to look, since most reputable archeologists thought it a long shot.

But Requin and a few others in The Faction did believe it. And they believed the tomb was the location not just of a *man*, but of the final secret the man carried to his grave. The very thing that had ultimately killed Alexander they already had in their possession.

But the object that could have resurrected him? The mysterious compound that could have saved his life? That was still missing.

Siwa was the best place Requin knew to look. Ignoring the popular archaeological and historical consensus — usually promoting an agenda pushed by the Egyptian government rather than by truth alone — all signs pointed to *something* buried there. Ancient historical texts, as well as apocryphal documents considered propaganda or poetic art, pointed to Siwa as the prime location for just what The Faction wanted to find. They had worked for years to uncover the real truth behind the conqueror's final days, his plans upon his death, and the political maneuverings of his followers and fans.

Most believed his body had moved at least once after his death, entombed in a casket and sarcophagus intended for someone else.

He knew the truth: this technology *would* change the world. The Faction had experimented with a related chemical compound over the past year and found its effects startling and surprising. This updated version, far more potent and powerful, allowed for the one thing the previous iteration did not: *control.*

No, he knew his employees were as shortsighted and naive as they were brilliant. He was not overstating the outcome: he was *underestimating* its true potential.

Even if this object was lost or stolen, the scientists down below had already created and began mass-producing synthesized copies of it. He needed to protect it, however, to ensure it did not fall into enemy hands. The object's power was immense, and anyone able to study the chemical compound inside it would realize this. Worse, they might then be able to understand The Faction's next attack and create safeguards against it.

It was a long shot, but he did not care. Right now, his only mission was to retrieve the tiny orb-like object and bring it with him.

He found the object where he had left it, hidden within a secret storage compartment locked in one of his desk drawers. He felt the hard ceramic orb inside the velvet bag it was in and placed both in his pocket. It felt heavier now, as if its weight was both physical and representative of his task.

Closing the drawer and leaving his desk just as it had been, he walked to the wall to the left of the desk. The opposite wall was made of glass and provided him a view of the laboratory and the scurrying hustle of his employed science team. Usually he kept the floor-to-ceiling curtains open, only shutting them when he had an important meeting, but these were rare. Most often, Requin simply kept the curtain open to let in the additional light.

The wall he stood in front of now featured a sole painting, an expensive piece he had procured in Italy, but he had no taste or desire for artwork. Instead, the piece hid a switch, which he flipped by swinging the painting to the side and revealing the recessed metal latch.

Immediately, the wall slid sideways, revealing an elevator. This shaft went from this office to the top floor of the three-story prison building, where there was a helipad on the roof. His chopper —

owned and operated by a full-time *La Guerre*-employed pilot — would be waiting.

He entered the elevator and pressed the button to bring him up to the first floor, at ground level. Phillips would be waiting for him, and he needed to see with his own eyes the preparations his chief of security had made. Requin estimated they had at least half an hour before the scuba divers he had seen were able to scale the cliffs. Hopefully Phillips' men could pick them off one at a time while they were still climbing.

Just after he pressed the button he felt a shift in the floor, accompanied by a slight popping sound.

He frowned, cocking his head sideways as the elevator righted itself and settled again, but not without a loud creaking.

What was that?

Through the elevator's open door, he could see across his office at the glass wall, and beyond, through the level to the floor below. Scientists and technicians were moving, faster than they usually did, and all in one direction.

Suddenly there were screams, muffled and faint through the glass.

And then... water?

He saw a thick vein of white rapids rushing through the aisles between the scientists' tables and desks. It seemed the entire open-concept workspace was suddenly *moving*. Tables and chairs shifted and slid in the same direction the people had begun moving, and then the water rose even higher.

Suddenly, another loud pop sounded, and he thought he felt the entire base shift beneath his feet. The water level in the laboratory chamber below shot upward by a few feet, almost immediately. The panic set in now, the screams elevated and echoed by everyone downstairs.

This is absurd, he thought. The elevator groaned again, and his eyes widened. He smashed the button for level three instead, pressing it numerous times until the elevator doors began groaning shut.

There were no stairs here. If the elevator could not get him to the surface, he would have to run out of the office and toward the stairs at the end of the hall. But he already saw white-coated lab techs running for the same set of stairs. It would be chaos out there, and the waters still did not seem to be slowing.

Finally, the elevator moved. It stumbled upward, then picked up speed as it rose. He knew the shaft would have to have been built into the foundation of the island itself, but there was no reason to suspect that it had been breached. The water would be kept out for a time, and hopefully that meant he would be able to reach the top level.

Phillips and his men would have to fend for themselves, he knew. His cause was far too important to be held up, and the object he carried needed to reach safe ground, away from these intruders who had somehow discovered a way to sabotage his company's head-quarters.

He was not concerned about the building itself — he had insurance for that reason. He would be made whole, and he could rehire scientists.

But he was *angry*. He had been irritated upon seeing the men outside the window in the room downstairs, but he had assumed they would be met with Phillips' full force.

But his frustration had grown to an incredible fury. His plans had been changed, and The Faction would not be happy about it.

If Phillips was able to take them alive, he intended to make these people pay in the most brutal and painful way possible.

CHAPTER 46
FREDDIE

SEPTEMBER 17, 2020 | local time 11:33 am
Sea of Marmara | Imrali Island, Turkey.

Freddie watched the harpoon lance outward from the mount hanging to the bottom side of the bubble-like shield.

But he didn't have long to wait. The harpoon shot forward, moving deftly through the water faster than he thought possible, and impacted with the glass window only a millisecond later. Its razor-sharp, reinforced tip pierced a half-inch into the thick glass window and then lodged there, unmoving.

A direct hit, but it was only half the intended payload.

A second later, Freddie let go of his own controls. They pummeled forward, the three men now holding onto nothing but the shaft of the harpoon rifle's chamber. Mounted beneath the propulsion system and designed to withstand immense pressures from whales and all manner of sea creature, the group had decided that it remained the single most structurally sound object to use to penetrate the glass wall.

Reggie's prosthetic arm, reinforced to hold up to thousands of pounds of pressure, as well as the sea itself, would do the rest of the job.

I hope.

Freddie discovered the answer to that question another second later. He pulled on the harpoon tube, sliding his body inward to allow the plexiglass bubble to better protect his head, then crouched into as much of a ball as the constricted space would allow.

The others did the same. Reggie rode on the rear end of the harpoon shaft, one hand gripping the trigger still, as if he planned on taking another shot at the glass-and-rock wall immediately in front of them.

Freddie couldn't help it. He squeezed his eyes closed just as the propulsion system impacted the glass. The harpoon itself was hit first, the plexiglass fighting against the alloy shaft of the harpoon, but the glass it was impaled in gave way first.

Freddie's body rocked against the plexiglass, the sudden jolt and stop nearly causing his bones to shatter. He held on, realizing that he had not come to a *complete* stop, which certainly would have killed them all.

Instead, the harpoon had finally been pressed through the glass, weakening the entire window and causing a ripple-like effect of cracks inside the glass window. The lattice shattered then, and the propulsion system now pressed inward as well, causing the glass to warp in on itself.

Finally, the entire thing gave way, and an absolutely *massive* wall of water suddenly existed where the *actual* glass did not. Freddie and his two remaining teammates tumbled into the dark room, now funneled along by the entire weight of the sea on their backs.

Freddie tried driving the propulsion system but found it too much a struggle to keep it pointed the direction he wanted to go. Thankfully, the water itself knew where it wanted to go, and it simply smashed through walls and doorframes to get there.

While the prison's subterranean compound had been constructed in the hollowed-out interior of the island, most of the concrete supports and reinforcements holding everything together were centralized and sat far apart from one another. That meant the raging seawater had almost no real opponent as it destroyed the interior of the place. Walls, doors, large glass windows made of thin, single panes — all decimated as the ocean roared into the space.

Freddie kept his scuba mask and goggles, and his head was thrust in and out of the water as they were pressed forward. It was a surreal experience, the chaos and noise and destruction his ears heard *out* of the water, then the relative calm, steady roar *in* the water.

They flew past hallways and into a large, open space. People wearing white lab coats turned to see a wall of water bearing down on them, but they didn't even have time to scream before the tsunami engulfed them. Freddie felt the heavy bodies impacting the front of the plexiglass shield, saw the bodies of drowning, scrambling men and women as their confused faces tried to recover and make toward the nearest pocket of air.

But there *was* no pocket of air. The sea had come in, and within ten seconds of entering had begun replacing all air with chilly saltwater. It churned and swallowed desks, chairs, laboratory experiments and people alike, with stunning ruthlessness and zero empathy. Freddie and his men were twisted sideways, crammed through narrow gaps between concrete columns, funneled around bends and corners, all while holding onto the harpoon's shaft and propulsion system's controls.

The shield held, and they were protected from the detritus that swirled toward them as they surfed the inside of the wave, and once the water had settled to a dull roar, Freddie found the controls willing to cooperate more.

The sea was still entering the facility and would until the inside reached equilibrium with the water level, and the team planned to ride it upward until it was done. He steered around a facedown man and woman near the surface, not daring to look up into their open eyes. The woman was holding a cell phone in a lifeless hand.

A few seconds later, and they were on the surface, skimming

along behind the propulsion system. Freddie killed the engine to save battery power, then let go and swam toward a stairwell that led up and out of the laboratory floor.

Two more far luckier scientists stood on the rail, pointing toward Freddie and his two-man team. The look of shock on both their faces told him everything: how could three men in scuba gear cause *this much* death and destruction?

Freddie wanted to wave, to smile and act brazenly arrogant, as if to shove their evils in their faces. None of these people would live through the day — Reggie would be sure of it, even if Freddie's conscience somehow got in the way. These people were obviously working for The Faction, and they would pay for it with their lives.

But he couldn't bring himself to have any other emotion but uncertainty. How could they know they hadn't already killed their friend just by coming here?

And if not, how could they know they hadn't killed him during their bold entrance? For all they knew, the prison wasn't just on *top* of the island — safe from their mischief down here. The prison complex up above them could be just a facade, a leftover artifact from the days when the Turkish government owned this land.

Harvey Bennett could be floating face down in one of the destroyed rooms or hallways here, just like the poor souls they had cruised by a moment ago.

But he would not allow himself these feelings, not yet. They had a job to do.

They would find answers here, one way or another.

CHAPTER 47
SARAH

Cairo, Egypt

The duffel *was* heavy, but thankfully the shooter who had attacked them before was nowhere to be found. Still, Sarah knew to be on her guard — the man was most certainly from The Faction, which meant there were *far* more men just like him, homing in on their location.

We need to get out of town, she thought. *But to where?* She had come for Marcia, and by proxy, her father. She had flown to Cairo because the last place he had been spotted was in Siwa, and it had been easier to smuggle the weapons into Egypt than it would have been to try to get them into Libya.

But... that had been the extent of her plan. *Get to Egypt, find my father's student, come prepared to fight.*

She had checked all of those boxes and was now feeling the stress of not having a more in-depth plan.

The younger woman walking next to Sarah apparently read her mind. "Sarah," she began, "we can't just walk around aimlessly. We probably can't buy a plane ticket, either, unless you've got a ton of cash. The Faction's able to track our credit card purchases, right?"

"Right," Sarah admitted. "And yes, we can't go to the airport. I was thinking we could get another rental, but we'll have another problem. The Faction will have people waiting close to any of the nearby rental outfits most likely. I don't want to take the chance."

She paused mid-stride, and Marcia copied her movement. Sarah sighed. *This is trickier than I thought.*

"What do Ben — Harvey Bennett — and your boyfriend, Reggie, do in situations like this?" Marcia suddenly asked.

Sarah grinned. "What, you mean situations like getting chased through a foreign country without any semblance of a plan?"

"Sure. That's a start, I guess."

Sarah's grin widened. "Well, usually alcohol's involved."

Marcia laughed out loud. "That's funny. But seriously..."

Sarah flicked an eyebrow up. "There's a cafe I've been to right around the corner. They usually have a few bottles on offer."

"Really? In downtown Cairo? I thought alcohol was *haram*."

Sarah knew the culture and society of Egypt — like most other places — was one of contradictions, traditions, and progression. For the ninety percent Muslim population that called Egypt home, alcohol in all its forms was forbidden, or *haram*. However, for the rest of the population that called themselves Christian, alcohol was just short of a necessity. Coupled with an increase in tourism to the country, it was impossible to ban alcohol altogether.

Beer brewing had been a part of Egyptian heritage for thousands of years, so it was more common to find bottles of local beers available in restaurants and cafes that catered to tourists and progressive locals.

They walked along the boulevard and turned the corner, finding the small cafe Sarah had mentioned bustling with people. Patrons spilled out onto the sidewalk, many of them shouting into the restaurant at the rest of their parties. It was an Italian-style espresso bar, featuring very few chairs and only bar-height tables. The place was packed, and Marcia hesitated outside the entrance.

"Are you sure we have time to stop?" she asked.

Sarah snorted a laugh. "Oh, sorry. You asked me what my boyfriend would do in this situation, not what *I* would do. *They* would act like idiots, relying on their strength and luck. I'm more of a planner, more of a thinker, admittedly."

"So we're *not* stopping here?"

"Not for a drink, no," Sarah clarified. "I want to meet someone."

"For what?"

"For a ride," she said, winking. "A couple nice-looking gals like us shouldn't have any trouble finding a guy who's willing to drive us out of town."

"That sounds... dangerous, Sarah."

She winked again. "I'm not planning on telling them what's in my duffel bag," she said. "And I didn't mention it to you earlier, but in case you're wondering — I'm not new to *using* them, either. I'd say we're pretty safe if we can stay together. The point is, we just need someone to drive us toward the eastern border, either to Port Said or even Sinai. Shouldn't take longer than an hour, really. Once we get there, we can —"

She cut herself off as her eye was drawn toward the side of the store near the entrance. A newsstand with the English-language paper *The Egyptian Gazette* face-out on the top rack.

"What's up?" Marcia asked, following Sarah inside the cafe.

Sarah pushed her way through throngs of men and women, many holding tea or coffee, and some with one of the copies of the very paper she was aiming for.

She reached the newsstand and grabbed the last copy of the *Gazette*. She pulled it up to her face, noticing the headline that appeared just above the page-sized image that had first caught her attention.

Ancient Sarcophagus Stolen From British Museum.

She held the paper out to Marcia, pointing at the image. "You recognize this sarcophagus?"

"I do," Marcia said, frowning. "It's a pretty popular attraction at the museum. It's Egyptian, right?"

"Nectanebo II," Sarah said. "The last pharaoh of the Thirtieth Dynasty."

"Who stole the sarcophagus?" Marcia asked, trying to read the article for clues. "And why?"

"I don't think they know yet. But it's interesting — I'd bet The Faction had something to do with it."

"Yeah?" Marcia asked. "Why's that?"

"Well, Nectanebo II was considered by some — at least according to an ancient, fictionalized account — to be the *true* father of Alexander the Great."

Marcia frowned. "I remember reading about that, I think. That's preposterous."

"It is, and I don't think any real historian believes it. Still, there are some close ties, which is why I think it's an interesting thread."

"Like what?"

"It's all stuff I've forgotten, to be honest. But I have a friend who works there, in London. Change of plans — *you* find someone to give us a ride, and I'm going to call her. She'll be able to fill in my missing details on the sarcophagus, and why it might be important to a group like The Faction."

Marcia nodded, and while Sarah saw a bit a hesitation in her eyes, she also saw the resolve. This young person was strong, and she would be able to commit when it mattered.

"You got it," Marcia said. "Let's figure this out."

CHAPTER 48
REGGIE

SEPTEMBER 17, **2020 | local time 11:38 am**
Sea of Marmara | Imrali Island, Turkey.

Reggie watched the brief standoff. The entirety of it lasted only a few seconds — Freddie staring at the two scientists, their shocked faces staring back. He knew what Freddie was thinking.

These people might not have known what they were getting themselves into.

Reggie disagreed. He had a feeling these people, and every other one of them, either dead and floating beneath the surface or escaped and safe elsewhere in the building, were well aware of what they had done here.

In the few moments Reggie had been able to piece together what this space might have looked like before the waters came in and remodeled, he saw that there had been a sprawling laboratory and research floor inside. Hidden from view by any prying satellite or terrestrial cameras, it meant that whatever had gone on here had been done in secret.

And there were really only two kinds of secret laboratories: those established by governments for testing weapons and science projects

237

they needed to keep out of sight, and those established by corporations that wanted to maintain some privacy.

And when those corporations were known Faction supporters and bought entire islands off the coast of Turkey to hide their operations, Reggie was less inclined to believe their motives were altruistic.

The scientist nearest to Reggie on the stairwell overlooking the laboratory floor, a man who looked to be in his late fifties, scowled at him. He rattled off something in another language, his voice and inflection telling Reggie he did not approve of their violent entry.

Freddie started to complain, but Reggie was quicker. Without bothering to look for more than a second, he checked the damage to his prosthetic. Incredibly, there was nothing but some cosmetic damage to the metal shaft around the wrist. He wriggled the fingers a few times and was satisfied. He had a rifle up and out of the water, and he pushed to the side, away from the plexiglass shield bobbing in the water. He fired two quick shots; the rifle set to single round fire. The man on the stairs stumbled backward and fell onto the rear railing, a blush of red spreading over his pristine white lab coat.

The woman screamed. Younger by about twenty years with yellow, frizzy hair that had streaks of gray running through it, her face contorted in agony, as if personally experiencing her colleague's pain.

Reggie recentered his aim onto her chest and started to squeeze the trigger.

"Hold your fire!" Freddie shouted at him. Besides the easing roar of the water filling the space, there were no other sounds, and Reggie's ear immediately started ringing.

"What the hell, man?" Reggie snapped.

"Stay there!" Freddie yelled now, directing his voice this time toward the woman on the stairwell.

The bottom of the stairs were completely underwater, and the level was rising at over a foot per minute. The woman's feet were already starting to get wet, the landing she and the dying scientist were on starting to disappear as well.

Reggie frowned, upset by Freddie's outburst, but he lowered his rifle. The tip hit the water, and Reggie instinctively pulled it back out. Waterproof or not, he had been trained that his gear was an extension of him.

"We can use her," Freddie said, his voice low enough for only Reggie and Chuck to hear. "She might know where that guy is. The one who shut the lights off."

Reggie cackled, biting off the laughter. He hadn't expected it from Freddie, who otherwise had been completely professional and serious this entire time. Reggie knew they were all thinking that the man they had seen in the glass-walled room was likely the man in charge of this entire base and prison.

Yet what bothered Freddie was that he had *shut the lights off*. He had made it difficult to ram their propulsion unit through the floor-to-ceiling glass window.

Reggie smiled. "Sure, man. Let's find that guy."

He looked back at the woman as Freddie guided the propulsion unit toward a floating, overturned table. He parked the bubble shield on top of it, added his dive gear, then pulled the table and its contents to the stairwell landing. Reggie helped him get the rest of their gear loaded on top.

"Figure we can let the table float everything up and keep it all together," Freddie said. "That way we don't have to lug it upstairs by ourselves. The water level will only go probably halfway up the second stairwell, anyway, so it'll be here waiting for us when we're back."

Reggie nodded, then turned to the woman. "You speak English?"

She shook her head, a bit too quickly for Reggie's liking. A flick of her eyes told him immediately that she was lying.

He stepped closer, toe-to-toe with her now, and leaned down, his towering, thin figure intimidating. Drops of saltwater fell from his brow onto her upturned face. "I asked if you *speak English.*"

She swallowed, but then clenched her jaw and set her face and eyebrows, as if about to lie again. "Y — yes," she stammered. "I do."

"Right," he said, sighing. "I figured. Where's that guy we saw? The one wearing the ridiculous smirk and a shirt that was too tight?"

He hoped he wouldn't have to painstakingly describe the man they had seen in the glass room.

She paused, considering her options. Finally, as the water reached their knees, she let out a breath. "Elevator." She tossed her head back and motioned toward the top of the stairs. "Private, goes from his office to the top floor of the prison building. There is a helicopter pad there, I believe."

"And does a helicopter live on this pad?" Freddie asked.

"I do not know," she answered.

"Fine," Reggie said. "Take us there."

"He will not —"

"*Now.*"

She let out a breath once more but started moving backwards until her feet hit the bottom of the second flight of stairs. There, she turned slowly and stepped up. Reggie was right behind her. Freddie and Chuck followed closely behind, and the group marched upward toward the elevator and hallway above.

Reggie gripped his rifle tightly as they raced the rising waters. He thought of the lab down below, wondering if this was the place where The Faction had cooked up an ancient cocktail to use as a chemical weapon — one they had trialed on his very team. One they had used to terrorize the entire world over the span of months of attacks across the globe.

A chemical that was potent and useful for disabling any and all enemies that got in their way. He thought about the stroke of luck — and a bit of similarly ancient wisdom from none other than

Napoleon Bonaparte, hidden for centuries — that had allowed them to escape the chemical's grasp and prevail.

All of that had been The Faction's fault, and if it had been cooked up here, in this laboratory, by these scientists, then he was more than happy to see it banished to an underwater grave.

He hoped they could end their terrifying reign today, here and now. But more than that, he hoped they would find answers to a question that had plagued the entire Civilian Special Operations team for months on end.

A question that had plagued and tormented one of his closest friends, Juliette Bennett. A question that had kept him and Sarah up at night, for countless nights.

Where is Harvey Bennett?

CHAPTER 49
MARCIA

Cairo, Egypt

It had taken a few minutes to find someone in the cafe Marcia was not afraid to approach, but she finally found her mark. In the opposite corner of the restaurant was a seated group of college-aged men, all laughing and talking loudly. A few of them were wearing the shirts designating their school, a university in Berlin.

She sidled up to them, hoping she looked at least a few years older than the kids, and smiled. "Any of you guys speak English?" she asked.

Two of the men raised their hands sheepishly, but the two others spoke up and confirmed.

"Good," she said. "I need a ride. Any chance I can bum one?"

"A ride? Where?"

"North, northeast maybe. Just need to get out of the city."

"Are you in trouble?" the man to her left asked. "Why do you just need to 'get out' of the city?"

"Trouble? No," she lied. "But we're in a hurry, and our car broke down."

"We?"

"Yes — me and that woman over there. All we've got is that bag on her shoulder, and we're supposed to be at port in two hours."

"Which port?"

She told him, and they continued for a few minutes, Marcia working up a believable story of how they had come to Egypt for an extended vacation, and nothing was going their way — not entirely a lie, she had to admit. They were on the last leg now, and their car had died, and they had no credit cards or enough cash to get them to Port Said. They needed someone who was heading that direction.

"We had not planned to visit that part of Egypt," the man said. "But we do have cars. We are here for the semester, so it really does not matter, I guess. We may be able to help you out."

Marcia let out a sigh of relief — this time not a lie at all. "Thank you," she said. "A rental car will cost another hundred dollars. We might have... half of that? I am sorry we cannot offer more."

The German kid waved it off. "No problem," he said. "We are happy to help a fellow student."

So I guess I don't look too much older, after all, she thought. Just then, Sarah walked over, a clear sign of uncertainty on her face.

While Marcia could certainly pass as a college student — after all, she *was* one — that ship had sailed for Sarah. She looked her age: at least a decade older than the university students sitting around the table.

The man who had conversed with her started speaking again. "I thought you said 'students?'"

"Well, *graduate* students," she said quickly. "We're studying archeology."

She hoped the change in subject was a point of interest for the young man and would stop the barrage of questions, but Sarah made that a moot point. "Did you find someone to help us out?" Sarah asked as soon as she had reached the table.

Marcia nodded. "Yes, this is —"

"Johann," the man said. "We are going to finish our drinks, then we can leave."

Sarah pulled out a hundred-dollar bill from her pocket and smacked it down on the table. "I'll have another one of these when we get to where we're going," she said. "But we need to leave, *now*."

Marcia chuckled as Johann looked her up and down. She shrugged, hoping the questioning would not start back up until *after* they had gotten buckled into the car.

The Germans were not entirely happy about leaving half-finished drinks on the table, but none of them argued. Johann slid the American bill into his jacket pocket and gathered his wallet and phone as they left the restaurant.

Sarah and Marcia walked ahead while waiting for the others to exit. "Did you find anything out?" Marcia asked Sarah.

Sarah's face had confirmed what Marcia already thought. "I did," she said. "And it's *big*. I can't believe I didn't realize it earlier."

"About the sarcophagus?"

"Yes — it's not Nectanebo II's sarcophagus."

"Wait, what?"

"Yeah. Well, I mean technically it is — that's what it's called, at least. The sarcophagus was made for Nectanebo II, who ruled Egypt from 360 to 342 BC. During Nectanebo's reign, Alexander's body was brought by Ptolemy to Egypt who, if you'll recall, essentially stole his master's corpse mid-journey. Since they had just built a grand sarcophagus for Nectanebo II, decorated and all, Alexander's remains were placed inside it."

"So it *was* Alexander's tomb?"

"Well, not really. He was probably *in* the tomb, but then it was brought to Alexandria, where Alexander had told at least some people he wanted to be buried. There, his remains would have been seen and observed while in the sarcophagus, up until Venetian merchants raided the tomb — sometime around 830 AD. As you might guess, they took the remains of Alexander the Great to Venice, where they remained in the Patriarchal Cathedral Basilica of Saint Mark."

"Wait — he was brought to *St. Mark's Basilica?*"

Sarah smiled as the university students filed out the door. None of them spoke to Sarah, but the young man in charge motioned for Marcia to follow him. They waited until the men had passed, and Sarah continued.

"Yes, which is where the rest of the world has gotten confused. You see, the Roman Catholic Church has *adamantly* refused to examine the remains that still exist at St. Mark's. They — and most historians up until about a year ago — believe that the remains brought to St. Mark's are not the bones of Alexander the Great at all."

"Of course not," Marcia said, suddenly understanding. "That would completely destroy their narrative. And they probably have plenty of reason to believe they're *not* Alexander's remains there. Most notably, the name of the basilica itself."

"Exactly," Sarah said. "The bones at St. Mark's have long been understood, not at all surprisingly, to be the bones of *St. Mark.*"

Marcia let out a breath. It was exhilarating, seeing archeology and history unfold in real time. But it did not add up for her — so far she had not heard good evidence as to *why* the Catholic Church may be wrong about St. Mark's.

"So what changed? Why does The Faction suddenly think there's something in this sarcophagus? And why do they think it has anything to do with Alexander?"

Sarah smiled, a mischievous look on her face. "Well, that's where the story gets *really* interesting."

CHAPTER 50
FREDDIE

Freddie followed the group up the stairs, Reggie leading the frazzled scientist. She did not speak, no doubt terrified and hoping she was not about to become a martyr for her cause, facing a fate similar to her coworker. Freddie watched her motions as she walked, trying to get a sense for her mannerisms. He thought he could see her body shaking slightly, and her feet seemed off-balance with every step. He wanted to believe she was rattled — confused and surprised, as well as terrified — but he wanted to stay vigilant.

Could she be hiding something? Was she about to make a run for it? Or worse, was she about to do something to Reggie?

Freddie shook off the feelings. *No*, he thought, *she's just nervous, running on adrenaline.* He was no psychologist and trying to interpret other people's emotional fortitude had never ended well. Reggie and Sarah were better at that sort of thing.

They would stay the course — Harvey might be upstairs, and if so, they needed to find him before the guards were clued in on what Freddie's team was looking for.

As they reached the highest floor of the subterranean levels beneath the prison building, the waters finally began to subside. It had filled the entirety of the laboratory floor and surrounding offices and rooms, reached nearly to the ceiling, and now seemed to be steadying at about three feet beneath the top of the stairs.

At the top, Reggie turned and corralled the group. The woman was breathing heavily, eyes red. Freddie took a quick glance around the landing to be sure they were alone, then followed Reggie's gaze out over the cluttered surface of the water. Gear and bodies were everywhere, floating upturned and in pieces.

Their own equipment, still floating on the table, had matched them in their ascent foot-for-foot, and was now waiting in gently sloshing water on the other side of the balcony. He was examining the overturned table to ensure everything was accounted for when he saw a dark shape just beneath the surface. Thinking it nothing but another body, he watched it for a second.

It darted forward quickly — too quickly for a human. *Far* too quickly for a live human.

It disappeared beneath the waves, and Freddie almost missed the slight splashing sound about ten feet away as the shape appeared again, this time revealing a slick, pointed fin and pummeling the side of one of the many bodies. The body and shape together sank a few feet beneath the surface.

Freddie's eyes widened. "I don't think we're going back out the way we came in," he muttered.

Reggie chuckled. "You're telling me *now* that you're afraid of sharks?"

Curtis laughed as well. "What's the old adage? 'You don't have to outrun the bear, you just gotta outrun your buddy.'"

Freddie shot him a glance. He was not at all sure the propulsion system could outrun a shark, and he wasn't interested in finding out.

He shook off the chilling feeling and focused once again on the large landing they were on. Reggie walked forward again, pushing open the single door in front of them. It led to a hallway, narrow and dark, with only one door along it. They hustled down the hallway, and Reggie pushed open the unlocked door as they passed.

A bathroom and a high window, but nothing else inside. They moved quickly down it until they reached another staircase — this one led up again to another hall that ran perpendicular to the previous one. The hall had two doors on either side of it — one leading to a conference room space about ten feet to their left, another heading a hundred feet down to a larger set of double doors at its end.

They ran now, Reggie nearly having to drag the woman along to keep up. At the end, Freddie joined Reggie at the doors, and he worked the bar handle. It, too, was unlocked, but before Reggie pushed it open, Freddie stopped him.

He turned to face the scientist. "Where does this go?" he asked. "What are we about to walk into?"

"Library," came the one-word reply.

Freddie frowned, aiming the silent question at Chuck and Reggie.

Chuck shrugged, pulling up his rifle and signaling readiness. "Only one way to find out, boss," he said.

Reggie nodded once, taking up a position in the corner of the doorway, wedged out of sight between the edge of the doorframe and the wall of the hallway. Chuck joined Reggie, and Freddie positioned himself on the opposite wall. He pushed the scientist out to the center of the doorway. "Open it," he said.

The woman looked from him to Reggie, then back again, and finally made a face that suggested she was growing tired of being pushed around. Still, she complied. She shoved the doors open — both at once, loudly — then stepped through.

There was a pause as all four people waited for the reaction of whatever was waiting for them on the other side of the door. Freddie tensed.

Finally, Freddie dared join the scientist at the entrance to the new room. He held his breath, then swung around, gun ready, and faced the new room.

He exhaled just as Reggie came to his side. "Well," he said. "She wasn't kidding."

CHAPTER 51
SARAH

SEPTEMBER 17, **2020 | local time 10:42 am**
Cairo, Egypt

They reached the group of two parked rental cars only a minute later. Sarah let Marcia get in first, then she slung her duffel bag into the seat next to Marcia. Happy to be rid of the weight temporarily, she rolled her shoulders and sat in the front passenger seat, offered to her by Johann. Sarah waited as one of the other young men got in the seat behind her, next to Marcia with the duffel bag on the seat between them.

She felt the small pistol pressing against her waist, comforted by the thought of a loaded weapon easily accessible. She had slid it underneath her belt as they'd walked up the streets after leaving the cafe. While she had no reason to suspect that these young university students were hostile, she had long since stopped taking unnecessary risks.

This risk — asking strangers to drive them a hundred miles — was calculated, and the best option, given their circumstance. Sarah knew Marcia was not trained to use the weapons in the duffel, but if things got out of hand, she felt confident in her own abilities.

Johann waited behind the wheel as the other three students

climbed into the other rental car in front of theirs. Together, the two vehicles pulled out onto the busy Cairo side street, heading toward the main highway that would take them north.

"Please, I would like to know what is going on," Johann said.

Sarah sensed a bit of urgency in his voice. "Sorry for the confusion, Johann," she said. "I apologize — I know this is not how you wanted to spend your day. I'm happy to tell you the truth, but first, I need to chat with Marcia about something."

He did not respond, looking straight ahead out the window instead. The young man behind her had not spoken a word since they had met, and he seemed content to keep it that way. Perhaps his grasp of English was not strong enough.

Marcia got right back to the point. "So you said the sarcophagus was made for Nectanebo II, used by Alexander the Great, but was brought to St. Mark's Cathedral in Venice?"

Sarah nodded. "That's what my contact at the British Museum in London said. The theft was definitely of Nectanebo's sarcophagus, but that the artifact itself has long been the subject of debate. There's pretty strong evidence that Alexander was at least *temporarily* inside of the sarcophagus, at least while he was in Alexandria. There, the Venetians stole the entire thing, dumped out the bones in Venice, and the sarcophagus was lost, eventually found again and brought to the British Museum."

"And the Catholic Church swears that those bones are the bones of the patron saint of the Venetian cathedral."

"Right. And for good reason. Apparently, around the time the Roman Emperor Theodosius I made Christianity the official religion across the entire empire, the temple where Alexander's remains were changed to the temple of St. Mark. No one knows if someone tampered with the bones at that point, but from then on the temple in Alexandria was referred to as 'St. Mark's.' Obviously, if Alexander's remains were there at that point, someone swiped them and replaced them with St. Mark's at some point on the journey from Egypt to Italy. *Or* before, while Alexander was supposedly entombed in the newly christened St. Mark's in Alexandria."

"*Or* the Catholic Church is wrong, and those bones are actually..."

Sarah picked up the thread. "The remains of Alexander the Great. Which is what I'm leaning toward believing."

Johann's eyes were wide, but he did not interrupt. Sarah smiled, knowing that he must be thinking the two hitchhikers he had picked up were absolutely insane.

"Is there evidence to suggest whose bones are at St. Mark's today?" Marcia asked.

"Yes," Sarah said, nodding along. "That's what my contact at the British Museum is studying, actually. She told me there is a man named Adam Chugg who believes these two tombs in Alexandria are actually the same one, just mis-named. He's been studying it deeply for years, and he's found some compelling evidence that the bones of St. Mark were *never* in the tomb or sarcophagus, and thus the bones in St. Mark's in Venice *are*, in fact, Alexander's."

"Intriguing — what evidence is that?" Marcia asked.

"Well, for starters, he found a piece of limestone in the foundation of the basilica at St. Mark's in Venice. It depicts a piece of a spear and a strange sun-shaped symbol on what appears to be a shield."

"A spear and a shield," Marcia said. "Not exactly what I would equate with the Biblical description of Saint Mark."

"Right," Sarah said, feeling the smile returning to her face. "And best of all, she sent me a text message a few minutes ago, confirming my suspicions. It's a picture of the piece of limestone, and the sun symbol is clearly depicted. Here."

She held up her phone, the picture her contact at the British Museum sent her in full view. Sarah noticed the man next to Marcia perking up a bit, trying to get a glance at the image as well.

Marcia's hand went to her mouth. "I'd know that symbol

anywhere," she said quietly. "We studied everything about that culture, and it's been a passion project of mine for years."

"I figured as much," Sarah said. "*This* is why Chugg thought those bones are Alexander's, not Saint Mark's."

"Of course he would think that," Marcia said. "That symbol is unmistakable. It's *Macedonian*. The same as Alexander. That's a representation of Alexander's shield and spear, without a doubt."

CHAPTER 52
FREDDIE

Sea of Marmara | Imrali Island, Turkey.

The doorway had, in fact, opened into what appeared to be an old library — low-hanging lights, bookshelves along every wall except for where two sets of windows let in light from outside, and ancient wooden tables in the center. There was another doorway at the far end of the room. One of its doors had been partially obstructed by more bookshelves, and in the few places no bookshelves stood around the room, there were old oil paintings on the walls. The look of the space had been completed by threadbare rugs over the floorboards beneath their feet.

"Wow," Freddie said.

Reggie whistled next to him as Chuck and the scientist came into the large room. "Yeah, they really nailed the period style, didn't they?"

"I wonder why," Freddie said. "This place looked completely inconsequential before. Concrete, metal, and glass. Maybe a bit modern. This is the polar opposite of that. It's like they airlifted an entire medieval library and dropped it here, down to the floorboards and all."

As if underlining his point, the wood beneath his feet creaked and groaned as he shifted.

"And the books," Reggie added, stepping close to one of the bookshelves. "I don't recognize any of them."

Chuck let out a laugh. "What — you expected walls full of Berenstain Bears books?"

Reggie shot him an annoyed glance. "I mean I don't even recognize the language of most of these."

"Wait, seriously?"

Chuck and Freddie walked over to where Reggie stood, examining the leather-bound tomes on the shelf nearest eye-level. The scientist woman, either amused or simply unsure of what they would do if she tried running away, joined them.

"Where are these from?" Reggie asked her.

She shrugged.

"Come on," he said. "You're hosed. Your cover's blown, your entire secret lair down there is filled with sharks and dead coworkers. The least you could do is give us a little hint."

She glared at him.

"Fine," he said. "We've got more important thorns to pull out of my side, anyway."

He pulled back from the wall and turned to face Freddie just as the unobstructed door at the opposite side of the room burst open. Three guards, each carrying subcompact machine guns, ran in. "Don't shoot unless —"

The guard's voice was cut off as Reggie immediately started firing, his rifle clattering with the bursts as he sent rounds toward the darkened edge of the opposite side of the room. The first two split off from the third and landed behind wooden tables. The third jogged forward toward another table, and Reggie got a shot off just as he ducked. The round sailed over the man's head.

"Get behind the tables!" Reggie shouted.

Freddie was already in motion, ducking behind a set of chairs and their corresponding table, yanking the scientist along with him. If she was going to be useful, it would only be if she was alive.

Flickering lights illuminated the room as the guards opened with return fire. Reggie moved again, barreling behind a large reading desk as one of the men's shots grazed his left leg. Freddie could almost feel the searing pain in his own leg — and fear for his friend's life — as Reggie stumbled. However, Chuck was there, grabbing Reggie under the arm and shooting toward the guard. His gun punched two small holes in the nearest table and sent the mercenary behind it diving out the way.

Freddie brought his rifle to bear on the third guard, but as the man was now in motion as well, he had to aim a half-second away from where the man was, and his first shots flew wide. He reset his shoulders, took a quick breath, and fired again.

There was a scream, and then silence. The man's legs poked out from behind a nearby table.

Reggie and Chuck joined Freddie. "You okay?" Freddie asked.

Reggie genuinely seemed confused at first, then looked down at his leg. There was a small gash, a bit of blood, but it wasn't deep. "This?" he replied. "Yeah, I've seen worse. In that same spot, actually, now that you mention it."

Chuck cocked his head toward the gate. "What now? They're moving up on us, trying to flank us around the tables."

Freddie stole another glance over the table at the guard on the ground, then at Reggie's leg. "You're good to keep moving?"

"You mean would I rather lay here belly-up and bleed out from a minuscule flesh wound?"

"Sorry I asked."

"Don't be. Just don't drag me if I trip over my ankle. Besides, I'm almost out of ammo."

Freddie noticed it as Reggie said the words. By opting for the harpoon gun, Reggie had been forced to take no extra ammunition for his rifle. Chuck and Freddie each had two magazines, and Freddie offered him one now. Reggie pushed Freddie's hand away.

Chuck sighed. "You could at least —"

A burst of submachine gun fire cut him off, and all four of them hit the deck, scrambling behind the only available piece of cover.

Reggie looked up at Freddie and whispered. "Thanks for the concern, but I'll live."

"Good, 'cause I need you. New plan: these other two assholes are flanking us as we speak, so we need to move up the middle. We run together, toward the dead guard up ahead. Chuck and I will pull back and use what's left of our rounds to cover you."

"Great," Reggie said. "Consider me your very own meat shield."

"That's not what —"

But it was too late. Reggie stood up, shouted something incoherent toward where they thought one of the guards had been hiding, and then broke into a full sprint toward the rear doors of the library.

Chuck stood with Freddie, both men watching the corners of the room where they knew the two remaining guards to be hiding, and then both released a quick burst of fire to keep them at bay while Reggie ran ahead.

"He always been like this?" Chuck shouted over the sound of the echoing and ricocheting bullets.

"No," Freddie answered. "He's usually worse."

CHAPTER 53
FREDDIE

SEPTEMBER 17, 2020 | local time 11:45 am
Sea of Marmara | Imrali Island, Turkey.

Freddie was prepared to fight his way up the stairs, following behind Reggie, whom they had met up with at the back doors of the space. Chuck and Freddie had followed behind him, each focusing on a side of the library. The men trying to flank them had been surprised to see Reggie, wild-eyed and shouting obscenities, and the extra second of shock had been their demise.

Freddie had punched two rounds through his man's chest and throat, and the guard had fallen unceremoniously to the floor. He felt a brief bolt of concern for the weathered, ancient flooring planks, wondering if they would now be permanently stained.

Chuck had dispatched his own man and together they reached the doors shortly after Reggie. The female scientist had calmly walked down the center aisle of the room, apparently no longer worried for her own life. If she was still miffed that they had used her as bait upon their entry to this space, it didn't register on her face.

In fact, nothing seemed to register on her face. Freddie finally recognized the signs of shock — the slacken, empty face, barren of feeling or emotion. She seemed like a blank shell of the woman she had been only moments before.

It wasn't that she's apathetic about all of this, he realized. *It's that she doesn't even know how to process it.*

Freddie had been a part of this crack team of civilians that called themselves the Civilian Special Operations for only about a year, and already he had started to feel desensitized toward the absolutely insane antics and situations they found themselves in.

Breaking into secret Antarctic facilities. Going toe-to-toe with Russian mercenaries. Fending off scores of trained killers, far outmatched and underprepared.

And now he could add to the list: Launching themselves like a torpedo into a glass wall to gain entry to a secret laboratory beneath an island prison.

He couldn't help himself. He shook his head, scoffing.

"Finally hit you?" Reggie asked. He stood leaning against the heavy closed back doors of the library, favoring one leg. Other than that, his injury seemed to have left him no worse for wear.

"Yeah," Freddie said, smiling. He threw a thumb over his shoulder. "But I think it's hit her just now, as well. And while I'm sure she had no idea what this day would bring, I can bet it wasn't us."

"She'll be fine," Reggie said, frowning at her. Her face didn't even register that attention had been thrown toward her. "And if she's not, well, screw it. She's one of them."

The Faction.

The group that had caused so much turmoil and strife for his new group of friends and coworkers. The group that had caused so much pain and suffering for the world through their terror and attacks. The group that, to this day, remained just out of reach.

And yet..

"You guys think we should take a look around here first?" Chuck suddenly asked. He was checking his rifle, reloading with a fresh magazine, and did not even look up at his teammates.

"What do you mean?" Reggie asked. "I already gave it a once-over when I ran like a crazed zombie through the middle of it. Ben's not here, so we move on."

Freddie shook his head. "No, I was just thinking... Chuck's right. This place is... weird."

"And the bottom floor just got filled up with dead guys and sharks. Even weirder. Let's go."

"Hold on, Red," Freddie said. "I'm serious." He hadn't intended for his voice to come out so strong and commanding, but, hell — it was his mission to command. "We should glance around. The Faction's a strange group — we already knew that much — but just how strange? I mean, we can assume they were using that lab down there to produce whatever chemical compound they used on us in Corsica. The stuff that renders us completely unable to move."

He knew he didn't have to remind him, but he wanted the scientist to hear. He wanted her to know what they had been through. What they had been subjected to, potentially because of something she may have helped create. Something she may have produced here.

If those things were true, it once again held no merit in her expression. Her eyes simply bore through him, even after his accusatory implication.

"Yeah," Reggie said, running a hand through his hair. "Thing is, I'm a simple guy, right? I got one thing I can really focus on at a time. I hate these Faction assholes as much as you do, but I'm not here to snoop around their cryptic old library. I'm here to get Ben back."

Freddie sighed. The last thing he wanted was an altercation amongst his own team, but he knew from experience that Reggie was stubborn to a fault.

"Make me a deal, Red," Freddie said. "We get our boy back first. We make sure he's safe — that means clearing this place out of all guards —"

"And scientists."

"And scientists, sure," Freddie said, noting how Reggie was

staring at the woman. "We clear out, we get Ben safe and accounted for, and then we come back down here to glance around. I don't need to read every book on the shelf, but there's something really fishy about this place. You do have to admit that."

Freddie expected an asinine response. Something akin to *I don't have to admit anything*, but instead Reggie just stared at the woman for a long moment. Finally, his eyes turned back to meet his.

And Freddie saw it then. He had known it was there before, he had assumed it existed, but he had not yet seen it manifested on his friend's face.

Pain. Remorse. Fear. Reggie was feeling the way Freddie felt about the loss of their friend, their leader. But it was inevitably worse for Reggie. He had known Ben from the beginning — long before The Faction and their experiences in Antarctica and Corsica and everywhere else. He had grown to love Ben, and their relationship had been one closer to a brotherhood than a friendship.

This man was in the deep stages of grief. The regret, the feeling of how things could have — *should* have — been different palpable in the air. Freddie had felt it before, but he had not considered how much stronger his friend's emotional reactions might be to the whole experience. He had not considered that everything he was feeling Reggie was also working through, only on an entirely different level.

Freddie saw the tear starting to form in Reggie's eye. He knew the man had been trying to hold it back, had been successful at it thus far. But now...

He lurched forward and wrapped his arms around Reggie, pulling him into a bear hug. He squeezed, not wanting to let Reggie wriggle away.

"It's okay," he said. "It's going to be okay. He's *here*, man. I can feel it. Okay?"

Reggie nodded. Freddie felt his chin move up and down on his shoulder. He squeezed harder.

"Let's go find him."

CHAPTER 54
SARAH

SEPTEMBER 17, 2020 | local time 10:48 am
Cairo, Egypt

The drive through the northwestern section of Cairo proceeded smoothly, a pleasant surprise for Sarah. The last time she had been here she had nearly been killed by commuters, this time she had nearly been killed by a psychopath trying to run her down.

Between The Faction and Egyptian drivers, it seemed Cairo wanted Sarah dead.

Thankfully, no such death had yet found her, and she continued sharing her thoughts to Marcia in the hopes that one of them would be able make sense of their situation.

"So the sarcophagus had a limestone encasement around it," Marcia said, "and *this* was the encasement that Adam Chugg found in St. Mark's, in the basilica."

"Correct," Sarah said.

"It would not be uncommon practice to build an encasement like this at the time. Especially since the tomb was designed and originally intended for Nectanebo II. Alexander's supporters and followers would have wanted a custom sarcophagus, but if his death was rather quick, they would have opted for an existing sarcophagus, adding the limestone casting around it later."

Sarah frowned, watching as Johann pulled the car around a speeding local. Apparently, the kid was a fan of German's *Bundesautobahn*, as it seemed the speed limit signs were nothing more than a suggestion to him.

"That's what's weird to me," Sarah said. "*Did* Alexander die quickly? I thought he deteriorated rather quickly once he started to pass, but it wasn't like his head got chopped off suddenly."

"Right," Marcia confirmed. "Historians and scholars say he got infected by something — bacteria, perhaps the same one that causes Guillain-Barré syndrome. So his death would have been slow, and painful."

"Guillain-Barre — that's the disease that causes a person to stiffen up, right? Makes moving muscles excruciating?"

"Exactly," Marcia said. "He died very young, but it was probably a blessing in disguise. Living with that would be terrible." She paused, looked out the window, then back at Sarah. "Still, your point stands — if he *didn't* die suddenly, unexpectedly, it seems strange that his closest friends would not have at least started the preparations for his passing. He was probably the most famous person on Earth at the time, so surely there would have been fanfare and widespread mourning. They would have wanted to be prepared for that with a custom sarcophagus and tomb."

"Another thing that doesn't add up is *why* The Faction would steal the sarcophagus. They came to visit you at the dig site in Siwa, right?"

Marcia nodded.

"And we assume they were visiting to find the tomb of Alexander the Great."

Another nod. The young man sitting opposite Marcia perked up at the mention of the great conqueror, but still did not speak.

"Yes — do you not think so?"

"I'm not sure," Sarah answered. "Perhaps they hoped to find him there, like my father and your fellow understudies. But if they went to the British Museum to steal a sarcophagus they *had* to have known was empty, I can't help but think they were after something else."

Marcia considered this for a moment, then nodded again. "Yeah, that makes sense. Of course, they knew there was no body inside the sarcophagus. And if we assume The Faction knows at least as much as we do, they probably suspect the bones at St. Mark's aren't actually Saint Mark's, either."

"Precisely my train of thought," Sarah said. "Which tells me they weren't coming to Siwa to find *Alexander*, but something else they thought could be there. Something that might once have been inside the sarcophagus they nabbed in London."

"Something they didn't find there, so they came to Siwa to look instead."

"Or the sarcophagus *pointed* them to Siwa."

"What do you mean?" Marcia asked.

"Well, we can assume the good folks at the British Museum would have checked pretty thoroughly, and anything still inside that sarcophagus would have been found and cataloged long ago. But they didn't just break in and *examine* the artifact, remember — they spent an ungodly amount of time, energy, and money setting up an actual *heist*. They wanted to *keep* the sarcophagus for whatever reason, and I'm guessing it's not because of something inside it."

"True. So they needed it for another purpose. I can't imagine an artifact like that fetching much on the black market, at least relatively speaking — they don't seem to be hurting for money."

"They're not, trust me," Sarah answered. "So they needed the sarcophagus for some purpose, and the best one I can come up with is that something about it told them to check in Siwa for... whatever it is they're truly after."

"Talk about being in the wrong place at the wrong time," Marcia said softly.

Sarah wanted to agree, but she knew there was a chance her father had been there when The Faction had arrived. Of course, that could mean that they had simply killed him, but she knew her father was far more resourceful than that. A man of his esteem and knowledge, as well as perhaps the man most knowledgeable about Alexander the Great currently living, would be attractive to The Faction. If what they wanted was at Siwa, her father might have been able to find it before them. If not, they could use his wisdom to find it.

Perhaps *he* was in exactly the *right* place at the right time. She knew what The Faction could do with their resources and left to their own nefarious goals. If her father had somehow gotten in the way of their plans, he may be able to save countless lives...

A vehicle swerved into the lane next to theirs, about three car lengths behind. It caught Sarah's eye, and she stared at it through the side mirror. Inside, she swore she saw the same man who had found them outside the embassy.

She turned to Johann, speaking quickly. "Listen, Johann — I need you to trust me, okay?"

His wide eyes told her everything she needed to know.

"Keep driving, but go as fast as possible. Your friend behind me needs to call the other car — tell them to get off the road for a bit. They're in danger if they keep next to us."

"Danger?"

"Johann, please. Someone is trying to chase us — someone you really don't want to meet. Your friends' lives really are at stake. Do you understand?"

The college student behind her started speaking in German, and she realized he was already on the phone. Johann swallowed, but to her relief she saw him grip the steering wheel tighter and accelerate even more.

"Sarah, what's going on?" Marcia asked. "Are they behind us? What do we do now?"

Sarah didn't break her line of sight with the side mirror. "Marcia, I need you to hand me something from that duffel bag."

She paused as she considered the plan.

"Something on the bigger side, please."

CHAPTER 55
REGGIE

SEPTEMBER 17, **2020 | local time 11:49 am**
Sea of Marmara | Imrali Island, Turkey.

The light from the midday sun nearly took Reggie's breath away. After navigating through the large, open laboratory, then through the ancient-looking library, and finally up a couple sets of dimly lit stairs, the natural light was nearly too much.

He stopped at the exit, blinking a few times to force his eyes to adjust. He sensed people around, people perhaps looking at him, though he couldn't quite see clearly enough to tell.

"Reggie! Get down!" he heard Freddie whisper from his right side. He had followed Chuck and Freddie up the stairs, grunting in pain but unwilling to slow the others down. Still, he had reached the doorway last, and was only now able to see outside.

He felt himself pulled to the right roughly, just as he heard a few shouts in a language he did not recognize. *Turkish? Russian?*

He crouched behind the large, wide concrete pylon that marked the edge of the building. It was offset from the corner of the prison complex, and he assumed the other side of it would feature some sort of electronic access keypad — otherwise, he knew no reason why the concrete block would have been there.

Makes good cover, he thought. He was glad for that. Almost immediately after exiting the building, two men began running toward them. One was the man who had shouted, as he was still yelling orders to other men farther away. Reggie's eyes could finally make out the shapes of the men, and the shapes of what they were carrying.

Assault rifles. He could not tell their makes or models, but it did not matter. He had been shot at by every manner of assault weapon over the years, and every time was a time he wished had not transpired.

He quickly checked his own weaponry, waiting for Freddie's words. He still only had a few rounds left.

"Now will you take this?" Freddie asked, once again handing him a full magazine.

Reggie nodded, raising an eyebrow.

"One left for me, two for Chuck," he said. Chuck nodded, farther behind them, crouching as well but facing the opposite direction. He had taken up a spot watching the western side of the building, while Freddie was guarding the approach of the men from the east.

"And her?" Reggie asked Freddie. He motioned toward the scientist, still gripped by fear as she hovered near the wall of the building, eyes wide.

He waited for the big man's response, wishing it would be something along the lines of, *let's just forget about her. Leave her here to die with the rest of them.* He wanted Freddie to be as pissed about all of this as he was. To be upset enough to just start shooting anything and everything until there was no one left alive except their team and the man they'd come here for.

Instead, Freddie's words came out calculated and controlled. "She stays with us. We'll eventually need to know what's been happening here. What they were working on down in that lab."

Reggie sighed. "We don't have room, man. We can't —"

"She stays with us, Red. We'll figure it out."

Reggie knew their remaining propulsion system was plenty powerful enough to haul four full-grown adults, even though it had been rated for three. Since they planned on leaving with *two* propulsion units, the six-man load after retrieving Ben would be split between the two devices.

Now, with only a single unit left, they would have to get four men — and now this scientist — on the craft. It would severely limit the speed with which they could run from this place, if they would even all fit.

"We got company, boys," Chuck whispered from behind them.

Reggie turned and saw two more men — wearing the black uniforms of the guards, he could now see — approaching from the west.

"Orders?"

Freddie did not respond. Instead, he stood up and began firing into the guards walking toward them from the eastern side. The guard on the left, the man previously shouting orders to his men, fell.

Reggie pulled his magazine into the rifle and started firing as well, but by the time he got loaded, the man on the right was running to the side, shooting above their heads. It was enough for his team to fall to the side, ducking out of the way.

The scientist behind him screamed in terror, and Reggie nearly turned and shot her. *I'm trying to have a nice, quiet firefight, and this lady's screaming my ears off.*

Three rounds peppered the concrete block, and Chuck shouted something unintelligible. Reggie heard his voice retreat, and figured the man must have also ducked away from the approaching threats behind them. The man in front of Reggie fired again, the rounds smacking against the building and the concrete block — all of which were far too close for his comfort.

He rolled to the side, landing just in front of the open prison door. He darted inside, coming to a stand just inside the frame, his weapon and head poking out.

Reggie popped off three rounds at the same time as Freddie, and the man in front of the building went down as well. He heard more shots, and saw Chuck stumble backwards, then fall back onto the hard-packed dirt outside the prison.

"He's hit!" Freddie yelled. He spun and fired wildly toward the other two guards, not trying to hit anything as much as scare them into hiding. Reggie stepped back out and copied the movement, trying to give Freddie time to regroup and aim a few well-placed shots.

He did just that, and the rounds hit their marks — the two guards scattered opposite directions, but Reggie saw at least two impact hits on one man, and a fine mist of red spray up from the other.

They may not have been dead, but they were probably down for the count.

He counted to three silently, then stepped closer to Freddie, who was breathing heavily, hunched over the prone figure of Chuck.

"He's... he's gone," Freddie said softly.

Reggie walked over, staying silent. There was nothing to say. Freddie had lost three friends — three fellow soldiers — already today, and so far they had nothing to show for it.

"What now?" Reggie asked. "We have to keep moving. We have to find him."

Reggie met Freddie's eyes. The younger man seemed to have just aged thirty years in front of Reggie, and it was heartbreaking that Reggie knew the exact feeling. He reached out and put a hand on his friend's shoulder.

"Come on," he said. "We have to find him."

He waited a moment, then Freddie nodded. "Yeah. Of course. I saw more people between those two trees, over on the far side of the island. Looks like they're prisoners, all wearing white clothes."

Reggie had not noticed, but he nodded and walked toward the building, where he could get a better glance at the people Freddie had mentioned. Sure enough, he immediately caught sight of a horde of white-clad men, all stumbling and walking slowly toward the building.

"They look like zombies..."

All the prisoners were men, but they seemed to be in differing stages of health and ages. Some seemed like they were already expired, waiting for the ground to reclaim their bodies, while others seemed slightly more alive, their eyes moving slowly side to side as they marched.

But all were moving slowly — far too slowly for normal, healthy men. Their feet trudged beneath them, as if they were in silent protest for being connected to their legs. They shuffled, bouncing against one another, and a few even fell. They got back up slowly, narrowly escaping getting trampled by fellow prisoners.

"What the hell is wrong with them?" Reggie asked. "They all look drugged out of their minds."

Freddie was next to him now, and the scientist woman had, surprisingly, joined them as well, standing directly behind them. Apparently she had chosen their side of the battle, either excited to hear Freddie's orders that they would keep her safe or just beyond caring, deciding that this group was a better bet.

But there was another option, Reggie realized. She was standing behind them, not out of submission.

Out of fear.

Whatever was marching toward them now was apparently far more deadly than the weapons Reggie and Freddie held in their hands.

CHAPTER 56
SARAH

Cairo, Egypt

Sarah looked over at Johann. The student was still gripping the wheel in fear. She wanted to comfort him, to tell him it was going to be okay.

But she knew the truth: there was no way to promise him that. The Faction had killed far more people for absolutely no reason other than to further their plans. If the car behind them was in fact the same man who had tracked them at the embassy, she could not lie to the young man.

"Johann," she began. "I am so sorry to put you through this. I did not think they would be able to find us this quickly."

"Who are they?" Johann asked. "Who are *you*?"

She nodded, knowing she owed him an explanation. "I promise you that I will explain everything, once we're safe. But right now —"

She heard the unmistakable sound of gunfire playing with the air. Two loud smacks reached her ears, telling her two things: the car behind them *was* out to get them, and they were using small arms — a pistol, most likely. Johann's vehicle was just a rental car; it would not have had reinforced glass.

275

That might be good news.

Sarah reached back for the rifle Marcia had chosen, and she couldn't help but notice the bug-eyed expression on the face of the other student along for the ride. She hoped he was not going to do anything rash to further complicate things, but she could not take the time to reason with him right now.

Johann seemed equally surprised by the sight of the weapon in the front seat, but he did not say anything. To his credit, he had not slowed down or attempted to get off the highway since discovering his occupants were crazed psychopaths carrying a bag of guns.

He's probably terrified, she thought.

She pressed the window down and started leaning out the side of the car.

"Oh, my God!" Marcia yelled. "What are you doing?"

She ignored the outburst, instead focusing on trying to keep her head and torso low enough so as not to provide an easy target for The Faction man trailing behind. The car swerved, and Sarah realized then that the man who had attacked them at the embassy was no longer alone — there was another man seated next to him in the car, also with the window down.

While Sarah was leaning far out the side window, passing other speeding, honking motorists, he was taking no such chances. He sat in the front seat, calmly holding the pistol out the front window and resting it on the mirror.

He even had his seatbelt buckled.

Well, he's got to be the safest villain I've ever been up against.

He fired again, and Sarah shrunk back a bit. The shots were just wide, fortunately missing her.

And *unfortunately* hitting another car Johann was blazing past. It honked, then swerved, as if unsure of what to do when the rounds peppered into the back windshield. The sedan then doubled back around, hitting the guardrail and popping over it as if it were not even there. The car skidded to a halt, safely off the highway. The driver got lucky — Sarah knew that the longer they played this crazed game, the more likely it was that an innocent person was hurt.

"Sarah, he almost hit you!" Marcia said. "Shoot him! I think he's reloading."

Sarah was watching the man in the front seat and noticed that his weapon had come back inside the car and was hidden from sight. She agreed with the assessment that he was reloading, but as she brought her rifle up, she shifted her focus.

I'm not aiming for him...

She popped off three shots, just like her boyfriend Reggie had taught her. The feel of a large weapon was still strange to her, but she had put hundreds of rounds through this exact rifle back on Julie and Ben's land. It was part of the CSO's ongoing training and conditioning regimen — since they were, by definition, civilians, they did not all have a background in firearms training and exercise. She was no sharpshooter, but she had a feeling these Faction grunts had been underestimating her.

At the very least, they had *not* expected their pistol fire to be met — in a big way — with return fire.

The sedan behind theirs pulled sharply to the left, banged against the concrete barrier, lost about 10 MPH of speed, and then swerved back on track. Her shots had missed their target, but they had certainly woken them up.

The driver's face registered complete shock and awe — a far better look on him than the smug smile he had given her and Marcia back in town.

Sarah pulled the weapon's sight back up to her eye, thankful at Johann's impeccable driving skills. He had kept the car chugging along smoothly, drifting left and right to pass the odd vehicle traveling slower than them.

She fired again, this time continuing to pull the trigger through eight rounds. The shooter in the passenger seat tried to react in kind, but two drifting rounds that sailed through the windshield and embedded themselves into his headrest forced him to cower.

Finally, her ninth round hit directly. The driver's head flew backward, a red smear behind it. The car lurched forward as his dead body's weight pushed harder on the pedal. His hands slipped off the wheel after a few more seconds, but his right hand took longer than his left, causing the vehicle's tires to shriek as they swerved into the next lane. The passenger looked frantically to his dead driver, then back at Sarah as the car bounced.

His face wore a look of pure rage, but it was short-lived.

The small sedan suddenly ceased to exist as an eighteen-wheeler reached it, hitting it dead-on as the two vehicles, perpendicular to one another, reached the same spot on the highway.

The driver of the eighteen-wheeler had no recourse — the car had driven into it, so there was nothing he could do.

The front half of the car simply disintegrated, and the eighteen-wheeler plowed on as if the lane had been completely empty.

Sarah pulled herself back into the car, placing the rifle across her lap like an extra seatbelt, protecting her from the dangers of highway travel. Johann was gaping at her, despite their car still flying down the highway.

She raised an eyebrow. "Sorry about that," she said. "Had to take care of something."

CHAPTER 57
GRAHAM

Sea of Marmara | Imrali Island, Turkey.

Graham walked slowly, trying to shuffle his feet like the others. He was not sure what they were doing, or why, but he had stayed alive so far by copying their efforts, copying their movements. If they were somehow drugged so that they could not understand their own motions and strange behavior, he would mimic them — if only to stay safe amongst them.

That had been his strategy so far: stay amongst the prisoners, and do not call attention to himself.

He recalled the events leading up to this moment. First, the helicopter with the men who had abducted him had flown him here, to this prison island. They had unceremoniously dropped him off, cutting his bound wrists and tossing a baggy white cloak over his clothing, then allowing him to stumble toward the waiting guards, all aiming rifles at him.

No one had given him any reason as to why. For what purpose had he been made a prisoner? And why had no one been here to greet him and fill him in? He assumed it was all part of the charade, part of the plan to keep him guessing, to keep him scared.

And if that were the plan, it was working.

There was a group of prisoners — all wearing white clothing like his new outfit — moving in rank and file, with more guards watching their march, heading toward the edge of the island. The prisoners, all men, had a jilted, half-dead look to them, and some of them even stopped and stood in place until pushed forward by a guard. They appeared to be suffering from some state of induced paralysis, as if each had just been removed from a high-octane chemical IV.

He only had a few moments to watch in fascination. As the waiting helicopter idled, the guards roughly dragged him toward the building. As they walked, the doors to the prison complex burst open, and two people ran out. These were not prisoners, though they were each dressed in white. They seemed to be wearing lab coats and wearing expressions that told him something terrible had just happened.

There had been commotion then — all the guards on the island it seemed had gathered together, each listening to their radios while the prisoners, nearing the end of their march, also gathered together like stunned cattle, milling about but generally staying in one area. No one tried to run back to the building, or otherwise leave the group.

Suddenly, he saw two guards escorting a well-dressed man out of the building. He spoke quickly with the guard on his left, who peeled off and joined the group of his comrades in front of Graham. No one had bothered to check with the professor, and if he had seen a way to get off this island, he would have taken the opportunity to duck for cover and head that direction.

As it were, there had been no sign of a way to escape his situation — and he could not for the life of him figure out *what* his situation was. Was he still a prisoner? Had they ignored him due to another more important threat?

It seemed that had been the case, as he saw the well-dressed man head directly to the waiting chopper, with one of the guards escorting him. They entered it without so much as a glance toward Graham. The chopper lifted off immediately and flew over his head, gaining speed as it sailed out of sight.

Strange, he had thought. He had expected at least a welcoming party — someone who might be willing to tell him why he had been abducted; after all, he had been ripped away from his dig site and told he would be brought up to speed upon arrival. For whatever reason, this was why his students had been threatened, and one killed in cold blood. He wondered if this had been because of his research. Because of his desire to explore the hidden wonders and antiquities of the world.

He had always been shocked at the heights others would go to keep these secrets hidden, but this was a first for him — he had never expected to be taken to a prison complex, dumped aside to wither away, just because he was a threat to someone's desire to maintain the status quo.

And yet here he was.

He eventually had joined the other white-shirted prisoners, hoping to at least fade into the mass of them and not be seen. If able, he would wait it out as long as possible and then try to work his way toward the building. He had had no plan to actually get inside, but if there were answers here, he knew they would be in there.

At one point, he had heard gunshots ring out, and he instinctively ducked. None of the other prisoners seemed to care — either this was a common occurrence, or they were more drugged than he had thought.

He tried to get a good look at what had caused the gunshots but could not see clearly the front of the building. He had, however, heard more shots. He even saw a few guards fall to the ground in the square in front of the prison complex.

Interesting, he had thought, *someone is firing at the guards. A little civil unrest in the ranks? Or has someone else arrived?*

He was terrified but had to admit his mind was stimulated. Why were these prisoners acting so strangely? Why had the guards hardly cared that he had arrived? Had they been planning to simply drug him into nonchalance as well? And why had the strange, suited man left in such a hurry?

Graham had waited amongst the prisoners until the fighting seemed to have died down, and then he had noticed a few of the prisoners begin heading back toward the building.

Strange again, he thought. *Is there some sort of signal controlling them? Perhaps they are responding to a noise being broadcast over a frequency, and they all have some sort of implant?*

He raced through the possibilities. If that were the case, did that mean they were being controlled somehow? Or, like cattle, had they all been preconditioned to respond a certain way, and they were responding out of their own free will?

He thought about this as he fell into place. His curiosity had finally won out, and he wanted to explore the interior of the prison. If the guards had fallen and the prisoners were being overlooked as simpletons who could be easily coerced, he might have a chance to break away and get a look at the place.

He walked beside a man who seemed to be in his late eighties. The man barely walked straight, and a few times Graham was almost tempted to help him along. His face was haggard, his hair disheveled. He refrained from touching him, for fear of retaliation or just playing his hand that he was not drugged like the others.

They walked in step for a bit, until the man beside him stumbled and fell. Graham instinctively jumped to the side, then he started to crouch to help the man up but thought better of it. *Can't risk it,* he thought. *Can't let them know...*

He caught motion out of the corner of his eye and looked over toward the front of the building.

There were two men standing there, both very tall. One thin and one larger, like a bear, with no neck and shoulders that seemed wider than was humanly possible.

He squinted as he continued walking, careful to stutter his steps and force his body to readjust after every step, selling the ruse that he was but a medicated prisoner.

There seemed to be someone else — a smaller person, wearing a white lab coat — behind them. *A scientist?*

But these two men were not guards. They were holding rifles, but their uniforms were different. And they were not aiming the guns at the prisoners, but simply watching.

He got closer, now able to see facial features and more details. He examined the men, starting with the larger man and then moving to the thinner —

Not possible.

There's simply no way. Graham thought his eyes must be deceiving him. The man standing there, watching him, was —

"Graham?" the man called out. "Professor *Graham Lindgren?*" He emphasized his name, sounding just as incredulous as Graham felt.

He swallowed, then smiled, pulling it back in half a second later, not wanting to trust his eyes.

"Is that you?" the man asked once more.

The second man turned, stunned, to his partner. "You *know* that guy?"

The slightly smaller man nodded, smiling widely. "Oh yeah, I know him. He's my girlfriend's father."

Graham could no longer help himself. He broke into a run, ignoring the grunts and shuffles of disapproval of the other prisoners around him as he split from the waddling group. He gathered speed, his old, aching body still spry enough to enjoy a bit of exertion.

The man ran over to meet him, and the two met in an embrace. Graham felt, for the first time, a sense of joy. A sense that his misfortune was soon to turn.

"Graham," the man said breathlessly, "What — what in the *absolute hell* are you doing here?"

Graham smiled, but his eyes betrayed him. "I am *very* glad to see you, son. And 'absolute hell' is a great way to describe this, Reggie." He shook his head, taking in the still-marching group of prisoners. "I — I cannot really answer that, either. Not well, anyway."

Reggie nodded. "Sounds like we've got that in common."

"Indeed. But, if you're up for some exploration, I would very much like to *find* the answer."

CHAPTER 58
FREDDIE

Sea of Marmara | Imrali Island, Turkey.

Freddie could not believe his eyes. Standing in front of him was Sarah Lindgren's father. He had never met the man, but Reggie had recognized him immediately.

"Why — why are you here?" he asked Dr. Lindgren.

The man looked pained when he answered. "I was taken — kidnapped — from my dig site in Egypt."

"By the guys that dropped you off here?" Reggie asked.

Graham nodded. "Yes, and they stayed in the chopper when that other man left."

"We saw him," Freddie confirmed, recalling their desperate and harrowing route into this prison complex. He could still feel the dampness in his hair. "I think he was running the place. We must have scared him off."

"And with it, my only ticket to understanding why I'm here."

Reggie swallowed. "Yeah... sorry about that. But trust me, we'll find answers. We'll figure out why the hell they brought you here."

"And who they are?"

Reggie shared a glance with Freddie. They had not spoken to

285

anyone outside the CSO about The Faction, and they had planned to keep it that way — there was no way to know who was working for whom, what secret ties outsiders may have to the evil organization.

Freddie cleared his throat as he guided the group, including the silent scientist stuck to his hip, away from the oncoming group of prisoners. "I think we know who they are. We can fill you in on that later; for now, we need to finish what we started. We need to find someone."

Graham smiled. "It seemed too good to be true that you would have come here just for me," the older man said.

"Trust me, we would have once we found out," Freddie said. "We'll consider this a stroke of good luck. But no, we didn't come for you — we're actually here for —"

"*Ben!*" Reggie suddenly shouted. "Ben — over here!"

A few of the prisoners' heads swiveled in their direction, but none seemed to care much about the strangely dressed men and scientist to their south. Freddie watched but could not see who Reggie was yelling at.

Reggie started jogging, then sprinting, toward a section of prisoners near the backside of the prison's main building. The group parted like a school of fish, a hive mind thinking and reacting together without a care in the world, never stopping their onward march.

He pulled up short in front of the thinnest, sickest-looking man Freddie had ever seen. Without realizing it, he had started jogging over as well, and was happy to realize the scientist lady and Graham Lindgren had followed him as well.

"Oh... oh my," Professor Lindgren whispered under his breath. "I... I understand now. You came here for *him*."

Of course, the professor would have heard from his daughter that the Civilian Special Operations was missing their founding member and leader. She would have at least informed him of his status, and that they were actively looking for Harvey Bennett.

They had decided to keep the details of the abduction to themselves, both because they *had* so few details and because they did not want to cause a worldwide panic that might further endanger their friend.

Freddie slowed as Reggie stopped in front of the prisoner he had called to. Freddie stared, taking in the details of the man standing there.

Tall, thinner than any man I've ever seen.

Brown, disheveled hair. Far longer than Ben's.

A beard, but a scraggly, scratchy one that seems to be struggling to stay alive.

On that note, the man himself seemed to be struggling desperately to cling to life. His eyes were more than half-closed, his mouth hanging open a bit, and he could see his tongue rolling side-to-side inside of it.

If there was any recognition in the man's mind, his eyes did not show it.

He swayed sideways, nearly falling, and Reggie reached out to grab him.

"Reggie, I —"

"Help me!" Reggie shouted. "Help me walk him over here."

"Reggie, I don't think —"

"Shut up and grab his shoulder, man," Reggie pleaded.

"It's *not him,* Reggie. Step back and look."

Freddie was trying to keep his own voice calm, trying to justify what his mind was telling him. The features were there, for the most part. Barely. Perhaps not.

He tried as hard as possible to recognize this man, to see the Harvey Bennett hidden somewhere on his face, but for the life of him, he could not. Reggie must have been projecting as well, forcing his mind to see what was not there.

Graham stepped forward and placed his hand on Reggie's shoulder. "Son, I'm not sure... I think we should at least —"

Reggie cut him off with a rough shake of his shoulder. He pulled the prisoner with him, mumbling under his breath.

The female scientist gasped as Reggie moved forward, and Freddie frowned at her. "The field..." she whispered.

"What? What field?" he asked. Unsurprisingly, she did not answer. Her eyes seemed to be trying to bore holes through this prisoner, who was now walking with a slightly better sense of balance.

Freddie had no choice but to follow once again. The rest of the prisoners had begun filing into the building, heading somewhere inside. He did not care — for the first time today, they were about to be alone out here. Perhaps they had more time now, to stop and figure this out and help Reggie understand —

"*Hold... hope...*"

Reggie nearly dropped the man, whoever it was. He set him onto the ground, letting the man collapse in on himself.

"*Hold... hope...*" the man whispered again.

"What — what was that?" Reggie asked.

"Reggie, we should take a second and come up with a game plan before —"

"He said 'hold hope,'" Reggie said. "What does that mean?"

He looked back at Graham and Freddie, who both shrugged.

"Hey brother, it's okay," Reggie whispered. Freddie could barely hear him. "We're going to get you home, okay? It's over. It's all over."

"The field..." the scientist said again, this time louder, her voice shaking.

Freddie turned on her. "*What* field? What are you talking about, lady?"

She shook her head quickly, not taking her eyes off of the prisoner. Reggie was stroking the prisoner's hair, pulling it away from his eyes.

Freddie felt the sense of losing control. Everyone in front of him was mad. The scientist, mumbling about a field, incapable of explaining herself, Reggie, convinced that this was his best friend, and the prisoner himself, clearly dazed and near comatose, based on the effects of some sort of chemical.

And then, with a sudden jolt that shot through him like electricity, Freddie sensed it. He *knew*. He knew he had been wrong. The way the man looked up at him, seated on the ground, face half-covered by Reggie's arm and hand. His eyes had somehow awoken in a moment, the haze of drug-induced lethargy allowed to lift for a split-second.

Freddie had seen it, and he knew. He felt tears starting to come; he did not bother to wipe them away. The emaciated prisoner on the ground in front of them had somehow broken through his silent chains and allowed his true self to shine through, if only for a moment.

But Freddie only needed a moment. He rushed forward, nearly blocking Reggie out of the way, and tackled the man in a bear hug. Careful to not injure him, he caught his balance and loosened his grip.

It really is him.

The prisoner's eyes glazed back over, and a bit of spittle fell over his lips, but Freddie hardly noticed.

We actually found him, he thought. *He's actually here.*

Reggie pushed him away and the two men wept together, in front of their friend who seemed to have absolutely no idea who they were, and Freddie felt the strange and beautiful sensation of relief and peace wash completely over him.

And in that moment, Harvey Bennett fell to the side, choked, and died.

CHAPTER 59
PRISONER 348

SEPTEMBER 17, **2020 | local time 12:02 pm**
Sea of Marmara | Imrali Island, Turkey.

I open my eyes. Or rather, my eyes are opened. I am not sure I was in control of their opening, or in control of my other thoughts, for that matter.

But now I see. I notice something distant, something a blur. My vision seems to have been reduced to a useless few feet of nearsightedness, no doubt because of what they have been doing to me.

I figured it out, eventually. The starvation — that great mind trick I had been playing on them — well, I had simply been playing right into their hands. Doing everything they wanted me to do, including keeping my stomach empty enough at all times for their drugs to have their effect.

No idea what was in the strange elixir they kept pumping me with, as most of the treatments had been done without my knowledge. Laying on the table, the cold hands of the glove-wearing scientists. A woman and man, sometimes two men. Always cold, always as lifeless as the way I had felt. They would force-feed me, and I would allow it only because I knew of no way to *not* allow it.

But they would not just force-feed me nutrients and protein and carbohydrates to keep me alive as long as possible. I realized soon enough that they were adding some other things to the mix. I overhead them talking about it. My mind was not in a place to parse the words, but somehow over the course of the next days and weeks the regimen became clearer.

Seeing what they did to The Poet — my friend, if I could still call someone that — finally allowed everything to click into place. He, like me, had been drugged. we all had been.

But for what purpose? I did not know what was in their medications, nor did I understand the reasons why they forced them into all of us.

Until it finally made sense. I watched as my friend suddenly clicked off, like a battery-powered toy, and became as lifeless as any corpse. Yet his eyes still worked, still saw, still took in information.

But his mind had been usurped. His mind had been taken over by these scientists and guards, and someone — I could not see who — had turned The Poet's mind against him.

He had stood there for an excruciatingly long time. Seconds? Minutes? We all watched, confused and hungry and probably scared, though that feeling had long since lost most of its meaning for me. And then he started to move.

His limbs pushed on as if controlled by an outside force, his body and head turning at the last minute to follow. He nearly fell, more than once even, as he continued turning until he straightened out and headed toward the edge of the island.

The cliffs.

I knew they were there, even though I had never stood at the edge. I knew what lay beyond this patch of hard-packed dirt — it was obvious from one glance. The sky met the ocean far off into the distance, and birds danced out beyond the edge.

He walked toward it. I wanted to yell for him to stop, to return and rejoin the circle of prisoners, but my voice did not work. It just opened and closed, over and over again as if I, too, was being controlled.

And then The Poet just disappeared over the edge, never even bothering to stagger his steps so that one foot would go over nicely before the other. His back foot simply tried to step up when the front half of his left foot hit the edge. It was a graceless fall, tripping over the edge and leaving our view.

I wondered if he continued the walking motion all the way down. I don't know — no one walked over to see.

There was disbelief, but it did not register. I thought I knew what they were planning. I had seen it... somewhere. A small device that emitted something that rendered men incapable of moving. I had seen the device, seen them try it out on prisoners.

But this... this was something else entirely. Something deep in my brain must have been triggered loudly enough to make even my conscious mind upset. There had been no device this time, no one in sight controlling The Poet. His limbs had not been rendered useless — on the contrary, they had been taken over and controlled remotely, or at least that is what it appeared had happened.

Perhaps he had simply decided on his fate, and this had been his preferred method.

I am thinking all of these things as my eyes suddenly start working again. I feel as though a fog has lifted, and in a way it has. My peripheral vision is back, I am no longer seeing the world through a narrow slat.

My friends are there — my old friends, the ones I thought I had forgotten, but somehow I know they are here for me.

One calls out to me, but I struggle to recall his name. He feels like a closer friend than the other one, but the other too must be here for me.

And there is someone else, and they are all waving and calling to me.

I stumble over, still fighting against the strange hold the starvation and the drugs have had on me. I wish I had not chosen that path — I wish I had not tried to best my captors, to starve myself and thus only accelerate their control of me.

But none of that matters now. I am in his arms, I am falling. He catches me, sets me on the ground. I feel emotions now, all at once, though they are a mix and a blur and a palette, a plate of colors I am not allowed to use to paint but only to see.

I want to speak, but I cannot. I want to hear, but I do not know if the words are my own thoughts or external voices.

"The field," someone is saying. It must be a thought or dream or memory because it is a woman's voice, and there are no women among the three men standing in front of me. *Who is the third man?* I feel as though I should recognize him.

There is commotion. Shouting.

I fall to the side. My breath hangs in my throat, and then I realize it is my *last* breath. My lungs fail to do their task — my chest is frozen in place. I choke, try to cough, but nothing happens except a rush of sweet air I could have used escapes my lips.

My mouth moves again, open and closed. And then my vision blurs again, this time sealing off even the single slat I had been in control of before.

I hit the ground, and the man is there again, crying and shouting and shaking me, but I cannot breathe. I cannot move, and so I do not.

Hold hope.

Strange, these should be my final memories. Strange that the words of a man I barely knew are to be the last that cross through my mind.

My eyes close, and this time I know it is for good.

ACT IV

"And fate? No one alive has ever escaped it, neither brave man nor coward, I tell you - it's born with us the day that we are born."

— Homer, *The Iliad*

CHAPTER 60
REGGIE

Reggie fought back tears; he failed. He beat on the ground with a fist.

Wake up, Ben.

"What — what happened?" Freddie asked. "How did he just... stop breathing?"

The scientist, the woman still hovering nearby, started up once again. This time, she barely got a single word out. "The f—"

"The *field!*" Reggie shouted. "What the *hell* is the field? Why did it do... this? Or did it?"

The woman did not even seem to hear him, but he was not finished. He pulled up the rifle he had set on the ground, holding it with a single hand as he stood and marched the short distance to the strange woman.

"Start talking," he shouted, aiming the rifle up and directly at the woman's face. "Now!"

"Gareth, please!" Professor Lindgren pleaded.

"Christ —" Freddie began, stepping back. "Reggie, let's —"

"*Enough!*" Reggie roared. "Everyone *not* employed by this prison

297

colony and insane science experiment, *shut up."* He turned to the woman. "Everyone *else,* you have ten seconds to tell me exactly what the hell this place is, and what you've done to *him."*

The woman swallowed, surprised, as if only now realizing that her life might be in danger. She waddled side to side for a moment, gathering her thoughts.

"Talk!" Reggie roared. He was feeling the stress of the entire day finally catching up with him, culminating with the death of his best friend. He had never handled anger well, and he certainly had never been able to handle the loss of a loved one.

And who could? In this moment, he felt justified — they had taken his friend from him. He seemed to be gone already, but if there was any way to save him — anything this woman could tell them that might clue them in on what had happened to Ben — he wanted to know.

She finally began to talk. "The field... it is..." she paused, as if trying to figure out how to explain it. "There is not a way... the methodologies we used to determine its existence are highly contested in ethical conversations, due to the —"

"What happened to my friend?" Reggie yelled, shoving the rifle tightly against her temple.

"He is out of the field," she said quietly. "The mind... the field is so closely incorporated it cannot..." her voice died away again.

"What field?" Professor Lindgren asked. Reggie backed away and nodded slowly. He was thankful for the help — he wanted to keep this woman talking, but he could not make heads or tails of her words.

"The thalamocortical network," she said softly. "It is an already interconnected group of —"

"Neurological modules," Professor Lindgren said. "Yes."

"You understand this gibberish?" Reggie asked. He glanced down at his friend. The frail, thin body beneath him looked almost nothing like the Harvey Bennett he had last seen nine months ago, but he trusted his gut more than his eyes.

As he watched Ben and listened to the two scientists' back-and-forth, he thought he saw the man's chest twitch.

He sank to his knees, frowning. He needed to get closer.

"He's — he's breathing!" Reggie said. "I think I saw his chest move."

"The field had control of involuntary functions," the woman said. "It would be impossible for one to regain control after such an extended time."

"I swear I saw him breathe," Reggie said.

"He is probably just in the final throes of death," the scientist said. She shrugged. "We have seen it in the laboratory as well. A twitching, a final gasp for air, that sort of thing."

Reggie ignored her clear nonchalance and carelessness and continued to pry. "What do you mean by 'extended time' in this 'field,' whatever that is?"

She nodded.

Reggie shook his head. They were getting nowhere.

Professor Lindgren jumped back in. "If I may — out of the interest of time. Is there any way to *revive* someone who has been, ah, pulled 'out of the field?'"

"No."

Professor Lindgren frowned. "If this —" he motioned to Ben. "If this is what I understand it to be, there should be a trigger for the neuronal *dis*connection, just as there was one for the connection."

"A trigger, yes," the scientist said.

"But you do not have one."

"Correct."

He squeezed his thumb and forefinger over the bridge of his nose. "How, then, did you come to find the connection trigger?"

She stared up for a moment, then locked eyes with the professor. "It is a bacterial infection, actually."

Graham's eyes widened, and Reggie noticed that Freddie seemed to be understanding a bit of what the two intellectuals were discussing. He wished someone would fill him in.

More importantly, he wished someone would tell him something that might help Ben.

"Bacteria," Graham said. "Of course."

"Specifically a long-lost strain of campylobacter."

"I've heard of that — is that the same strain that's believed to cause Guillain-Barre Syndrome?"

She nodded.

"My God," he whispered.

Reggie stared at him a moment, then placed his hand on the professor's shoulder. "Graham," he began. "Sir, please. Do you know something that might help us?"

Graham frowned, deep in thought. Finally, he looked toward Ben and whispered. "I do not think I do, unfortunately. She is correct — if this is the same bacterial infection that causes Guillain-Barre Syndrome, and they have found some way to aerosolize or electrically charge a 'field' with it, I cannot think of another way to bring him back without the disconnection trigger."

"What about bringing him back into this field?" Freddie asked.

Reggie watched Graham shaking his head. "Too late," he said. Reggie looked toward the doors. The last prisoners had stumbled inside. "It's somehow moving with them," Graham continued. "They must be using near-field technology to somehow control the dispersal. It's incredible, and I never thought something like it could be fabricated."

He turned now and faced Reggie. "However interesting a science project it may be, I'm afraid it's too late for Ben."

CHAPTER 61
GRAHAM

Sea of Marmara | Imrali Island, Turkey.

Graham Lindgren watched, helpless, as Harvey Bennett thrashed once more and then lay still. His mind raced with the scientific ramifications of what he was seeing.

Somehow, this scientist and her coworkers had created a way to inject a bacterial infection into the air — one that immediately and powerfully took hold in the neurological networks inside the human brain. Individually, these pieces made perfect sense to him. He had read reports of biologists and neuroscientists performing the individual components in a laboratory environment, but it seemed that these people had perfected the science and were now testing it on a grand scale.

He knew the grim repercussions of testing on human lives — people would be killed. There was no doubt in his mind why they had chosen to use prisoners and had chosen to conduct their research on a remote island.

And if he understood correctly, the mechanism to safely disconnect the human mind from this 'field' had yet to be discovered or created by these scientists.

Graham looked down at Ben. He was no doctor, but he knew that some of the man's involuntary functions had been shut off, and thus his lungs refused to inhale and exhale. Without air, he had minutes to live — the danger of brain damage could sneak in far sooner, however.

"Tell me what you have done so far to find the disconnect," he said to the scientist. "And tell me quickly."

"Our laboratory is — *was* — making progress," she said. "But we cannot create what we do not know. Our progress has been hindered due to the lack of an existing sample."

"Meaning you based the bacterial infection — the trigger — you've created on an existing, real-life bacteria: campylobacter."

"Correct, yes," she said.

"And this bacterium shuts down the nervous system's ability to pass on commands to the body, essentially. But there should be a *disconnect* trigger somewhere as well. Something natural, or at least not laboratory-created."

"Yes."

"And without it, you have been forced to work to recreate this trigger in the lab."

She paused, as if considering her words carefully. Graham watched her, knowing there was more she was not telling him.

"Do not hold back," he said, urging her on. "I believe you know the risks here." He was above empty threats, but the rifle in Reggie's hands told him this threat was far from empty.

"Yes. And not just the lab," she said, finally. "But it is too late. There is a team — more than one team, I believe — looking for a natural substance that will work as the disconnect. A counter-bacteria, if you will. Something that will at least cancel the hold the campylobacter has on the thalamocortical network. As I said, it is too late. By now —"

"Where? Where have they been looking?"

She frowned, and Graham was suddenly worried she would not

be able to help them. Perhaps this group had kept their teams isolated, working without knowledge of the other teams' progress.

"A tomb," she said. "One that has been mythologized and turned into a legend."

Graham's eyes widened. *Of course.* "Because the person inside this tomb was believed to have been buried alive, right? Because at the time, the best doctors had no explanation for the strange phenomenon that befell the tomb's sole inhabitant."

She nodded profusely; no doubt impressed by his knowledge.

"And it just occurred to me that this person may have actually been suffering from Guillain-Barre Syndrome."

He reached into his pocket. *Could it really be true? Could it be so simple?*

Reggie and Freddie were speechless, watching on in awe as Graham brought his hand out of his pocket. "I... found this..." he stuttered, pulling out the tiny, round object he had carefully removed from the ceramic pot. The tomb at Siwa had defied all explanation, except for one.

It was not a tomb meant for Alexander, he thought. *It was a tomb meant for Alexander's savior.*

If it were true, this object contained the very cure for Guillain-Barre, the disease thought by some to have afflicted Alexander the Great in his early thirties. Some scholars speculated that the disease actually stiffened his body so much that he was unable to move, speak, and even breathe. His aides and assistants therefore would have been confused by their leader's behavior, eventually deciding that the man had perished.

Graham knew the truth now, in this moment. The speculation and rumors had been true — Alexander the Great had been buried not *after* he had died, but while he had been *alive.* He had been rendered unable to move, and his breaths would have been so slow, so small, that his aides had thought he had passed away. And Graham postulated that Alexander had poisoned himself — a grand illusion that would have worked flawlessly had his partner carried out the rest of the trick successfully.

A poison and an antidote. By faking his own death, only to rise again somewhere distant, Alexander could have become more than just a great man — he would have been seen as a *god*. It was fantastical, but Graham knew the truth now.

He shuddered as he handed the scientist the object. Her eyes had widened more, and she cocked her head to the side, not understanding.

"There is no more time," he said. "Please, take this and use it, if you can."

She hesitated, but Reggie grabbed the object and placed it into the scientist's open hand. He nodded, and she stepped up and crouched to Ben's motionless body.

"I — I am not sure what this is," she said. "Surely it is nothing but —"

"Do it," Reggie said.

She shrugged and twisted the object. Graham watched as two sides of the orb-like device fell to the sides and revealed a hollow chamber inside, just large enough to hold a marble.

As she worked, she mumbled reasons why she believed the cure would fail. "It is too late, as I have said," she began. "They are already working to —"

"Keep going," Reggie said. "Please."

Graham sensed the man's urgency had shifted from a basis of threats to that of worry.

"They will be near the mainland by now," she continued. "This is but *one* cure, if it works. Perhaps it is the thing we have been looking for, but as I said, it is too —"

"Enough," Reggie snapped. "*Do it. Now.*"

In this hollow crevice, Graham saw a stack of tiny white disks. Each flat, circular. They looked like miniature communion wafers. The woman gingerly peeled the stack out of the tiny device and put one into her hand, holding it between two fingers. Without fanfare, without hesitation, she placed it between Ben's lips.

"I do not know what is in this," she said. "It could be a poison far more deadly than the campylobacter."

"It doesn't matter now, does it?" Reggie said. "Too late — it's our only option."

"Where did you find this?" the woman asked as she pushed the wafer down and let it fall into Ben's throat.

"In a tomb near Libya," Graham said solemnly. "I did not understand what it was, why it should be there. The tomb was never occupied by a person."

"No, it would not have been," she said.

They watched the man lying on the ground. He did not move; in spite of the pill-shaped object they had just force-fed him.

"I don't understand," Graham said, trying to keep the conversation going. "We had enormous trouble finding it, and when we did… it was as if it had been built as an afterthought. Most tombs are elaborate, ornate, designed in a way future civilizations can appreciate."

"It makes sense," she said quickly. "This tomb of yours was *not* meant to be seen by anyone. It was built not as a way to present this tiny object to the world, but as a way to *hide* it from the world."

"Okay," Freddie said, "we can talk about all of that later. For now, can we go back to what you were saying about this all being *too late*? What the hell was that supposed to mean? You were talking about Ben, right?"

The scientist looked over at Freddie as if seeing him for the first time, frowning strangely at him. "No," she said. "Not him. Too late for the rest of us. For the world."

"What the —"

Suddenly Ben's mouth opened, and he coughed violently. Spittle and a bit of blood shot from his lips and landed partially on the scruff on his cheeks.

CHAPTER 62
REQUIN

SEPTEMBER 17, **2020 | local time 12:14 am**
Istanbul, Turkey

Requin walked through the doors of the *La Guerre* facility in Istanbul both fearful and enraged. This was his company's office building, purchased with the money his company had earned from a lifetime of service and savvy business sense, and yet he had been summoned here like an insubordinate schoolchild on the way to the headmaster's office.

After taking off from the prison building's helipad, he had made a few calls to other Faction members to inform them of the break-in at his island laboratory, eventually receiving the news that there was also a contingent at play on the mainland. An American group was in Egypt, currently being tracked by Faction-loyal mercenaries.

He had clenched the phone tightly upon hearing the news. He knew the American group they were referring to, even if they had not yet identified the exact people.

Civilian Special Operations.

During the attacks nine months ago, the final plot had been thwarted by this same group. They had somehow discovered the properties of the chemical compound Requin's ancient object held, and somehow created a way to offset the effects. A final showdown had left Faction members dead, the CSO unharmed and still at large, and — whether they knew it or not — in possession of one of the world's most impressive technologies.

He hoped they had not done further research into the bacterial compound, but he had always suspected they were slowly making progress. Americans were curious by nature, and this group — seemingly not under the purview of the United States government and not having to answer to any direct organization — would be working hard to understand the technology.

And so, Requin had taken steps to slow their progress. He knew that the basic bacterial infection that caused immediate rigor mortis to set in was just the beginning. His scientists had perfected a version of the chemical that was so far beyond the scope of the original, unaltered recipe that its effects seemed indistinguishable from magic. He had no doubt the Americans had not uncovered these secrets yet, but he had not wanted to give them the chance.

He had worked quickly to discover where the Americans would be headed next, and by stringing together world-spanning Faction resources, he had eventually had a mercenary group travel to Corsica, find the group's leader, and capture him. The man had been unarmed and completely unaware of the Faction's presence.

And why should he not have been? He was visiting the CSO's founder and secretive benefactor, a man he trusted implicitly. He would have had no reason to believe the benefactor himself was somewhat partial to The Faction.

In all, it had been too easy. Harvey Bennett had been snatched from the grounds while his benefactor watched on, surely upset and confused but no doubt agreeable to his loyalties. After bringing him in for questioning and finding that Mr. Bennett was as tough as any trained soldier, Requin had threatened the man one final time.

Tell us what your group knows about the compound you found in Elba, or I will have no choice. I will lock you up, torture you daily, and slowly replace your memories and destroy what you remember of your life. I will keep you alive long past the average lifespan of a man your age, and it will only serve to pull you apart, piece by piece.

Requin had been uncharacteristically cruel, but he had meant every word. To allow the chemical compound's secrets and potential to land in the wrong hands was a fate worse than death. It would reveal The Faction's play, and it would spell disaster for its future plans.

What Harvey Bennett had told him next was, at first, laughable. But after time, the man's simple response began to haunt Requin's sleep.

Good luck.

Usually men cracked under the weakest of pressure. Even those trained in combat. Only the men whose character had been born of a lineage of strength, then tempered in the fires of experience, could stand up to certain torture.

Harvey Bennett had not only stood up to it — he had made a mockery of it. He knew the man's history, and — thanks to a recent revelation — he knew the man's ancestry as well. It was almost unbelievable, but the proof had been found in his immutable courage. Not once had Bennett given in; not once had he balked. His guards had told him that Bennett would die before giving in to Requin's demands, and now Requin actually believed it.

He reached the facility's block of offices on the second floor and walked briskly down to the end. He had reserved this corner space for himself, and even though he had spent no time here over the last five years, he had been livid when he had heard this was where he was supposed to meet the Faction member.

He felt it was an invasion of his privacy, as well as a significant slight. A power move that upset him to no end, but one he at least understood. He was not in charge here. Sure, it might be his company, but this was *Faction* business.

And the man on the other side of this door was the most important person Requin would ever meet.

CHAPTER 63
BEN

SEPTEMBER 17, **2020 | local time 12:15 pm**
Sea of Marmara | Imrali Island, Turkey.

There was light. Bright, stunning light. He tried to force his eyes to focus, but found it hurt just about every muscle in his body to do so.

Strange.

He had little recollection of how he had gotten here. He could only remember the procession of men, like him — prisoners? They had been wearing white. Was he still dressed like that?

If so, it meant he was still in the same place, that little time had passed.

His head felt about to split down the center; a migraine the strength of which he did not know to be possible. He wanted to scream, to pull his hands up and break the two sides of his brain apart and rip them out of his skull cavity.

He did none of those things, for his arms and hands simply would not work. None of his body would, it seemed. He could hardly breathe, his lungs seemed compressed beneath the back tire of a truck. He focused on this problem first, homing his attention on the careful, slow rise of his chest.

He felt the air going in, but there was a massive amount of pain. He sensed fluids draining and being forced away by air, the shock to his system massive and surprising. *How long has it been since I have not been breathing?*

Ben's esophagus and throat tilted back now, more fluids falling away back to wherever they had come from. His eyes shifted, the lights finally beginning to make sense, becoming shapes and forms and shadows.

One of these shadows leaned down toward him. He was scared, tried to move away, but his body was locked in place. Apparently, his being was slowly coming to life again, and his mind had pulled all available energy away from his extremities to focus it on his involuntary functions.

The shadow said something to him, but he could not understand the words. He felt his stomach lurch now, the bile rising up, but he did not flinch. He could not have vomited if he wanted to, so he simply lay there, the hard earth on the back of his head screaming for attention. He must be resting on a sharp rock, but again he could not move, even after trying to voluntarily divert energy back to his arms and legs.

He was being observed now, three massive alien shapes staring at him, a smaller one standing off to the side, behind them. They were mumbling, their voices underwater.

He frowned, then was surprised that he had been able to frown in the first place.

The headache grew to an insane intensity, and he wanted to scream. His vocal cords' main function had not been reinstated yet, so he stared upward as the pain shuddered through him, the body he barely recognized coming to life around him, as if he were a corpse floating in water, the flowing liquid surrounding and pulling him.

"—he needs a hospital," one of the voices said.

Ben recognized the voice, but he could not recall their face. More importantly, the words made sense to him now.

He tried nodding, tried agreeing with the voice, but no sound came out and his head still did not move. *Hurry up,* he thought, now succumbing to an arguing match with his inner psyche.

"There is no hospital here," another voice said. Lighter, higher pitch.

"He needs *something*. There must be a place inside we can —"

"It's too dangerous."

There was a pause, and Ben sniffed, that sense popping back into his mind as if a switch had been flipped. The air was tart, crisp with a salty feel. The sky came more into focus now, and he saw faint wisps of clouds flying high overhead.

And the sun.

The brightness of it had been turned up, a dial simply thrown all the way to the right.

He squinted, his eyes now attracting some of the pain away from his head.

"Ben, are you with us, son?"

He stared at the shadow, watching it melt into focus and suddenly realized he recognized the man. Again, he had no recall yet, but his mind was shouting that he knew this person.

He tried to nod, but instead a grunt fell out of his mouth.

One of the shadows, the largest one, covered his own mouth with a hand. A gasp. "He's — he's alive," he said.

"I cannot believe what I am seeing," the smaller shadow said from farther away. "It is... stunning. Our missing piece."

Ben did not understand this part of the conversation, but it did not matter. He *was* alive. He did not know what that meant, but he assumed that it implied he had previously *not* been.

"Can you sit up?" a voice asked. "Do you want to try?"

No movement from his body. *I guess that's answer enough,* he thought.

"Ben, do you know who I am?" the first voice asked.

He frowned up at him, waiting for the recall that never came. He squinted harder, the memories coming into focus much like the shadows had.

His lips parted, the strange grunting rolling into sounds and words. "R — Re... Reggie."

His eyes closed, exhausted, as the pain once again swelled to an epic surge. His body reacted violently, rolling over on its own accord and leaving him on his side.

Then the bile reached his mouth and he vomited.

Reggie was laughing hysterically the entire time.

CHAPTER 64
SARAH

Port Said, Egypt

Sarah's cell phone rang, and she struggled to pull it from her pocket without moving so quickly it sailed across the front seat.

"Hello?" she said breathlessly. "Reggie?"

"We got him, Sarah. We actually found him."

Her heart soared. For the first time in a long time, the world was starting to feel normal again. There were still problems to solve, still issues she would be forced to deal with, but for now, everything was right in the world.

She let out a long, deep sigh. Her eyes were closed, and for a moment she forgot the rest of occupants of the car were there.

"Ben — you found him?"

"Yes."

She pumped a fist in the air as Marcia let out a small *whoop* from the back seat. "Reggie, that's — that's amazing, I can't even... how? Where?"

"We'll have time to talk through all of that when we debrief," he said.

She frowned. He was not speaking as Gareth Red, her boyfriend, but as Gareth Red, Civilian Special Operations. She recognized the same cold, calculated accuracy in his voice that meant he was still a man on a mission. Sure, he had found the target, but until said target was back home, safe and sound, his mission was far from over.

"I understand. Everything okay?"

She knew the team members who had gone to Turkey had brought with them a satellite-enabled waterproof communication device. In a sense, it was just a fancy cellular phone that had a connection no matter where in the world they ended up. It was also heavy, weighing in at nearly ten pounds, which is why they had chosen to only bring one. And she knew the parameters for Freddie's mission had them using the device only when necessary — either life-or-death, or otherwise a situation that might turn into a life-or-death scenario.

"No. The Faction is looking for us — we already know that much," Reggie said.

Yeah, you can say that again, she thought. Even though she had taken out two of their operatives, she was not naive — there were countless more after them, and when they discovered what had become of the two men dispatched to take care of her and Marcia, they were not going to be happy.

On the phone, Reggie continued. *"Look, they might be after you, Sarah. Professor Lindgren is here and — "*

"Wait — *what?*" Sarah could not hide the incredulousness from her voice. "Are you — *how* is that possible? Is he okay?"

"Sarah, yes — sorry, can't get into details, since we're running out of time."

"Running out of time for what?" she asked. "You found him, right? Are you able to bring him home? What — how is he?" She hadn't meant for the questions to dump out all at once, but she was a bit frazzled. All of this was happening so quickly, and she still did not understand *what* it was.

"I think something's about to happen," Reggie said. *"Something big. Bigger than... the events."*

Sarah shuddered. She knew exactly what 'events' Reggie was referring to. The terrorist attacks that had transpired nine months ago had been The Faction's entrance onto the world stage. After the CSO had foiled their plans to crash all the currently flying commercial flights around the world, saving close to a hundred-thousand lives, Sarah and her friends had been thrust firmly onto The Faction's list of top priorities.

When Ben — the leader of the CSO — had gone missing in Corsica, the group had determined that The Faction was not only interested in wiping the CSO and its members off the map.

They were going to do it in a way that was unequivocally decisive.

The four Faction-led terror attacks were not just the way the organization had decided to become known to the world. They were not intended as one-off events to scare a population into submission.

No, Sarah and the others understood now: those attacks were the opening salvo to a much larger — and longer — battle.

The Faction had declared war on the world, and it intended to win.

"What do you think it is?" she asked. "Can you give me any details? I'm in Egypt, so I might be able to help."

"All we know is a guess. But that guess is that they are planning to launch an attack... somewhere in the world."

She sighed. "Yeah, that's not much to go off of." While waiting for Reggie to continue, she turned on the speakerphone mode, knowing that the others in the car were anxiously awaiting what this conversation was about. She had nothing to hide from Johann and the quiet kid behind her, so she figured it might save some time to just let them listen in.

"Well, I think it's related to what they were trying before. The

compound they discovered that causes a rigor mortis-like effect in subjects, remember that?"

She nodded and confirmed, feeling the previous high she'd had dropping to much lower levels.

The chemical compound The Faction had weaponized had rendered anyone in the near vicinity of its detonation completely unable to move. Some sort of dust-like particle, when breathed into the lungs and then sent throughout the body, caused a person's mobile musculature to completely stop responding to brain signals. The involuntary functions of the body still worked, though they were forced to strain heavily against the rigid exterior skeletal frame.

The CSO team had intimate knowledge of these effects, and though they provided an interesting scientific study, none of them were interested in repeating the experiment.

"It seems like they've perfected it," Reggie said. *"Although it's probably bacterial now, or at least bacteria-based. The difference is that the affected area is probably ten, maybe twenty times larger. The potency of the drug — wherever it is that they've made airborne — is so much higher than anything we've dealt with yet."*

She shuddered when she imagined how Reggie had come across this knowledge. *At least he's safe,* she thought.

"We found Ben — he was... affected by... whatever this is. So were the other... uh, others. Anyway, there's a woman here who was working on it. I guess the laboratory she was in created this weapon based on an ancient bacterial compound. The details are a bit lacking, admittedly, but I've seen the effects."

Reggie paused, and Sarah tightened her grip on the phone.

"Sarah, this is going to be... this will be big. And not in a good way."

She swallowed. "Okay, let's try to get in front of it. What can we do?"

"I don't think we're in front of it at all, actually. They knew we'd be looking for Ben, and even though me and the guys caused some havoc

here, there was a guy — I'm guessing the main Faction asshole behind this place — who left in a chopper right after we arrived. I've got no idea where he's heading, but I have a feeling we just kickstarted their plans."

Sarah had no idea what place it was Reggie was talking about — she had not gotten many details about their leg of this mission, including where, exactly, they were heading. Somewhere off the coast of Turkey — but that was all she really knew. "Reggie, don't you think it's likely we caught them with their pants down on this? You found an *active* research laboratory or something, right? And the guy leading it hustled to get out of there in time. So could it be that we *interrupted* their plans? Why do you think they're still so far ahead of us?"

There was another long pause, and Sarah squeezed her eyes shut. Her boyfriend was never a quiet man, so the fact he was being hesitant told her everything.

This is worse than we thought.

CHAPTER 65
MARCIA

Port Said, Egypt

They had reached the city of Port Said, but Johann was either too engrossed in the conversation playing out between Sarah and her boyfriend, or he was too terrified to interrupt.

Marcia listened intently from the back seat, leaning forward so she did not miss a word.

"This chemical — whatever bacterial infection they've weaponized — I'm guessing they already have stockpiles and stores of it, since it's all but perfected. That means they can attack with it at any point."

"Then why haven't they?" Sarah asked. "What are they waiting for?"

"A cure," Reggie said. *"They want to perfect the cure — the treatment, or antibody, whatever the right term is."*

"Why would they care about that?" Marcia suddenly asked. Sarah turned to look at her, but she motioned with her phone for Marcia to repeat the question. She did, continuing. "If this is a terror attack, why would they even *want* a cure?"

Reggie responded immediately, apparently not fazed by the new voice. *"We decided before that The Faction has lofty goals far above* simple destructive terror. They don't care to scare people — they actually want *something*."

"Any idea what that is?" Marcia asked him.

Sarah answered instead. "Control. Power. Money. Acknowledgement. All of the above?"

"She's right," Reggie's voice said. *"They have a plan, a purpose far beyond simply terrifying innocent people. I don't have a clue what it is yet, but I can bet it's something far more nuanced and complex than just blowing shit up."*

"Okay," Marcia said, "but how does their control of a cure play into —"

She stopped herself. *Of course.*

"Yeah," Reggie said. *"Sounds like it just hit you, too."*

She nodded at Sarah. Johann met her eyes in the rearview mirror. If the college student was in the dark before, she had to think he was starting to piece things together.

"It's a ploy to control the demand *and* the supply," Marcia said. "It's an old pharmaceutical company trick."

"It's a government *trick,"* Reggie clarified. *"They probably think they can get away with it, too."*

"They're going to give the world a plague — one that's so incredibly dangerous and impossible to slow that nations will *have* to pay attention to their demands," Sarah said.

"Precisely our thoughts," Reggie said. *"I think they'll release this somewhere very soon. Probably in a very populated place. It has enough similarity to the protein-based compound they used before for their relatively small-scale terror attacks that this will be a perfect allusion to them. A much larger, far more deadly attack."*

Marcia remembered what he had said earlier. "It has the potential to completely incapacitate millions of people," she said. "Possibly hundreds of millions, worldwide. They just need a small sample to send through central air systems, water supply, really anything that disperses chemicals through a system."

"Exactly," Sarah said. "And since they want to control the cure as well, they can claim to be the world's saviors."

"How would that play out?" Marcia asked.

"Easy," Reggie said. *"Freddie and your old man have a theory. We haven't really spent much time discussing it since we've had, uh, other things to worry about, but essentially they think The Faction's going to be releasing this under the guise of some actual terrorist group. Someone who's long been known to have a bone to pick with modern society."*

"And then they'll come out with their cure?"

"Maybe," Reggie said. *"But not as* The Faction, *most likely. They'll use their ability to compartmentalize. They'll send the cure to a tiny lab somewhere and use modern media control to spread the message that the small-time lab cooked up a cure that works to heal the population. That message will snowball, around the same time other small laboratories and research outfits, universities, around the globe will miraculously come across the same cure."*

"All given to them by The Faction, in secret," Sarah said.

"Right. No one will really care, because their cure will work. But after the dust settles, they will have exactly what they want — attention, eyeballs, and reputation. They will be able to claim they not only saved the world with their cure, but they'll be also able to point to the way they tricked the population. The bad guys won't be The Faction, they'll be the media moguls who turned a blind eye to the truth. Society's institutions — governments, academic networks, media organizations — will be thrown under the bus, and the average citizen won't give a shit about it, because they were lied to. Finally, the proverbial wool will have been pulled away from their eyes. They'll see whatever The Faction wants them to see as pure, unadulterated truth."

"That's far-fetched," Marcia said. "You really think they can pull a fast one on humanity? Won't we remember that they were literally *terrorists* only a year prior?"

"No," Reggie said. *"They won't. People have been duped from the moment news stations found out they could make money selling a*

narrative, and from the moment politics became big business. The only difference is that there has never been a large enough group willing to throw themselves under the bus and take blame long enough to burn down the curtain."

Marcia took a moment to parse through the metaphors and implications, but she could not disagree with the man speaking. "So you think The Faction is ready to do that? To become the scapegoat only long enough to prove to the world that *they* are the good guys, and the systemic institutionalized bullshit we've been fed through mass media is the bad guy?"

There was a pause, but not a long one. *"Think about the words you just used to describe the modern civilized world. You think people need a really compelling reason to burn down the society they've been a part of? You think they want a well-reasoned argument, presented by lawyers in a judicial system they understand only enough to know they don't agree with it?"*

"Good point."

"Thanks. But the point really is that this is happening, uh..."

"Marcia."

"Right. Heh, sorry. We'll have time for proper introductions later. Anyway, Marcia, yeah, this is happening. We know The Faction is not above killing scores of people to get what they want. We've just been confused as to what they want. What, exactly, they hope to accomplish? Sure, saying 'power' and 'money' is part of it, but that doesn't really describe it in detail, right?"

"Right."

"So we need to figure out how they plan to release this cure, and exactly where. Then we can try to stop the spread of it before it hits major news sources. If we're right about this, we can nip it in the bud before it hits worldwide news."

"Wait a minute," Sarah interjected. "Why the hell are we focused on the *cure*? Shouldn't we try to figure out where they're going to launch this next attack? Stop that, and we stop the spread of this outbreak that you think might happen."

"*Yeah, as much as we can, we should. But the focus should be on the cure.*"

"We don't *have* a cure, Reggie," Sarah pleaded. "Right?"

"*Well... not exactly.*"

Sarah blinked a few times, and Marcia's mouth dropped open. "Wait — you guys *have* a cure?"

CHAPTER 66
REQUIN

Istanbul, Turkey

Requin was reeling.

His conversation with his superior, a man whose name he did not even know, had been both enlightening and terrifying. He had left the office almost as quickly as he had entered, the conversation brief and one-sided.

He had been right about one thing: The Faction *was* planning an attack that had been rushed along by the CSO team who had somehow discovered the *La Guerre* island facility, as well as by the woman named Dr. Sarah Lindgren, daughter of Professor Graham Lindgren. Both had been in Egypt, and Requin knew from his own team that Graham Lindgren had been brought to the prison complex only moments before Requin himself had left to come here.

But he had been wrong about everything else. He had underestimated The Faction's preparedness for an infiltration like this. He had jumped the gun by leaving on his private helicopter, and he should not have been surprised to receive the in-flight orders to visit his office building in Istanbul, where a Faction leader would receive him.

And he had *severely* underestimated The Faction's scope and

327

breadth. Long ago, when he had been a young recruit, he had made that mistake. After that, he had vowed to never again underestimate his benefactors and the organization he had sworn fealty to. But he had done just that, and during the meeting he had not been able to contain his surprise and shock.

Just when he thought he was protecting The Faction by alerting them to the infiltration and breach of his complex, he had been playing directly into their hands. Sure, they were ultimately on the same side, but their ability to hold all the cards close to their chest meant not revealing any of their larger plans even to high-ranking members like Requin.

And the plan was immense. The scale was terrifying, even though he knew they had been planning it for decades.

He had anticipated a regional attack, similar to the ones carried out by some of his own recruits less than a year ago. Those attacks had been The Faction's planned reveal, the multi-pronged synchronized display meant to terrorize and frighten the world. More importantly, it was meant to scare citizens of nations into believing there was another sinister terrorist organization out there, working to convince the world of their religious or political beliefs.

Instead, the true nature of those attacks was far more calculated: The Faction *wanted* people to believe there was a new terrorist group working against the governments of the world, but the governments themselves — the top-secret programs and special operations teams that actually paid attention — knew the real truth: The Faction was playing chess, not checkers.

But by convincing the world that they were merely terrorists that could be eradicated with a focused effort and some strategic military movements, those same citizens afraid for their lives begged those same governments for protection.

The result had worked as expected: militaries the world over paid lip service and made empty threats against a terrorist organization they knew did not exist. They wasted resources and energy and money coercing the masses into thinking they were really working to bring the terrorists to justice.

All the while, The Faction had maneuvered into place right where they wanted to be. They were a fractured-yet-organized, secretive yet too-large-to-miss group, working both in the shadows and directly in view of the public. They finally had the attention directed toward what the public *thought* they were, and that was the ultimate sleight-of-hand. The misdirection had worked flawlessly, and now they were poised for an even bigger and better play.

Requin had not been shocked that they were planning something bigger. Instead, he had been shocked to hear that this play was not a stepping stone to an even bigger attack — this next phase *was* the endgame.

It was all-out war, and The Faction was preparing to drop a figurative atom bomb.

He walked back down the hallway quietly, his head full of thoughts and realizations, finally seeing clearly how this last move was going to play out.

He shook his head once again, still in near disbelief. The CSO team had been so stupid. *He* had been so stupid. They would all be dead soon, and there was not a thing he could do about it.

He had originally thought his own life had been spared because of his actions, because of his loyalty and his offerings through his company *La Guerre*, but now he knew the truth.

He was alive because someone still needed him. That was it — the long and short of it. He was alive because *they* had decided it was not yet his time to go.

That reveal had been even more terrifying than the details of the attack. He knew he was a pawn, and though he felt like a bishop or a knight, he was being placed on the board as bait. His life was in their hands, and there was not a thing he could do about it.

Except one.

He needed to find the group his leader had told him about. His next mission was potentially his last. If he could survive the attack, figure out the next moves, and play his cards correctly, there was a chance they would have mercy on him.

It was inevitable The Faction would eventually discard him like they had so many other pawns; he could see that now. But he would continue his work, continue his drive toward their shared goal.

And that started with locating the ones who would ultimately be responsible for bringing The Faction's vision to life.

A group, taking a Latin moniker, one that was fractured around the world similarly to The Faction. They were currently allies, though this had been new information to Requin.

He didn't know where to start, but he would start, nonetheless. He needed to find them.

He needed to find *Draco Medicinae.*

CHAPTER 67
REGGIE

Sea of Marmara | Imrali Island, Turkey.

"Yeah, I think so," Reggie said. "And that's the reason I called — the reason we're now in a huge hurry. We know for a fact they have an agent of destruction. But we got here too fast and probably jump-started their plans. Before they could cook up a replicable treatment for this infection. So that means they're probably going to launch their attacks, as planned, anyway. But without a cure ready to go. That tells me they probably have full faith they'll find a cure, right?"

"Oh, my God," Sarah said. *"You're right."*

"And if they do," Marcia added, *"it means they'll still get what they want. They can prolong the attacks for as long as they need. Years, even. If they know they'll somehow find or develop a cure, they can just start infecting the population now. It'll get so much worse the longer we go without a cure, but for The Faction it will only further their cause. The more strife, the more of a hero they'll be once there* is *a cure."*

"Yeah," Reggie said, sighing. "Which is the conclusion we've come to as well. Essentially, by even coming here, we've started the ball rolling before The Faction was planning to, but that only plays into their plans."

"Shit," Sarah said. *"And we don't even have a cure."*

Reggie looked over at Freddie, who was walking next to him, carrying Ben with a hand over his shoulder. "Well... not exactly."

"Wait, what?"

"I think we might have a cure, actually," Reggie said. "We need to sample it and study it, of course, and then figure out if it can be synthesized to be mass-produced, but I think we — or your dad, actually — may have stumbled onto something that'll work."

"Reggie, that's incredible. How do you know?"

"Ben's alive, that's how I know," Reggie said. "But we can talk it over later. If you're safe, stay that way. If not, get that way. I'll do the same."

"You're bringing Ben back?" Sarah asked.

"Absolutely. Though actually performing that act may be the most complicated part of this entire mission."

"Why?"

"Well, let's just say we didn't expect him to be in the state he's in."

"Will he... be okay?"

"If he's not, I'll kill him."

She didn't laugh at his attempt at humor.

"Reggie, please be safe. Please come home to me."

Reggie hung up the call and turned to the others still gathered around him. "Okay," he said, "we're all on the same page."

"Uh huh," Freddie added, "except for one thing."

"What's that?"

"Exactly *how* the hell are we supposed to get off this rock?"

He knew it would come up, but he knew they had all been putting it off. The plan had originally been to use the same SubCarts they had arrived on, adding Ben to the Cart that had one fewer individual. However, they were down to a single submersible vehicle and now they had *two* extra people to bring home: Professor Graham Lindgren and Ben.

Reggie frowned, then shrugged. "You're in charge of this mission, bud," he said. "That's a commander problem, not a Reggie problem."

Freddie laughed. "Yeah, we've got three extra bodies to bring back."

"Three?"

He nodded, matching Reggie's frown. "Sure — this woman, the scientist — we're not going to just leave her here, right?"

"Well... yeah." Reggie had not even considered bringing this stranger back with them. Why would they? She was the enemy, after all. She had been complicit in aiding The Faction in their work to create a weapon that could kill potentially hundreds of thousands of innocent people. Sure, she had helped *them*, but that did not mean Reggie wanted the extra baggage of trying to save her life.

Besides, what would happen if they just... left? They did not have to kill her outright, but simply abandon her and the rest of the prisoners, as well as any other guards and scientists who may have survived. He had not thought that far ahead, but it seemed Freddie was working on this very issue.

"We can't just leave her, man," Freddie said, laughing. "She's not — I mean, if she's Faction, she probably didn't have a choice in helping them. But she *did* have a choice in helping *us*, and she chose to. We wouldn't have been able to save Ben without her."

"Still — we can't afford the extra weight."

"We can't take the SubCart at all if we're trying to get Dr. Lindgren and Ben back to our boat."

Reggie let out a deep sigh. He knew Freddie was right. Their boat was anchored far enough away that trying to swim back from here would be an impossible feat even for an Olympic long-distance swimmer. Add to that the extra baggage of an older gentleman who was not in as good shape as the two ex-soldiers, and the eviscerated, thin corpse of a man still lying on the ground at their feet.

As if hearing his thoughts, Ben opened his eyes and looked directly at Reggie. "Are — are we alive?" Ben asked.

Reggie smiled. "Yeah, man. We're alive. Unfortunately."

"What's going on?"

Reggie knew his best friend was going to need significant medical treatment at least, and possibly physical reconditioning and mental health care as well. All of that would have to take place after they got off this island, and that was proving to be a difficult feat. He knew that even with perfect conditions, a perfect situation — having two SubCarts and enough operators for each of them — Ben's physical state made a water-based exit a very precarious scenario.

"We're just trying to figure out how to get you home, man," he answered.

Ben seemed like he was processing this, but then his eyes closed. Dr. Lindgren leaned over him, inspecting his vitals. Reggie watched, and finally Ben's eyes opened.

"I like planes," Ben said. "Airplanes are fun."

Reggie couldn't contain his laughter. "Right, you *love* airplanes." He smirked at Freddie. "He seems to have forgotten his only phobia."

Freddie smiled back at him. "And, apparently, he forgot about that little plane crash in Antarctica."

They had all been together in Antarctica, looking for a Russian station they believed had been operating illegally. Before they could even land, the Russians had shot their plane out of the sky, killing four of their crew, including their two pilots.

"We don't have a plane, bud," Reggie said. "We're stuck on the island, and I doubt you're able to swim in this condition."

Ben writhed a bit on the ground, then responded, talking to no one directly as his eyes opened and closed. "I — I like to swim. I could go for a swim. Heated pool?"

They kept laughing, but there was a hesitation in Reggie's. *We still don't have a plan to get out of here.*

"I may have an idea," Freddie suddenly said. "Let me see that sat phone."

CHAPTER 68
FREDDIE

SEPTEMBER 17, **2020 | local time 1:10 pm**
Sea of Marmara | Imrali Island, Turkey.
"They should be on their way by now, right?" Reggie asked.

Freddie nodded. He had used the phone to connect to the modern-day version of an operator, choosing this option rather than try to mess around with setting up an internet connection and performing a search. Thankfully, the operator had been able to speak English and had gotten him directed to Bulgarian authorities.

After a ten-minute back-and-forth, Freddie had used his family's name to convince the Bulgarian customs representative to transfer him to someone in the military. He had not wanted to use his uncle's name as leverage, but he'd had no choice. It was better than destroying his uncle's credibility by calling the US authorities and admitting they had disobeyed official US-Turkish relations agreements.

The alternative to that was even worse — had they decided to call the Turkish government, it would be asking them for help in spite of having infiltrated a Turkish prison, killed Turkish guards, and caused a major headache for a Turkish-based business. It would have been, at best, a tough sell.

Since Bulgaria neighbored Turkey, it posed the best option for Freddie: they were geographically close to their current location — by flying over a small strip of Greece, easily reachable without having to cross over Turkish land — and they had reasonably healthy, albeit strained, relations with Turkey.

Best of all, since 2006, Bulgaria and the United States had established the U.S.-Bulgarian Defense Cooperation Agreement, providing necessary intelligence for the protection of both nations' citizens.

Because of that, Freddie knew his uncle's name *would* have an impact with someone high up in the Bulgarian Army, yet it was far enough removed from his homeland that he assumed that news of his being here would not reach the States.

He hoped.

But it did not matter — they had no other option.

"They would have scrambled at least a couple of choppers based on what we told them."

"It's still a long shot," Reggie said. "You have to admit that, at least."

Freddie flashed him a glance. "Still seems to be a better plan than what you came up with," he said.

"I didn't come up with... oh, right. Okay, I guess you got me there."

"Besides," Freddie said, smiling, "this is a straight-up CSO-special."

"CSO special?" Reggie asked.

"Totally. A half-baked, untested, dangerous mission with so many glaring holes and a complete lack of parameters it would make a Marine happy."

Reggie raised an eyebrow.

"Which is, far as I can tell, *exactly* the kind of missions the CSO ends up on."

"That so?"

Freddie chuckled. "Yeah. That's so. But it's the best we've got, so we go with it. You all know your jobs?"

He turned to the others still gathered around. Or, rather, to Professor Lindgren. Ben was seated now but rocking back and forth on the ground. The scientist woman was pacing nearby, looking up at the gathering clouds.

Professor Lindgren at least was paying attention, and he nodded. "CSO special," he said.

"Great," Freddie continued. "I'd say we've got half an hour. Most likely they're going to do their best to go through proper channels, which means red tape and bureaucracy, and lots of wasted time before they can —"

"They're here," Reggie said, cutting him off.

Freddie's neck snapped sideways, looking in the direction of Reggie's voice. He squinted, trying to see what it was that had caught his friend's eye. For all the training Freddie had been through, nothing trained a man like experience, and Reggie had that in spades. He should not have been surprised that the older soldier could hear an inbound chopper from miles away.

He waited a while and didn't see it, but finally he *heard* it. The unmistakable sound of stampeding hooves, rotor wash pounding quietly but in a rising, dramatic way. At least two flying machines, fighting for dominance in the air as they powered forward.

A minute passed and he saw them then, the two helicopters breaking through the clouds at a blistering pace. They descended at speed; their noses aimed toward the tiny island.

"Shit," Freddie said. "That was *fast*."

"And they're still *moving* fast. Time to go," Reggie said. "Let's roll."

Freddie still wanted to talk through the plan — at least, the half of it they had formulated. He knew there were far more variables and options to discuss, far more details he wanted before he felt comfortable with his plan.

But this was not the military, he reminded himself. This was the Civilian Special Operations.

The CSO special. A half-baked plan was about twice as baked as their plans usually got cooked.

Reggie was already scooping Ben off the ground — at least he was so thin and scrappy that Reggie hardly had to strain to lift the grown man. Freddie ran toward their scientist tagalong, who was still looking at the clouds above. She seemed to not care at all about the diving choppers growing closer by the second.

He pulled her arm and yanked her to the side, aiming for the building the rest of the prisoners had disappeared into. He had not seen anyone else come or go, but they could not save everyone.

That was part of the reason they wanted some government authorities here, and the main reason they wanted it to be someone *besides* the Turkish government. For all they knew, the prisoners inside — like Ben — were innocent, just enemies of the state or The Faction. By inviting another country's military to this outpost, he hoped they would provide some relief and rescue efforts for the men they could not take back with them.

He had questions about The Faction's involvement with Turkish government and vice-versa. Were they working together? Planning their attacks together? Or was their relationship serendipitously just based on corporate cooperation?

Again, these were questions he did not need to find answers to, at least not right now. They needed to get off this rock, first and foremost. And they needed to do it in a way that was safe for Ben.

The choppers slowed their descent and hovered over the long strip of land that must have at one point been a small runway. Freddie knew the type of chopper immediately, knew either of them would work for their purposes.

Phase One was about to begin, he told himself. *And this one should be the easy one.*

He ran toward the landing chopper closest to him, the scientist in tow. Thankfully, she was fast enough, and he did not have to stop and pick her up off the ground.

He was not sure if having her on his arm would help sell their story or work against it. He was not sure if her presence would convince the Bulgarians they were the good guys or the bad guys.

He was not sure if having her with him would make it *easier* or *harder* to steal a Bulgarian Army helicopter.

CHAPTER 69
SARAH

Port Said, Egypt

"Any word yet?" Marcia asked.

Sarah shook her head, still glancing down at her phone. The last she'd heard from Reggie was that they had a plan — a half-baked, likely-to-fail plan — but a plan, nonetheless. He had said that it was better than having *no* plan, but she figured that remained to be seen.

Right now, however, she was not worried about Reggie and his team. She was worried about *her* team. The ragtag group consisted of her, a CSO-trained operative, a graduate student, and some under-grads who barely spoke English. Johann and his friends were still surprisingly with Sarah and Marcia, even though she had told them to leave.

They had seen firsthand the danger that Sarah and Marcia were in, the destruction caused by the killers who had chased them on the Egyptian highway, and they had seen Sarah fight back with an arsenal of high-powered weaponry.

Yet they promised Sarah to stay by her side, at least until Sarah and Marcia were safely away from The Faction. She had tried to explain to Johann that there *was* no way to be safe from The Faction,

343

at least not while a single member of the deadly organization still lived. Still, Johann had convinced them that he and his friends would escort them to their next destination, see them off, and then carry on with their lives.

Sarah had reluctantly agreed. Having more people in their group might make them a bigger target, but nothing would be more notice-able than two American women traipsing around a small port-side city. Besides, Johann and his friends were young, and would likely not attract attention from The Faction members who had not already seen them.

So they walked slowly through the streets of Port Said, keeping close to the docks. Johann and the driver of the second vehicle had parked their rental cars in a paid lot at the edge of this fishing district near a large open-air market, and together the group headed the opposite direction — toward the water instead of away from it.

Sarah was looking for a very specific target: a boat large enough to make the crossing to Greece, or at least halfway, to the large island of Crete. Worst case, they needed a fisherman to take them to Turkey, but she wanted to avoid Turkish customs for the time being, at least until her boyfriend and his group got away safely.

Up ahead, she found the boat she was looking for — a fat, tall fishing vessel abuzz with activity. With luck, it would be a boat nearing its departure time, and with a bit more luck, she could glad-hand the skipper with a few hundred-dollar bills. It's not like they would be eating the group out of house and home — a journey to Greece would not take more than a day, even if they were traveling slowly and stopping to fish along the way.

But first they needed to convince Johann and his friends that they were safe, convince the captain to even let them on board, and then hope that The Faction had not tracked them into Port Said.

And that last item was proving to be tricky. Already Sarah had seen two men suspiciously watching their progress along the docks. They were seated innocently enough at a cafe, but their eyes followed her every step. Just before they were out of sight of the men, she saw one of them lift a phone up to his ear.

She was not one to be paranoid, but this was certainly a time that called for a bit of situational awareness.

"Time to go," she whispered. "Get to that boat, about 2 o'clock. Got it?"

Marcia did not argue. She nodded, picking up her pace. "See something?"

"Maybe," Sarah said, raising her voice a little as she saw Johann's ears perk up. She turned to the younger man walking next to her. "Johann, I think it's time we part ways. We're getting on that boat, and we'll stay belowdecks if possible. No need to follow us all the way there."

"But Sarah," he began, "we are happy to walk with you until —"

A powerful ripping sound tore the air above her head. She ducked instinctively as three more shots rang out. Johann's eyes grew wide, and two of his fellow classmates began running toward the buildings across from the docks.

"Go!" Sarah shouted. "Now — get out of here!"

She did not wait to see if Johann had heeded her advice. There was no time. The Faction knew she was here, and they had probably known all along. But how? Sure, she had been on a long-distance, unsecured phone call with Reggie during their drive to Port Said, but there was no way they could have tracked her cellphone without knowing her number.

She and Marcia bolted forward and to the right, ducking between gigantic spools of rope, piled fishing nets, and dockside workers shuffling around to prepare for the next shift. She jumped over a cart, the man pushing it wide-eyed and frazzled at the sight of a woman hurdling over his equipment, as a few more rounds from the small subcompact fired her way.

Two of them landed on the side of the cart and the man froze.

Sarah and Marcia did not, however. They sprinted toward the

large boat she had identified earlier, now cutting the distance to it by half. She vaguely recognized Johann's tall, lanky figure running as well, but he had veered off to the left across the street and was now aiming for a break between the restaurants and buildings on that side of the road.

Sarah did not turn around to see if it was the two men she had noticed earlier shooting at her or someone else. It really didn't matter — she was not interested in getting shot, no matter who was doing the shooting.

She reached the fishing boat just as two fishermen hoisting a massive rope up and over the side of the vessel stepped aboard. Marcia was in front of her, and the younger woman lunged over the dock's edge and onto the boat's ladder. Sarah was close behind and heard the shocked cursing of one of the Egyptian fishermen.

A second later, two more gunshots sailed into the dock, peppering the air with splinters and sawdust. These shots rang out loud and clear and were unmistakable to all present. The two fishermen involuntarily ducked, hearing both the impacts and the delayed shots themselves.

Sarah did not stop there. Her mind was racing as fast as her feet. She needed to get to the bridge, where she knew the skipper would be preparing their imminent trip. "Marcia," she yelled over her shoulder. "Stay here — try to convince these guys to cast off. *Now.*"

She knew she did not need to express the gravity of the situation to Marcia and was pleased to see she was already pointing wildly at the men approaching from the east of their position. The fishermen, for their part, seemed equally uninterested in getting shot at, so they bustled around to prepare, heads down, while Sarah ran toward the bridge.

On the stairs, the captain met her halfway. He spoke smattered English. "What is — who you? Why you are here?"

CHAPTER 70
REGGIE

Sea of Marmara | Imrali Island, Turkey.

Reggie was a trained pilot but was currently only licensed up to multi-engine recreational flights. Even if he had been certified as a commercial pilot, he was mostly useless in the pilot's seat of a helicopter.

As the Bulgarian choppers descended, Reggie analyzed the situation and thought through Freddie's plan. As he had mentioned, it wasn't much — but it was better than nothing.

Or was it?

He shook his head. This would be seen as an act of war, but that was assuming they could even get away with their lives.

That was his job.

While Freddie would be working to convince one of the chopper pilots to allow them to commandeer his aircraft, Reggie had to find a way to prevent the other chopper from just following them as they escaped.

Not *one* hare-brained plan, but *two*.

At the same time.

He sighed, shrugged, then started walking. He had left Ben in the care of Dr. Lindgren, hoping his girlfriend's father had the strength to carry Ben to the chopper. He did not want to risk Ben's waning physical strength any more than necessary. He also knew Ben would be safest out of the way of the soldiers soon to be exiting the choppers as well, so they had agreed upon a spot nearby that was within running distance.

The chopper nearest him set down, and the door slid open before it had even settled on the ground. Two Bulgarian Land Force commandos jumped to the hard-packed dusty island surface and started toward him.

He held his arms up, having left the rifle he'd brought with behind a tree, and motioned for them to come closer.

To his right, Freddie and the scientist were performing a similar song and dance in front of the other helicopter.

Hoping the two soldiers standing in front of him understood English, he began shouting over the sound of the chopper's rotor wash. "My name's Reggie," he began. "We called in the alert."

"Where are they?"

Reggie was surprised to hear the man's voice in perfectly accented English. "Who?" he asked. "The guards? They're all inside currently. We've got them locked in a central room; don't ask how we managed it."

Don't ask, because it's a lie, he thought. While they *had* visited the central room — the strange, stone-walled library filled with towers of books and ancient texts — they had killed all the guards they had found. Since the prisoners had entered the facility once again, Reggie had not seen anyone else outside.

They had considered checking inside the prison complex to see what had become of the rest of the scientists and prisoners but had decided against it. They needed to keep control of the situation as much as possible, and if they could convince the soldiers to head inside to check for themselves, it would only help their plan.

And that's exactly what these two soldiers did. Giving him no more than a cursory glance, the two men jogged off to the doors of the complex, followed by two more soldiers who had come from the other chopper.

Reggie looked over at Freddie and the scientist, who were looking his direction. They exchanged a quick nod, and Reggie smiled. *So far, so good.*

Another commando — an officer — ran up to Reggie and extended a hand. "You are the one who called us?" the man asked.

"Yeah," Reggie said. "We, uh, got ourselves in a sticky situation."

"But everyone is still inside the building?"

He repeated himself, as this man was obviously their leader. "I believe so — we were able to fight our way out, then lock the remaining guards inside. There are also prisoners, but we think some of the guards may be dressed up, disguised as prisoners themselves. That's why we waited out here for reinforcements rather than head inside and risk getting shot."

The man nodded as he listened. Reggie hoped he had picked up on his inflection of the word *reinforcements.*

He had. Reggie had been correct in assuming that by reminding this man that they were soldiers, helping American *civilians,* he would not want them in the way. "We need you stay out here, got it?"

Reggie swallowed, feigning surprise. "We can help," he started. "Maybe even —"

"Stay *outside.*"

Reggie nodded, then smiled as the man trotted away. *Perfect.*

He had convinced all of these Bulgarian Army forces to head inside the prison building — far enough away from their ride that Reggie and Freddie would have time to do what needed to be done — *and* convinced their leader that they were all helpless and useless civilians, best hidden out of the way.

He walked up to the chopper and met the eyes of the pilot inside. As expected, this last-minute excursion for them had meant a paper-thin crew — five soldiers in the unit, one unit leader. Two choppers for extraction of innocent bystanders, scientists, and civilians, with one pilot for each bird.

He nodded at the pilot, ignoring the man's confused expression. Without hesitation, he walked beneath the bird's extended tail, pulling out the handgun tucked inside his belt. He found the reinforced panel door that housed the critical hydraulic arm connecting the main rotor with the tail and smiled.

On a civilian chopper, this entire panel would have been aluminum or fiberglass. On a craft designed for battle, it was reinforced with steel so that any stray bullets, from the ground or another craft, had a hard time piercing the door.

But it was no match for bare hands.

Reggie reached up, calmly squeezed the tiny door's latch, and the cabinet lid popped open. He was immediately looking into the lifeline of the mechanical beast.

He raised the pistol and fired three rounds at near point-blank range, severing the line with the second and third shot and causing extensive unknown damage beyond. There was a tiny hiccup from the idling aircraft, but nothing that would immediately alert the pilot to sabotage.

He stepped back, trying to stay out of sight of the pilot and not accidentally get clipped by the tail rotor, and calmly put the pistol back in his belt.

The job was finished, and no one was the wiser. When the pilot tried to move the cyclic for liftoff, he would be met with no response. The chopper would simply idle in place, unable to tilt the rotors whatsoever.

Hopefully.

CHAPTER 71
FREDDIE

Sea of Marmara | Imrali Island, Turkey.

Freddie pushed the lithe, rail-thin scientist up and into the belly of the chopper. He had not paid attention prior to now how small the woman actually was. She seemed to weigh less than a hundred pounds soaking wet, and he thought it a rare miracle she'd survived this long, but he chalked it up to "right place, right time." In his previous line of work, there was no doubting the fact that luck was often a major factor, no matter how well someone was trained. This woman seemed to have all the former and none of the latter.

As she pulled herself up and into the passenger bay with a lanky, scrawny arm, he thought of the strange way she had presented herself. Almost as though she spoke no English until she had been forced to comply, forced to admit that her team had been overrun. Her help had been crucial, however hard it had been to pull it from her. He wondered what her role had been here at the facility beneath the prison's floor. She had seemed distraught seeing her coworker shot, but otherwise had been the picture of aloofness and eclectic behavior.

He was a soldier, however, and these thoughts were quickly

pushed aside in favor of more pressing concerns. He and the rest of the team could debrief and discuss the weird scientist lady later.

He had seen Reggie duck behind the tail end of the counterpart Bulgarian chopper that had landed nearby. Since then, he had not seen his friend, and they were going to run out of time. The Bulgarian forces, save for the two pilots still here, had all disappeared into the complex, likely searching for the guards he and Reggie had alluded to.

That there *were* no guards dressed up as prisoners was something they would discover sooner or later, and they would not be happy to find out. Likewise, they would not be happy to discover that one of their rides had been commandeered and the other left stranded.

If everything worked as planned.

He sucked in a breath and pulled himself inside the chopper, immediately looking toward the cockpit, where the pilot was turned in his chair, staring at him.

The pilot muttered some words in Bulgarian, and Freddie could hear by the inflection it was a combination question and a string of obscenities. He pulled out a sidearm and swiveled around more.

Freddie was already ready for the motion. He had a pistol out and pointed directly at the man's forehead, maintaining a six-inch distance in case the pilot wanted to get handsy.

The pilot, as Freddie had hoped, had not expected much resistance from his safe perch watching his bird. His eyes grew wide, the pistol falling and dangling from his trigger finger.

Freddie quickly disarmed the man by tossing the sidearm out the open door behind him and addressing the older man. "English?" he asked.

The man nodded quickly. "Y — yes."

"Sorry to do this," Freddie said. "I really am. There was no other way, and we aren't sure we can trust you." He paused, noting the dazed look in the man's eyes. "You getting this so far?"

The man nodded again just as Freddie noticed his friend slink over to the still-open door. He motioned behind him, and in the distance he saw Dr. Lindgren holding Ben over a shoulder, the taller, younger man seeming to consume the older, stouter one, but to his credit Dr. Lindgren did not stumble. Reggie waited by the door, guarding the clearing with his found rifle, then ran out to help the last ten feet.

"Anyway," Freddie said, turning back to the pilot, "we need a lift. I hate that it has to be under these terms, but I figure there are two outcomes — you disagree, in which case I know for a fact you're against us, or you agree, fly us back home, and we can explain everything then."

The pilot swallowed.

"I promise you'll be able to phone home once we land again, but for obvious reasons I'm gonna need you to refrain from doing that, got it?"

The pilot stared daggers into Freddie, but he finally let out a sigh. "We are not enemy," he said, nearly shouting over the rotor wash. "But if you believe this is the only option, and you are adamant..."

"Oh, we're adamant, all right," Freddie said. "Great. Glad you'll be a good sport — think you can spin 'er up and have us wheels-up in sub-five?"

The pilot frowned.

"Think you can get us flying in five minutes?"

The pilot responded by turning back in his seat and gripping the cyclic while flipping a few switches. Freddie was no pilot, but he noticed that one of the switches the man had flipped to the *OFF* position was the radio transmission receiver.

That's a good sign, he thought. Satisfied the man was not going to pull a fast one, he turned and helped Dr. Lindgren and Reggie get Ben into the chopper, laying him across the back row of seats. The scientist was at his feet, crammed into the window seat, while the other three men sat facing the rear seat, side by side.

Reggie pulled the door closed just as the helicopter lifted off from the island, this time with far different personnel than when it had landed.

He watched as Reggie hovered by the door's rectangular window as they pulled away from the island, the second chopper still unmoving. He knew the man was concerned his ploy would not work, but he had faith.

CSO Special, he reminded himself. *They only work because there's no way in hell they'll actually work.*

As he smiled at his silent joke, he was even more satisfied to see the second pilot jump from his chopper and start running toward the prison. He was obviously alerting his crew that they had been duped, but there was not a thing any of the Bulgarian troops could do about it. They would be out of range of their assault rifles in less than a minute.

As their chopper dipped into a sharp turn, he watched the water below over Reggie's shoulder. His friend had finally sat down, no doubt as satisfied as he could be that they had actually pulled it off. Ben was with them, he was alive, and it was looking like he would stay that way.

He couldn't be sure, but when the light glinted off Reggie's face just the right way, it seemed as though his friend was crying.

Freddie's smile widened, just as a pinprick-sized boat crossed their view on the water's surface. He recognized the boat — it was the same one they had left afloat before taking their underwater approach to the island. He remembered leaving the boat only hours before, with more than twice as many teammates.

He remembered losing each one of them.

And his smile faltered just a bit.

CHAPTER 72
SARAH

Port Said, Egypt

She understood enough of the words to know that between his command of the English language and her crazed expression, she thought her odds were good she could convince this man to drive away from the dock, as quickly as possible.

She started to do that, but her mind was elsewhere, putting the pieces of the puzzle together.

Sarah knew that she had been a target with the rest of the CSO for some time now, and that The Faction had near-infinite resources. The fact that they had not been captured up to this point was incredible, and she had just assumed that they had fallen off The Faction's radar for whatever reason after Ben had disappeared.

Unless, of course, The Faction had chosen not to catch them. Unless The Faction had been lying in wait, hoping to spring a trap for them. They had Ben already — she had to assume that. Perhaps Reggie and Freddie and their team had caught a lucky break in finding the island where The Faction was holding Ben, but she did think it strange that only *now* — only after her father had been taken — did The Faction have interest in capturing Sarah as well.

What had Reggie told her? They were running out of time. He could not know how much time was left, nor what it would mean if they ran out of time completely. But it did seem strange that just when Reggie and Freddie and the others had flown to Turkey to rescue one of their own, Professor Lindgren had disappeared at Siwa and one of his students killed.

Then, almost immediately after landing in Egypt, Sarah and Marcia had been attacked.

The captain ushered her inside the bridge, apparently deciding this woman was less dangerous than the gunmen still making their way toward his boat.

Once inside, the man began checking his systems. The engine was already running, the idling motors humming calmly beneath the two-storied craft. He pulled the boat away from the docks, glad to discover that Marcia's encouragement had worked, or else the deck-hands had been spooked enough to simply take her word for it.

And then the final piece of the puzzle fell into place.

Ben. Reggie. Freddie. My father. Me.

All of them, including herself, had been either taken or coerced into the locations they had ended up in. They had been tricked, duped. The Faction knew their exact moves, each and every time they had decided to act. Ben had flown to Corsica after the CSO team had foiled The Faction's plans to enact a global terrorist plot.

They had spent months trying to find him, months of having no luck whatsoever. Months of Julie's suffering, bemoaning the loss of her husband.

And then, with a stroke of amazing luck, they had found the island. Freddie had gotten the information from somewhere — he had refused to explain to them exactly *how* he had come across this data — and they had found the tiny island off the coast of Turkey. He and Reggie hatched a quick, rash plan, and they were off.

At almost the exact same time, her own father had been pulled to Egypt for a dig. A dig *he* had planned, no doubt, but one that serendipitously coincided with the exact timing of Freddie's and Reggie's trip. And how had he finally gotten approval from the Egyptian Ministry of Antiquities? She knew the woman in charge had been a newer agent, someone whose political interests seemed far shy of the typical competitive streak found in high-ranking government employees.

Had The Faction orchestrated this? Had they put their own person in power in Egypt, ready and waiting for Graham Lindgren's attempt to gain access to the ancient sites at Siwa? It was a strange grant, she had to admit. The Egyptians typically denied *any* claim that had no direct benefit to the country or people, and her father, renowned or not, had no ties to Egyptian heritage.

Finally, the realization struck her that men had been following her — and trying to kill her — not from the moment she had *landed* in Egypt, but from the moment she had entered the U.S. Embassy.

Had they put someone there as well? It seemed plausible — likely, even. Her cell phone had obviously been tracked, both when she had run with Marcia through the streets and parks of downtown Cairo, and on the highway with Johann, and finally here in Port Said.

She had thought before that the only way to track her phone was by having already given her number to someone. Perhaps this was true, perhaps not — maybe there was another way to track a cellphone. She didn't know. But she *had* given her number to the desk clerk at the embassy. When she had arrived, she had wanted to stay in the public eye as much as possible. She had hoped that by keeping a higher profile with the federal government, her chances of being targeted by a terrorist cell would be lessened, or at least she would have more protection while abroad.

But she had not considered that the same terrorist cell was *already* prepared for this scenario. That they had *waited* here for her, knowing she would come to Egypt to find her father, knowing that she was part of the organization they wanted to kill most of all. She had walked into their trap. The person at the desk at the embassy in

Cairo was working for The Faction, she was sure of it. At the very least, someone there was, and had access to the daily check-in records.

She shook her head, knowing this was far worse than she had previously thought. It was far worse than *Reggie* could have thought, and far worse than any of them could have imagined.

This was not just a petty fight. A battle on the way to the war.

This *was* the war, and she had helped The Faction get exactly what they wanted. The Faction was preparing for something massive, that much was clear. But she had not considered the fact that *she* might be the target of that very thing — that her group, the CSO, might actually be the main playing card in the deck The Faction was holding.

She had assumed they were an annoyance, a deterrent, to The Faction, not the ultimate *target*.

Now it was clear — whatever they were planning, it was going to be huge. But it was not going to be innocent lives at stake — unknown civilians around the globe. If they were killed, they would be collateral damage.

No, it wasn't the impersonal masses that were the target of whatever The Faction was planning. It was *them*.

It was *her. Reggie. Freddie. Ben. Julie.*

It was the CSO.

With a trembling hand, the sounds of gunshots and a revving engine filling her ears, she pulled the phone out of her pocket and turned it off completely.

By using it once more, she knew that it would alert and update The Faction to her exact location. They already knew, judging by the sounds of the gunfire still nearing the docks. But this boat was old — not a technological marvel by any stretch. With luck, The Faction would not have the means in place to track a boat like this, and they would be able to drift freely for days.

But she didn't have days. Reggie and Freddie — as well as Ben and her father — were out there, waiting to hear where she was. She needed to get to them, to get home.

Julie was waiting for them. Julie and —

"Sarah," Marcia's voice called out.

She whirled around, not realizing she had been caught up in her own thoughts. "Hey," she replied. "How are you holding up?"

Marcia's eyes widened as a smile fell over her face. "You mean, am I still alive? Yeah, for now. I guess. Any word on where we're headed?"

The captain's eyebrows rose at this question, and he muttered a response. "Near Tel Aviv. Fishing."

"Okay," Sarah said. "Any chance we could convince you to go a little farther north?"

"Where?" the man asked.

"Cyprus, maybe?"

If they could reach Cyprus away from the prying eyes of The Faction, they might have a chance at getting home unmolested. There, she could use a burner phone to reach Reggie and update him on their progress.

"Okay, Cyprus, yes. On our other route. I tell crew."

He immediately pulled a radio mouthpiece off the wall and his groveling, deep voice carried through the onboard intercom system.

She understood only the words Tel Aviv and Cyprus, but after he was done, she wiped a tear from her eye. "I cannot thank you enough," she said. "I owe you an explanation, too. I promise I will —
"

"No explanation," the old captain said. "Men shooting guns, two innocent ladies. My crew take you wherever you need to go."

She swallowed, then ran across the bridge and embraced the man.

When she finally pulled away, he was holding an ancient-looking cellphone. "Use phone, please. Will still have connection near docks, but not for long."

She smiled broadly and nodded, taking the phone. This was even better — she could reunite with Reggie and the others far sooner than she had expected, and she had no doubt Reggie would work out transportation home.

She started dialing her boyfriend's international number. Sarah walked over and squeezed her shoulder as she pulled the phone up to her ear.

For a moment, one she hoped she could hold forever, all was right in the world.

CHAPTER 73
BEN

SEPTEMBER 24, **2020 | local time 4:13 pm**
Anchorage, Alaska

Ben took a deep, steadying breath. It did nothing to calm his nerves, and almost nothing to actually steady himself. He had already gained seven pounds since his friends had found him, but the recovery ahead of him would be long and painful. He was in a wheelchair, being pushed through the hospital wing by Reggie, Freddie and Sarah by his side. Professor Graham Lindgren, Sarah's father, and a younger woman named Marcia, who he had heard was working with Professor Lindgren on some Egyptian dig site.

His head was still swimming, the effects of forced starvation and dehydration, combined with the medications he had been pumped full of, still taking a toll. He could not speak well, and his sentences usually clipped off or fell into strings of incoherent garble.

Ben vacillated between feeling elated and frustrated. Elated that he would — hopefully — return to some semblance of normalcy. His doctors and nurses had already marveled at his speed of recovery, but he was starting to think it was a canned response they gave anyone in the hospital. But he had to admit he was feeling better. His memories were still sparse and unhelpful, and he relied on his friends to fill in the details.

And he was frustrated that they seemed to be holding back. He had not heard *why* he had been in a prison, nor had they told him how it had happened. He supposed it was for the best, as the neurological expert who had seen him earlier that week had told him his own memories would start crashing back soon, and it was very likely that the traumatic ones would be crippling and exhausting. Better to wait for that than to strain and try to make sense of the trauma as explained by someone else.

But he was most frustrated not by *what* they were holding back from him, but *who*. He knew who they were keeping him from, but no one would tell him why. No one could even maintain eye contact when he would ask about her. He wanted to stand up and simply march out, to find her for himself and ask her why. But there was no way he could do that, not in the state he was in.

At first it had been easy — he was in no position to function, much less speak and walk and think. The first three days of his hospital stay were like hallucinogenic dreams, drifting in and out of consciousness and being force-fed calories and nutrient-dense meals on a strict plan.

Then he had spent two days sitting up, listening to Reggie and Freddie explain bits and pieces of their harrowing rescue, but leaving out tantalizing details that Ben knew were important, but could not figure out why. He had listened as intently as he could, but often found himself waking up to an empty room, nothing but the beep of the monitor and drip of the IV to keep him company.

And his own mind seemed hell-bent on torturing him. He could conjure up visions of white-clad scientists and evil guards, strapping him to a table and then blinding him to sleep with bright overhead lights. He would convulse, then sweat, then somehow eke out a scream or a loud enough groan that a nurse would rush in and check his vitals. Eventually, he would drift away into a dreamless sleep, no doubt helped along by even more drugs and sleep aids, then awake to his friends once again regaling him with more impossible tales.

As they rolled down the hallway, there was a distinct silence in the air. He knew he was no celebrity, but he had been told that many of the hospital staff here knew of him from numerous news accounts and articles, none of which he had any memory of. All of them stood solemnly by as they passed, their backs to the walls. Anyone on phones hung up and nodded slowly as he rolled by, as if he were a parade of one.

But there was no fanfare. No cheering, no smiling. Everyone seemed to be rooting for him silently, using only their eyes, but it still felt more like a dirge than a celebratory procession.

He was confused, and the frustration was growing. *Where the hell are we going? What's wrong with these people?*

They rode an elevator, the four of them, and still no one spoke. He could not see their eyes, could not tell if they were communicating silently between one another, trying to talk while keeping him out of the loop.

Hold hope. He heard the words of The Poet, the nameless man he had befriended in the prison — and he knew now that it *was* a prison. That he had been taken, brought to the island, and undergone strange and brutal tortures. The Poet had been like him — an enemy of an unknown force, someone the powers that be at the prison simply needed to silence. He knew he was on the road to recovery but wished he had already traveled that path. He needed to be healthy once again, because he needed to know who they were.

He needed to avenge The Poet's death. To hold them accountable for their sins. To make right the wrongs he had seen and felt.

They had tried to take everything from him, and they had nearly succeeded. Reggie had said something about a way they had controlled him, something they were still perfecting when he and Freddie had arrived to save him. He could not understand the details, but he knew he would.

Eventually, the doctors told him, his mind would be back to normal. His body, with work, would be as well.

And he needed to get there as soon as possible.

But first, he needed to understand what *this* was. Why he was here — why they were pushing him around, silent, keeping him scared and confused and hopeless.

Hold hope.

The ding of the elevator doors startled him, but he was moving again before he could react. They wheeled him down a new hall, this one brighter, more inviting. It had a different smell — not one he liked, but one unfamiliar to him. He had always hated hospitals, almost as much as he hated flying. But he was told he had survived a plane crash in Antarctica, so he supposed he could survive this as well.

Whatever *this* was.

They stopped outside a door, and his eyes were too out of focus to see the lettering on the panel next to it. A larger sign hanging above him told him nothing: A3.

Reggie rapped on the door a few times and he caught his friend wiping a tear from his eye. *Strange.* He had more memories of Reggie available to him than almost anyone else, and none of them alluded to the fact that this man cried often. Something was bothering him. Or were they tears of satisfaction, of resolution?

The door was pulled open by an unseen person, and he was pushed inside. He glanced around, his involuntary functions like focusing and blinking back moisture in his eyes apparently failing him. He forced them to take in the room, to allow perspective and depth once again, so that the dimly lit interior of this large room was presented in his mind.

And it *was* a larger room. Almost twice the size of the room he had been in. He rolled forward and suddenly felt as though he was alone.

He stretched his neck and saw that he *was* alone. The others had left, waiting outside the open door. The nurse who had opened the door was also outside, and he pulled the door closed again.

He was now alone inside this room, and he waited a few more seconds to see if his eyes would provide any more support.

Not much — everything was blurry and out of focus, an effect of the drugs, he assumed. He tried listening, hearing a gentle buzzing sound after almost a minute.

No. Not buzzing. A whisper. Something so faint he almost thought he was imagining it.

A voice, one that was weak and almost nonexistent, but definitely a voice. Coming from right in front of him. On the bed.

A hospital bed, like the one he had been living in. A form, tiny, laid across the sheets, and he knew then it was the source of the whisper. He centered his eyes on the body's form, the head coming into focus.

Julie.

But she was not alone — he could see something else, something in her hands. Her arms cradled it, a small mound, impossibly small, swaddled in pink.

The whisper fell out toward him again, and his ears picked it up better now, tuned in to it.

"Ben..." the voice said. "Ben... it's me."

CHAPTER 74
BEN

Anchorage, Alaska

Ben sat next to the bed, his frail, weathered hand in hers. He watched the hands, for the moment the only thing his eyes allowed him to focus on. Julie's hand was thin but seemed larger and healthier than his own. Strange, considering what the doctor was now telling him.

"...and there is nothing we can do, Ben. I — I'm sorry. It was like cancer, but far faster. There was no time to even run diagnostic tests."

He heard someone else talking, a muffled voice from behind him. *Sarah's?* "So it *wasn't* cancer?" she asked.

"No," the doctor said. "And I can't believe I'm saying this, but... I wish it *was* cancer. At least then we'd be able to look at surgery, treatment, chemotherapy, whatever it would take."

Another voice. Reggie's. "I don't understand how you *can't* know what it is, Doc," he said. He must have re-entered the room along with Sarah, but Ben did not turn around as his friend spoke. "There's got to be *something*. I mean, shit. Come on, we made it all this way, just to —"

"I really am sorry," the doctor said. "Truly. We saw it last night, when her vitals started to register anomalous responses to... whatever it is that caused it."

"And what caused it?"

Ben squeezed Julie's hand, but he was not sure if the impulse his brain sent to his hand could even trigger the muscles to move. He felt weak, both physically and mentally, more tired than he had been even before, on the island.

There were tears now, streaming from his face. He felt Sarah wiping them away, whispering something to him. Or Julie. He did not know. He could not know.

Instead, he stared down at the small, bundled form on his lap in the wheelchair. He could not really hold it, since his hands were clasped around Julie's, and he was afraid they were not strong enough to handle even just the seven pounds of it.

Of her.

He sniffed. Blinked back tears. They came anyway.

He was so scared. So confused. So full of joy, and yet plagued by the worst sorrow he had ever felt. He remembered his father passing away after the bear attack, dying in a wing of a hospital that looked no different from this one.

He remembered his mother's death, standing by her bed, next to Julie.

And now Julie.

"How long, Doc?" Reggie asked.

Ben saw the man shake his head. "Minutes? I don't know; we *can't* know. It seems like it's already won, whatever it is, and now she's just holding on with whatever she has left."

"*'It's'* already won?" Sarah asked. "You say that like it's... like it's *poison*. Is that even a possibility?"

"At this point, I won't rule anything out," he answered. "But it's not anything common or easy to spot. It's not acting like a poison, either. Rather than shutting down her systems one at a time, as a poison would as it reaches her organs and gets into her bloodstream, this seems to have worked its way through her body and *then* started attacking. It's part of the reason why there's nothing we can do but watch and pray, but even then..."

Ben looked at Julie. The death was there already, in her eyes, waiting to claim its next victim. She tried to move her lips into a smile, but a tear escaped her left eye instead. She finally formed words.

"Ben..." her voice had weakened considerably. He knew it was only minutes, as the doctor had said. Perhaps less. He leaned in a few inches, careful not to disturb the sleeping being on his lap. "Ben, I need... I need to know."

He frowned, waiting.

"The name. *Her* name. Tell... tell me."

He had not realized her head was raised a bit, but it fell deeper into the pillow. He sensed the others around him dispersing, the doctor leaving with Reggie and Sarah. The door closed behind him.

The tears fell freely now, one of them landing on the sweet child's face, causing her to stir.

He thought for a moment, allowing himself a few precious seconds to consider. He did not have time to waste, and he was surprised that he needed hardly any time at all. Suddenly the name was there, already on the tip of his tongue.

Hold hope. Hold Hope.

"Hope," he whispered. He repeated the name, a bit louder, as he looked down at his daughter on his lap.

"Hope," Julie said, her voice barely audible.

He watched his daughter's face as she cooed and squinted, then squirmed a bit. He pulled her tighter, the tiny ball of warmth filling him. He heard beeping, an accelerating distraction that tried to consume his attention. Stirring around him as people came and went, white coats that reminded him of the scientists from the island.

Suddenly, a hand was on his shoulder. He looked up, seeing Reggie, his eyes red and filled with moisture. He frowned.

"It's time, Ben," he said.

The words pulled him away from the room, away from his daughter. He looked back at the hospital bed, saw his wife still looking at him, though her eyes were strained, nearly shut. Her mouth hung open slightly, turned downward, and he knew it was true.

He could not stop the tears now, could not even try. He gripped her hand tighter while once again shifting their daughter on his lap. He wanted to crawl up on the bed with her, to experience this last moment the only way he knew how: not alone.

Instead, he sat, feeling useless in a wheelchair, holding her hand as she passed.

"Ben —" she started.

"I love you," he said quickly. "I love you so much, Jules. Just fight it."

"Ben, I —"

And then she was gone.

EPILOGUE

SEPTEMBER 24, **2020 | local time 4:25 pm**
Anchorage, Alaska

The young man entered the cafe and found his girlfriend sitting near the back wall, hoodie over her face and crouched inward, focusing on her tea. He knew better, though — there was something on the table she was using as a mirror to watch the front door. A spoon, perhaps, or even the surface of the tea itself.

She had always been this way, always paranoid and waiting for someone to attack her. And that was not a surprise to him, knowing her past. She killed people. For a living.

And while she always said that past was far behind her, he knew the truth: that sort of past was *never* left sufficiently in the past. No one fully recovered from that sort of thing. No one ever let their guard down.

In those brief moments of vulnerability when they shared a bed, he had seen flashes of her true self — her beauty, the internal kind. He had seen moments of clarity, when she would allow him beyond her eyes and into her soul.

But never in public, never out like this.

She shifted when he started toward her, no doubt seeing or

sensing his presence. She pulled the tea up to her lips and sipped, her eyes still lowered and refusing to look at him.

How could she look at me? he thought. *I can hardly stand to look at myself.*

Thankfully, there were no mirrors in sight, so he did not have to worry about it. And he tried to brush off the feelings of insignificance, the feelings of self-deprecation. She would not feel this way; she was a professional. Or at least used to be. She would know how to feel, know how to compartmentalize.

It was a skill he drastically needed improvement in, especially now. It did not matter, the logical conclusion he had come to. The rational answer — the solution, even — to the problem they had faced. It did not matter that the decision that they had reached was the correct one — *had* to be the correct one.

It hurt. A lot. Nothing could have prepared him for the emotional toll this was taking.

He approached the table and started pulling out the chair across from hers. He sat down, heavier than necessary.

She looked up at him and cocked an eyebrow. Nothing on her face reflected his own feelings about this, and why should it? He reminded himself, once again, that she was a professional. This was her sort of thing.

He felt a flash of anger then. *She* was the professional, so *she* should have done it.

"Did you do it?"

He nodded once, his eyes falling.

"How?"

He sucked in a breath. "Just like we decided. Through the IV line's attachment, just unscrew the cap and pour it in. Quick, too. Just like you said."

"I don't like doing it that way," she said. "I *didn't* like doing it that way."

"But there was no pain?"

She shook her head. "No. There wouldn't have been."

"They'll eventually figure it out."

"They'll figure out what killed her, yeah," she said. "But they won't know how it got into her system, and I doubt they'll know in time to do an autopsy. Hell, even if they did, they won't be able to figure out what the stuff even *did*. They won't know it was a reaction."

He nodded. He knew her words were accurate — they had talked about it at length, for days. Weeks. Over and over again, working out the details, trying to find another way.

But there had been no other way. *This* was the way.

"Did you... did you see him?" she asked.

Was there hesitation in her voice? He couldn't be sure.

He shook his head. "No. I couldn't." She frowned, but he ignored it. "It was too hard. You have to understand —"

"That's why *you* went, and not me. Remember? If they saw me, they would have known I'm not family. You were supposed to see him, to make sure they knew you were there."

"But if *no one* saw me, we're still in the clear, right?"

"Can you be absolutely sure no one saw you?"

His head fell. She was right. Of *course* he could not be sure no one had seen him enter and exit the hospital. In fact, it was more likely he had been seen by *multiple* people. Sure, he hadn't signed in or made it obvious he was patrolling the maternity wing, but he would at least show up on security footage, should it come to that.

"Sorry," he said.

She did not acknowledge his apology. "Whatever. It's done. We *had* to; you know that. Right?"

"Right."

He took in another breath, this one deeper, longer. *Since when had doing the right thing felt so incredibly wrong?*

He answered his own question immediately after. *When you have to murder good people for it.*

His heart sank, and he felt a pit in his stomach. It was like his body was shutting down, taking his life away from him just as he had taken it away from —

"Stop it," she said. "Knock it off, okay? I know how hard it is. Shit, I did it every day for years. It gets easier, but not by much. And not by pouting."

"I'm not *pouting*."

She waved a hand over his sullen face. "This — whatever you want to call it — stop it."

He felt the anger return. "He won't ever be able to forgive me, Ember. You had to know that."

She looked at him closely now, a half-grin on her face that wasn't matched by her eyes. "Yeah, of course I know that. But it won't even get to that."

"Why?"

"Because, Zach. He can never know what you did."

ABOUT THE AUTHOR

Nick Thacker is a thriller author from Texas who lives in Hawaii and Colorado. In his free time, he enjoys reading in a hammock on the beach, skiing, drinking whiskey, and hanging out with his beautiful wife, two dogs, and two daughters.

For more information and a list of Nick's other work, visit Nick online:
www.nickthacker.com

AFTERWORD

If you liked this book (or even if you hated it...) write a review or rate it. You might not think it makes a difference, but it does.

Besides *actual* currency (money), the currency of today's writing world is *reviews*. Reviews, good or bad, tell other people that an author is worth reading.

As an "indie" author, I need all the help I can get. I'm hoping that since you made it this far into my book, you have some sort of opinion on it.

Would you mind sharing that opinion? It only takes a second.

Nick Thacker

BOOKS BY NICK THACKER

Jake Parker Thrillers

Containment (Book 1)

The Patriot (Book 2)

False Allegiance (Book 3)

Six Assassins Thrillers

Primary Target (Book 1)

Subtle Target (Book 2)

Unstable Target (Book 3)

Captive Target (Book 4)

Vendetta Target (Book 5)

Final Target (Book 6)

Mason Dixon Thrillers

Mark for Blood (Book 1)

Death Mark (Book 2)

Mark My Words (Book 3)

Harvey Bennett Mysteries

The Enigma Strain (Book 1)

The Amazon Code (Book 2)

The Ice Chasm (Book 3)

The Jefferson Legacy (Book 4)

The Paradise Key (Book 5)

The Atlantis Artifact (Book 6)

The Book of Bones (Book 7)

The Cain Conspiracy (Book 8)

The Mendel Paradox (Book 9)

The Minoan Manifest (Book 10)

The Napoleon Job (Book 11)

The Embers of Siwa (Book 12)

Harvey Bennett Mysteries - Books 1-3

Harvey Bennett Mysteries - Books 4-6

Harvey Bennett Mysteries - Books 7-9

Jo Bennett Mysteries

Temple of the Snake (written with David Berens)

Tomb of the Queen (written with Kristi Belcamino)

Harvey Bennett Prequels

The Icarus Effect (written with MP MacDougall)

The Severed Pines (written with Jim Heskett)

The Lethal Bones (written with Jim Heskett)

Gareth Red Thrillers

Seeing Red

Chasing Red (written with Kevin Ikenberry)

The Lucid

The Lucid: Episode One (written with Kevin Tumlinson)

The Lucid: Episode Two (written with Kevin Tumlinson)

The Lucid: Episode Three (written with Kevin Tumlinson

Standalone Thrillers

The Atlantis Stone

The Depths

Relics: A Post-Apocalyptic Technothriller

Killer Thrillers (3-Book Box Set)

Short Stories

I, Sergeant

Instinct

The Gray Picture of Dorian

Uncanny Divide (written with Kevin Tumlinson and Will Flora)

9 781959 148227